THE BANSHEE OF CASTLE MUIRN

THE BANSHEE ALONE 1

SHEILA CURRIE

To Colleen,
Please enjoy!
Sheila
29 June 2019

eBook ISBN: 978-1-9994918-2-6
Print ISBN: 978-1-9994918-1-9
Audio ISBN: 978-1-9994918-0-2

The Banshee of Castle Muirn is a work of fiction. The story is loosely based on historical events, but names, characters, places and incidents are the product of the author's imagination.

Cover design by Steven Novak

Neart nan tonn leat truime trèine!
Bho 'Taladh Dhòmhnaill Ghuirm', gun urra

Might of the waves be with you, of the highest and strongest!
From 'The Lullaby of Noble Donald', anonymous

PROLOGUE

Singed by gunfire as she flew over the foreign warriors among the oaks and beeches, Crow dived through the smoke hole of the first house in the village. She flew only at night to escape notice, but they had spotted her and opened fire. The strangers were hiding near Castle Muirn. She had learned that the news from the south was not good when she had agreed to deliver a message to Morag the Wise.

The scent of fragrant heather mingled with the smell of soot in the thatch and the herbs drying in the rafters. All seemed well, but Crow knew otherwise. The bird took a few moments to warm herself on a large stone radiating heat from the banked fire in the central hearth while she examined the burnt tips of her feathers. Nothing serious.

No sign of Morag—she must be asleep behind the oaken doors of her box bed. She prospered as ever. Her clothes chest brimmed with linen and plaids, her food kist with oatmeal and barley. Four low chairs waited at the fire for her clients.

No doubt Morag preferred to stay abed under a quilt on

a cold night to keep her old bones warm. "Morag, get up. It's time to go, lazy one! You have business." Crow flapped outside the doors of the box-bed and pecked the wood repeatedly. A few black feathers scattered in the air.

Crow heard a grunt, and the doors swung open.

"So I'm still alive in the world." Morag swung her legs out of bed. The firelight shone in her eyes, two wells of youth in a face ridged with age. "*Dòlas!* Blast!"

"You've to warn them tonight." Crow ignored her anger and hovered out of reach.

As the wind rattled the stones anchoring her roof, Morag looked toward the rafters as though bad omens might bring down her house. "So one of them will change sooner than we thought."

"Yes, one will die at sunse. Didn't you see that yourself?"

"Not clearly. Your Sight is better."

Strong visions of what might happen didn't come to the bird either, but she took pleasure in the compliment. "Best hurry."

"One death in an ocean of life." Morag the Wise unbound her hair and pulled her fingers through it to separate the strands of black and grey. She rubbed her hands, swollen with the joint sickness. "But there are many in this glen who will die before their time."

Poor woman. Her old bones made her short-tempered, but with the Crow's help she'd prepare herself for her night's work. From her kist, she scooped up a handful of fine oatmeal to powder her hair white. She put a bleached sheepskin mask to her face and tied it at the back of her head. Then she cut her hand with a small knife and darkened the mask's lips with her own blood. She winced as she bandaged her hand and massaged her knuckles afterward.

The bird had a more important task—to find out if Morag had secured her apprentice. Only one other of Morag's kind lived in the district—Shona, the chief's daughter. Both women had silver-grey eyes, a sure sign.

Crow nibbled the seeds spilled on the kist. "Keep your mind on your business, old dear."

Morag put on a worn linen shift and an *earasaid*, a mantle of grey and white, and belted them with a sash of green silk, the emblem of her calling.

"You're dragging your tail feathers." The bird jumped from chair to stool to chest.

"You'd know more about that than I."

"Someone's outside. Stay here. I'll go see." The bird flew out the smoke hole, and found a young man with his arm about a girl by the garden wall. They thought birds had no power to understand human speech, and they'd ignore her. Then she saw dark shapes moving beyond the church. The ones who had fired at her. Must be. She rushed back to Morag's and landed sideways on the chain holding her old bronze cauldron over the fire.

"A young man. And the men in dark coats and breeches nearby. Too bad the young one will be caught up in this. But this death is the beginning of change in Gleann Muirn. I saw it."

Morag pinned her garment with a silver brooch so big that the bird could have built a nest on it.

"Let's go," Crow squawked. "It is destiny. Let's get it over with."

"Hush, rude bird. You'll wake the dead."

"They'll want to meet all the new people joining them this year."

"I know. I'm ready."

Crow enabled the old woman to keep her nocturnal walks a secret. Morag skirted the edge of the village. She had to appear from the west, the direction of the Otherworld, and the bird flew overhead to make sure no one encountered her while she was working. In all the years the old woman had done her job, the villagers had remained ignorant of who among them predicted death.

The people of Baile Leacan knew Morag only for her knowledge of herbs and simples. And so they should. Now Crow's duty was to help her find a replacement. "Only one silver-eyed woman has the copper in her blood. Only one person sickens with iron."

"You're nagging." The old woman, her hand on her back, straightened and groaned.

"My people have seen what may come. A generation of blood and death—unless we do something."

Morag's shoulders sagged again. "I knew evil was gathering."

"Did you take something for the pain?"

"I did."

Only a sliver of moonlight cast light on the path. Although Morag knew the way, she stumbled and muttered a curse. Her bad leg had collapsed under her.

"You must ask Shona. With her father away, there's a chance she may agree."

"You think I haven't thought about it?" Morag picked herself up and rubbed earth and tiny pebbles from her hands. "Her father won't allow it. He wants her married." She leaned on the wall of a house.

Crow hovered above. "You'll think of something."

"So I will." Morag smoothed her *earasaid*. "I'm all right for a few years. Just do your part." A tinge of anger coloured her words.

"I'll help you when I can." Crow wondered how long Morag would last. She lighted on the woman's shoulder and nuzzled her neck.

"Blessings on you, kindly Crow."

"Go now, dear one. Perform your sad task."

After a short rest, Morag straightened, her hand on her back, and walked to the house where one soul had less than a day of life.

From inside the house a woman sobbed and, at his door, a man uttered a stream of invective. Quick as a ferret, he darted out before Crow had time to warn Morag. He almost hurtled into her. "Woman, what are you doing out here in the dark?"

Morag's white hair hung unbound below her shoulder blades. By the light of the moon, Crow saw her turn her pallid face slowly toward the man. She said nothing. *Clever woman.* She let the man speak.

"It's *you*! It's me you're warning? Someone in my house? A guest?" He dropped to his knees. "A little more time. Just a bit. To make things right."

Morag's face shone white in the moonlight. She stared at the man.

He covered his face and wept. "I'll never argue or shout again. Let us be and I'll be a good man to my wife. The best. Please give my family more time."

"Too late." Morag raised her palms and pushed the air. The man flew up and landed on his back; then he lifted his head and shook it. Fear warped his face. "Go home," she said.

Above her Crow screeched, and the man scuttled away on all fours. He never stood until he reached the safety of his threshold. *Silly man.* Fear would keep them shut tightly in their little houses, but those tiny wattle doors wouldn't protect them from what the bird saw. Not now. Not ever.

From the direction of the setting sun, Morag the Banshee trudged between the houses and cried a warning of death to the living.

CHAPTER 1

Scottish Highlands 1638

"Not wise. Not wise at all, Alasdair Dubh. We shouldn't be here." The old man scanned the crowd and the wide bay round them.

"I see no danger at all." Alasdair saw people of all ages, but most youths and children stood close to the water while the older adults sat talking quietly on plaids. Alasdair could still see faces clearly even though it was close to midnight on the feast of Saint John, the longest day of the year. He saw girls playing a counting game. The girls laughed and squealed, but the adults nearby hushed them.

"It's what I can't see worries me." Ruari had been his tutor and had followed him as a soldier to the Low Countries to fight for Spain.

Alasdair pressed his lips together. Ruari was cautious and that's why he'd reached a great age. Better to pay attention. "What do you mean?"

"No fighting men."

Alasdair looked for men of his own age, but could see

nothing but women, children and older men. "So the rumour is true. The young men are all away in the south."

"Or waiting for us in the trees or behind the church wall."

"If they are truly away, we may have a chance to bring our cattle through at little cost for each beast." Maybe this was a mad foray into enemy territory, and maybe it wasn't. "If we pass through Campbell country, we save ourselves a couple of weeks on the road."

The crowd talked in low voices and people hunched down as they went from group to group. As if something large and predatory were about to come out of the sea.

"We could have stayed safe at home." Ruari used the voice of instruction Alasdair knew from his youth.

He did not look at the older man. "And we'll see another starving year. I'd rather do something about that. And if you're here at my back, so do you."

"Most of the time, Alasdair Dubh, but they don't look happy." The other man shook his head and said no more. From all directions, hosts of people crept slowly to the white shore of the Tràigh Bhàn. Alasdair and his tutor stood on a ridge of sand built up by centuries of coastal tides.

Two rocky headlands defined the curve of sand beach, with the graveyard on the east side and the castle in the west. The wind strengthened and the waves drowned the speech of the crowd closest to the water.

At midsummer the sun, a disk of red crystal, hung low in the western sky, softening the hills to the curve of a woman's back, the marram grass waving like the fringe of her plaid. The midsummer festival was the best time for the MacDonalds to come among the Campbells, when they would neither expect nor give injury. Twilight on the longest day of the year.

He drew a long breath to calm himself. *Nothing will happen.*

A file of women approached from the village and parted the crowd. The leader, her grey-streaked hair loose on her shoulders, processed to the sea, followed by young women. They wore what women wear: linen shift, red wool kirtle and the *earasaid*, a mantle of three loom-widths. But their belts and brooches glinted with precious stones while most of the women wore a simple pin and a plain belt over the *earasaid*. Two women carried cloth-wrapped bundles.

A light-headed cousin had tried to persuade him that the Campbells might look like ordinary people, but they shape-shifted into black boars with bloody tusks at the full of the moon. Few MacDonalds were willing to believe they were that accursed. Alasdair had fought in the Wars of Flanders, and in his opinion men were much alike and the good ones weren't all on one side. It was unlikely that the Campbells had horns, tusks or tails. Despite that, Ruari was one of only five men to join him on his quest.

They'd left their claymores with the other members of their band, who waited beyond the western headland. He and Ruari had come to the shore without sprigs of heather in their bonnets, which would identify them as MacDonalds even in poor light. If Ruari and Alasdair lost their lives, the four men and six boys who waited beyond the headland could do nothing but avenge their deaths.

Alasdair half expected the Campbell men near him to shout "To arms!" as though they could recognise MacDonalds from their shape or scent. To his surprise, people nodded and praised the day. Of course. He passed for a Campbell gentleman because of the fine stuff of the *féileadh* wrapped round him, his carved belt and jewelled brooch. He stood straight in his supple shoes, while many went barefoot on the warm sand. He was indeed a gentleman, although he didn't have a title from the king like a few of the Campbell gentry. Still, he was a MacDonald, descended from the kings of Ireland, while the Campbells were a people arrived yesterday from nowhere. Or so the *seanchaidh* said.

"*Éistibh!* Listen!" A woman put her finger across her mouth. Others repeated the gesture till all were silent.

"They're starting!" A man's voice. "Finally."

The woman wrapped her arms round her chest. "High time. What a dark thing it was for the banshee to cry the evening before the midsummer festival. However beautiful her song, she brings sorrow." She addressed Alasdair. "At least you know she didn't lament for you. You won't die. You're not from this glen."

Several people hushed her.

"No. I'm sorry for your trouble." *Mac an Donais!* Damn! He hadn't chosen a good time to come through Campbell country after all. He had bought cattle with the money he'd earned in the wars and raised them on good grass. He'd get a high price for them in the Lowland cattle markets, but Campbell country lay between himself and his goal.

"We don't yet know who among us must prepare to bury a loved one." The woman shivered and blessed herself.

"Will you not listen?" The man placed his arm around the woman's shoulders. They must be a married couple.

"You're welcome here, stranger. But it's a sad time when it should be happy." She said that pleasantly, then glowered at her husband.

"Thank you. Perhaps the ritual will bring fortune for the rest of the year." Fond hope. The spirits of the place were angry at something. The MacDonalds had been luckless for over a hundred years and didn't need more bad times.

The Campbells looked like his own people in their bonnets and plaids, and they sounded the same, most kindly, a few impatient. It was easy to pity them the loss to come.

When the crowd surged forward behind the celebrants, Alasdair and his tutor followed. The grey-haired leader raised her arm, and the crowd made room for her. She stepped up on a flat rock while five young women made a line at the water's edge. One of them stooped, then held out a tall silver cup to her elder. Alasdair caught his breath. While the old one poured ale, the beautiful one stared in his direction, her face shining and her hair gold-blond in the light of the red sun. She might notice him, a head above most men, as she surveyed the crowd. Unlikely. She'd be too busy with the ritual. The wind blew tendrils of hair across her face; she pushed them back and faced the water.

A Dhia. Dear God.

Who was this fairy queen at the mouth of the sea? A *sìtheach* must have used shape magic to transform her from a swan or a mermaid. She must be a Campbell woman, so there was no question of befriending her ... or anything more. That would not go down well with the Campbells or his own people. But he wanted to see her again. Studying her lovely form wouldn't hurt anyone, and it would make him very happy indeed. When the crowd shifted, he made his way through.

"You'll excuse him," Ruari said to a heavy woman who complained at his rough passage. "An impetuous young man for sure. That lad has boundless energy when most of us want our beds. Be careful, lad. Someone may be offended by your swift movement."

"I was careless indeed. I apologise." How thoughtless of him, the so-called leader of a new enterprise that would save the MacDonalds of Duacha. But he discerned no resentment—they were as gracious as if they were all under a spell. Ever on the alert, Ruari scanned the fields beyond the beach and the church walls. Since Alasdair's seventh year, Ruari had stood at his back to defend him.

"Who is the lass with the silver cup?" Alasdair stared at her in the distance.

"I hardly knew her myself," a man replied. "She has become round and ripe in the last year. Very sweet to look at."

"You! Avert your eyes and mind your tongue!" The woman who'd spoken before pushed the man.

"Who is—?" Alasdair tried again.

The woman pointed in the direction of the magical creature. "That's Shona Iain Glas, of course. Our chief's daughter."

The chief's daughter. He'd spend little time in her company.

At the sea's edge, the women unpinned their brooches and removed their *earasaid*. As the dying sun touched the edge of the world, the old woman walked waist-deep into the blood-red sea, lifted the silver cup high above her head, and sang:

A Shionaidh na mara,
Nach toir thu dhuinn biadh?

O Ancient One of the sea,
Will you not bring us food?

She poured the libation of ale into the sea. Then the fair-haired woman gave an offering of oats. The sea rippled as the women sang, hushing the beholders while the peat torches crackled.

Ancient One, work the magic of transformation:
water into seaweed, seaweed into corn,
and corn into people and their beasts.
Give us life, Shionaidh.

Those behind took up the song.

He barely heard the words as he filled his eyes with the sight of her. If he spent more time studying the Campbell woman from the top of her head to her heels, he'd be spellbound and forget his purpose.

No, he would not. Nothing he could do about his racing heart, though.

Suddenly the ocean shivered in front of them, and the Ancient One formed a large wave, which grew higher until it split to form columns of water, silvered in the sun with crystal streamers spinning off the tops. The water rained on the women and onlookers. The golden-haired woman lifted her arms and the pillar grew higher. On every person near the shore, the hair hung long and lank, but a silver cage of water kept the golden woman dry. When Alasdair saw her, perfect and dry, he knew she had Sionaidh's favour. But the sea spirit had captured her for a purpose known only to himself.

He stared at the shifting sea. Ruari shook his shoulder and he came to himself. The old woman on the stone nodded as if she had expected the action of the waves. As the water quieted, the young women began to sing again, and those behind took up their song, until hundreds of voices filled the curve of hills round the bay. The water calmed, the only sound the waves drumming on the rocks. Still on the large stone at the water's edge, the old woman lifted her arm, and signalled her permission to leave the shore. The fair-haired woman followed the grizzled one, and the crowd flowed into the falling darkness.

Alasdair stood alone at the edge of the sand, sea salt stinging his lips and his damp *féileadh* chafing his neck. He thought about the woman whose hair had blazed with the setting sun behind her, her linen shift wrapped her round like waves in the wind.

Then he remembered he was among Campbells. He looked round, but all eyes were on the women. No sign of any hostility.

"An unusual thing has happened here tonight, sure enough." Ruari watched the backs of the retreating Campbells.

"Have you ever seen the sea waves twist and turn like that?" said Alasdair, not sure the spell had ended.

"I've never seen such portents in the sea, and I saw the evil winds that blew across Kinsale, and destroyed the great men of Tyrconnel and Tyrone."

"The golden woman?"

"Never seen her like."

Alasdair stared in the direction she had taken. "We'll follow them and ask for hospitality."

Ruari opened his mouth to say something, but he held his tongue.

The power in the sea would make any man hesitate to interfere, but Alasdair had come too far among his clan's traditional enemy to walk away now. He would find out where they held their assemblies and make his offer. He and Ruari joined the last of the crowd walking from the shore.

A half-grown woman had dazzled him. Campbell or not,

chief's daughter or not, he'd trade his cattle for another sight of her and his hope of heaven for words with her.

He huffed at his wild thoughts. He'd do nothing of the kind. Foolishness. Many MacDonalds depended on him. He'd make his request and leave.

Likely he'd never see her again after he left Gleann Muirn.

~

Knowing that the crowd watched her, Shona, daughter of Iain Glas, chief of Clan Campbell, walked with as much decorum as she could muster. Below the peat torches, people talked and laughed, but kept a few paces away from her and Morag the Wise. Of course, they respected Shona as the chief's daughter and Morag as the healer. But tonight there was something else in the way they kept their heads down and turned away if she looked at them.

When the old woman had asked her to assist, she'd felt like prancing round the hearth fire like a young child. But she replied gravely that she'd be honoured. Every part of the ritual had gone well. If the feast to honour Sionaidh were as perfect as the ritual, then Gleann Muirn would have good crops and prosperity for the whole of the year to come. But the banshee had cried the night before, and that meant someone would die. She had done what she could to prevent further bad luck. She would stay with the celebrants for the feast and then go back to the castle.

And face her stepmother.

Shona hadn't thought of her new stepmother for hours. A little dart of guilt shot through her, prodding her to return to keep the newcomer company. The Campbell gentry always attended the festivals, but her stepmother had told her to stay away from the "low folk of the farm toun" who attended the ceremony. Shona knew Priscilla was lonely in her new home, and thought the festival would brighten her mood. Yet she had no interest in joining Shona. She, however, would stay and enjoy the company of her people regardless of her stepmother's disapproval. Her stepmother didn't understand that many of them were distant relatives. They weren't low people at all. Their blood was as good as Shona's.

In a field above the shore, spits turned with venison and beef while broth simmered in cauldrons. Tables overflowed with dishes of hare, fresh salmon, and partridge while flagons of ale and whisky cooled in the stream nearby, ready for the festival crowd. The smells of the outdoor kitchen made her mouth water.

The figure of a man, standing as strong and tall as the stone called Fionn the Giant, caught Shona's eye, and she pulled the top of her *earasaid* over her head so that she could study him without his seeing her. Like most men present, he wore the *féileadh* of two loom-widths, belted at his waist; the lower half hung to his knees and displayed legs as strong as pillars. An ample brooch on his left shoulder held the top folds of cloth away from his right arm. Although he carried no claymore or targe, she knew he was a warrior.

He turned toward her, his black hair framing a golden face she remembered from the crowd at the shore. She followed him with her eyes until he disappeared past the churchyard.

"Fine figure of a man," said Morag.

"What man?" Now, that was a silly thing to say. Morag saw so much—no one got away with anything around her.

"Ha! You know."

"His clothing becomes him." Harmless words. She had said the same about many good-looking lads.

"Shapely calves and thick thighs." The old woman held her arm. "You be careful with that one. Aren't you meant for a fine Campbell gentleman?"

"I know. I'm to choose between Cailean or Ailean. Or perhaps Niall of Fearann Mòr. This man is a stranger of no interest to me." Because he was a stranger, she couldn't think seriously of his courting her. In these dangerous times, women had to be careful of the men with whom they were friendly. But she could dream … a bit.

Morag seemed to weigh her words. "You have so much to learn. And you may have another destiny."

Another destiny? Shona saw fear in the old woman's eyes. "What's wrong?"

Morag took her by her two hands. "I see trouble coming to this glen. Terrible tragedy."

Shona looked down. Her fingers were hidden by Morag's. "Is it the death to come? The banshee has cried, but perhaps for one person only. A person who is ready to leave the earth."

Morag's face told her that the old woman meant more than that. Those dark eyes flicked up and pleaded with her. "Many deaths."

Shona's heart had not space enough to beat. She loved her home, its lochs and high mountains, and wanted unhappiness banished from her glen.

"You may turn the tide as surely as the moon." Morag guided her away from the crowd nearby. "We'll speak later. We should join the others and help serve food. People fear me enough as it is. Will you go with me?"

"Of course."

As they walked toward the feast in the church grounds, the crowd allowed them to pass. The wise woman helped the sick, the lovelorn and the cursed, and they feared her—or at least her knowledge. The healing arts were dangerous, so they thought. They avoided contact with her and tonight with Shona as well, for the first time since childhood. Because she was with Morag? The old woman's words were so strange.

"What happened at the shore?"

"There was great power in the sea," said Morag.

"Sionaidh was pleased?" Perhaps, like storms, the Ancient One made a better display some years. A good omen.

"He recognised power—in one on the shore." Morag uttered her words slowly and carefully. "Yourself."

"Me?" She studied Morag, who didn't smile. Her face looked like it did when she had to tell someone about a death, her head tilted as if she were waiting for the right moment. For acceptance. "How do you know? Perhaps Sionaidh honoured the village itself. Perhaps he was reassuring all of us in the *baile* that one death was all that was necessary for him."

So it was the ritual caused the distance the between herself and the people of the *baile*. People thought she was favoured by Sionaidh.

She didn't want her people to be afraid of her. Uncomfortable with her new stepmother in the castle, she was now uneasy among her own people. "Not me. I know so little about healing. I could never learn—"

"Power. You have the power to make things move." Morag took her two hands once more. "I'm old. I'll have no more ability than I have now. Less."

"What on earth do you mean?" Surely Morag was

wrong. She looked strong and fit. Tomorrow she'd collect plants and visit the sick as always. Tomorrow Shona would do her duties and forget this. Tomorrow everything would be as it was. A week or a month later, she'd barely remember the events of this night.

"You have a decision to make."

"Please, answer my question. What power?"

Morag looked all ways and smiled and waved to those passing by. Some returned the greeting. "Too many ears. Later."

"You know I have little say in what I do. Not even my father determines what I do at present. My stepmother rules our house." Shona had some freedom to make a decision about her future, but eventually she must do as her family expected—to keep Clan Campbell strong.

"Not what I meant."

"The course of my life has been plotted by my father. I'm not unhappy about that. I will marry a Campbell gentleman and have children and a hospitable house." She forced herself to smile as if she were carefree. "I don't want to leave Gleann Muirn, but hopefully I won't be far away."

"No." Morag leaned closer. "You have little time to learn so much. I'll teach you everything I can."

"You've taught me much about herbs and healing and housewifery. I'll learn what I can. I'll help when I can." She had a quick mind and more strength than most girls her age, and she would put those abilities to work for her clan. People treated her differently, but only because she was a chief's daughter.

But then there had been the ritual at the sea ...

"Whatever you think I can do matters little. I must obey my family in the end."

Morag placed her hands on each side of Shona's head.

Images flashed through Shona's mind: the fountains in the water, her stepmother, and a dark-haired stranger. Loch Muirn shimmered and turned red. The castle, the sky all black. Evil portents. "What does it all mean?"

"Your father in Edinburgh won't protect people here from those who have come from the Lowlands." Morag lowered her arms and her breathing made Shona raise her head. "Listen, young one, you may be strong enough to fight and defeat it."

She had more confidence in Shona than she had in herself. "What will happen to Gleann Muirn? Tell me."

"As you did, I saw red blood and black death. I saw evil men. And this I know." The old woman looked at her gnarled hands. "I can't fight it—I'm too old."

"How can I deal with it? It's men's work. My father's warriors will fight and protect us." Shona drew in a deep breath.

"Warriors are needed, but also people like us. You and me."

"What could we possibly do? We are only women."

The fire flashed in Morag's eyes. "Women we are ... and much more!"

They spoke quietly, but intently. Morag looked about her. People averted their gazes and steered clear of them.

"You must learn the ways of the sisterhood."

"The sisterhood?"

Morag slowly turned her head each way. "Later." And that was all Morag would say about her future that night.

Shona heard a man shout, "Fight!"

CHAPTER 2

In the torchlight Shona saw the violent movement of grey and black shapes among the tartan *féilidhean*, and heard harsh breathing. Her heart clenched as an image of hot blood burst into her mind. *A violent death on Sionaidh's Day.*

No, surely not. Everyone must know about it, and everyone would prevent its happening.

Men scuffled with each other. A crowd had gathered and obscured her view.

Another woman struggled to see above the crowd. "Pushing and shoving, looks like." People turned in the direction of the disturbance. Shona saw her friend. "Una, over here."

Una hesitated and looked about. "A fight! On Sionaidh's Day! I can't believe it!"

"A bad omen for next year. We have to sort it." Shona needed someone with her. "Please, come with me."

Una pulled away and wrapped her arms around her chest. "We are women. How do we fight men? We can do nothing." She looked wildly about her.

"We can talk to them!" Shona took her friend by the hand.

"They're men! They're too big."

"Come on! We'll be safe enough." Maybe. Shona was breathing hard, and beginning to shake. But she had to do something, say something.

Una's eyes widened, her mouth gasped for air. She shook her head no. She wouldn't stop any wickedness on that day. Shona was on her own. Her heart flipped about in her breast like a fish in a basket.

Without looking back, Shona threaded through gaps in the crowd. The coarse wool of a man's *féileadh* scratched the skin of her face. She started and quickly lifted her hands to pluck at his sleeve, but he jumped back before she touched him. Yet she was slow getting through the crowd.

"Let me by! In the name of Iain Glas." When she invoked her father's name, the crowd shifted to let her pass, their faces looking fearful. No time to think of that.

"Please, go ahead, daughter of Iain Glas," said a man who backed himself into others to make room for her.

"Thank you, Niall Calum."

He was a *filidh*, a professional poet who made poems to praise the great men who led Clan Campbell. If he liked them. He would always do the right thing and expect the same.

Shona spilled out of the mass of people and faced a group of Campbell men who wrestled with strangers dressed in grey coats and baggy trousers. Foreigners—the likes of which she'd rarely seen before. Everything the strangers wore was tattered, the black rusty and the grey faded with sun. She had no idea how to stop them.

Farther away by the tables, the foreigners stuffed oatcakes and cheeses into their pouches, and others filled skin bags with ale from wooden casks. Shona avoided a Campbell who held one ragged man around the chest, and a second who threw his opponent over a stone dyke. Wheezing for air, men rolled on the ground and struggled to grip each other's throats. The crowd receded as the fighters rolled toward them.

"Stop it!" she yelled. "No bloodshed on Sionaidh's Day!" None of the fighters paid any heed.

The Campbell men tried to wrench staves from the hands of the intruders. One of her people held the wrist of an opponent armed with a club, when a second enemy hit his legs. He collapsed on the sand and they kicked him. Suddenly knives flashed in the hands of two strangers—but iron was forbidden at the festival and the Campbells weren't armed. Shionaidh, the Ancient One, hated iron, which is why he pitted blades with the salt from his sea.

"Anndru, Seoras! Go to the castle and bring men and weapons!" she shouted. The two men pushed through the crowd. "Donal, I can't be heard. Will you shout to them?"

One Lowlander sliced the air with his long knife, and a Campbell fell back over a fire and screamed at the flame's bite. Her belly tumbled with fear. Sacrilege. The Lowlanders didn't understand. She had to tell them.

Shona strode forward. Two older Campbell men caught her. "Be wise, Shona Iain Glas. They're wild with fighting. They won't listen to you." They blocked her passage. She was about to struggle out of their grip, but didn't. They were only trying to help.

"We must do something," she said.

One of the strangers was dressed in a rough leather coat over baggy breeches. He shouted orders at his fellows, and they did as he ordered. Must be their leader. His sword banged his side as he ploughed through a stack of freshly baked bannocks. One after the other he buttered them with his fingers, and stuffed them into his maw. The crumbs frosted his dirty linen shirt.

Shona shouted at the big man. “You!” Startled, he almost dropped his knife. He whirled about. “You dishonour the Ancient One! Tell your men to stop.”

He stared at her. She repeated her words in Inglishe.

He laughed. “We are puir and hungry men. A’ this lovely food.” He crunched a large bite from an apple with the few teeth that he possessed. “Aren't ye a pretty piece. Mmm.” The leader bent down to her, licked his lips and laughed again.

Shona recoiled from him. “If you had waited, we’d have shared what we have.”

The leader wiped his fingers on the breast of his greyed shirt. “Weel, it’s done and there’s no much ye can dae, a wee lass like ye. We need it a’.” He put his knife between her and the food in his left hand.

She had never been threatened with a blade in her life. Her chest froze and her breath stopped in her throat. Suddenly she realised what she had done. She was a woman against a ring of armed men. She felt dizzy. About to faint.

She refused to let herself swoon.

“Bad luck for us and for you.” When she needed a voice like a lion, she squeaked. The man shrugged and resumed eating enough to feed four men.

“Hey! Bring this lassie along wi’ us.” He kicked two men toward her. “Go get her.”

“I won’t go with you.” No one appeared from the castle. Most of the crowd had run out of the churchyard and hidden behind the wall. “You will regret this.” Her words rang hollow, without strength.

The two men approached her slowly. “Calm yerself,

dearie. We might treat ye kindly." They grinned widely.

She couldn't control these men. She knew it.

"Smells nice, does she no?" The strangers thrust their arms out to grab her.

Shona felt herself grow cold, then warm and a tingling crept up her spine. Her arms pulsed with weird power.

As they approached her, she lifted her arms, palms outward. "Stop there!" As if that would stop them. But the men fell backward as if struck by an invisible force. Shona didn't understand what had happened, but she intended to make good use of the time it took the two men to stand up. Desperate, she ran to the church wall. She'd have no time to jump it before they reached her.

When she was a few feet from the wall, she faced them. "Come no closer!" She raised her arms and pushed the air. Would it work a second time?

Suddenly the two men flew back ten feet. Dazed, they lifted their heads and looked round them.

No time to think. She glimpsed other strangers by the wall of the ruined church. One of them she remembered from the shore. They must belong to a branch of Clan Campbell unknown to her. Shona ran to them. "Please help us."

"Not our concern, Alasdair Dubh. Come away." An older man spoke to the tall one.

Alasdair. Not a common name among her people. Perhaps they weren't Campbells. These two could be in league with the strangers. She studied the younger one, and his eyes, beneath wide brows, bespoke kindness. *Please help me.*

The old man spoke over the younger man's shoulder. "We can't interfere."

"We'll help," said Alasdair. "If we leave now, we leave

with their curses. We stay."

"Too dangerous for us," said the other man. "You are blinded—" He put his back to her as he tried to persuade the younger man.

Ignore him. Please ignore him.

"Some fool may kill a man unless we intervene," said Alasdair. "And bring bad luck to this glen. And beyond."

"We may finish by fighting them all. Not good odds at all."

"Not for the first time, old warrior."

Enemies. But not Lowlanders. They were dressed in *féileadhean*, bonnets and good linen shirts, like her own people. "Any violent death on Sionaidh's Day is an ill omen for all of us who live by the sea. Yourselves as well. I beg you. Stop them." She couldn't read the tall stranger's face, but his nearness disturbed her. "In the name of my father, Iain Glas, I say no harm will come to you from any Campbell of Gleann Muirn from tomorrow till—"

"You'd best be careful what you promise." The tall man held up his hand. He said to his clansman, "Bring the others. Hurry!"

"Do you know them?" She indicated the intruders.

"I know the type of man with the sash and the endless capacity to fill his stomach—their headman." The leader's eating and laughter caused his belly to shake, and his dangling sporran to dance. "As a drover, I've met many strange men." A table overturned, catching his attention. "And heard many strange things about soldiers returning from the Wars of Flanders. They have no money and no food. They're used to taking what they need."

The strangers' leader threw the remains of a bannock to the ground, unsheathed an old dented sword, and held it up to the night sky. "Show some steel to these Campbell men!"

"Excuse me." The Lowlanders turned round, and Alasdair threw two of them over the wall of the church enclosure. He fought three men one after the other; he tapped their heads hard enough to put them out but not to bloody them. He seemed comfortable in the middle of the skirmish.

A true warrior. Hope grew in Shona's heart for a bloodless end to the fight.

A Campbell picked up a broken knife and glanced at her. When she shook her head and mouthed, *stad*, he threw the knife over the church wall away from the fighters. Alasdair prevented a Campbell being attacked from the rear.

Then a Lowlander plunged his knife into the neck of Niall Calum. The spurting blood sheeted over Shona. She screamed and fell to her knees. The blood pressed against her face and chest and heart like a drowning sea.

"Ruari, see to him!" shouted Alasdair. Then, suddenly close to her, he said, "Listen to me. You're all right." He wiped her face with his sleeve.

She gulped air. And tears came and she wept.

"Can you stand?"

She croaked, "I can."

Strong arms raised her slowly to her feet. She could barely see through a haze of blood and tears. Frantically she wiped her eyes. Was she safe? Grunting men surrounded her. "What's happening?"

Alasdair guided her away from the fighting. "We'll find out. My men are here to help."

New voices.

"We should leave before anyone blames us." She heard irritation in one of the new voices. "We should never have come here. I knew today was a bad day when I rose. I shall never prosper and get land."

"If I say fight, you fight!" said the old man. "If you're

pricked by one of those rusty blades, you'll die of lockjaw, and we'll all benefit from a period of calm."

Alasdair's voice sounded over her. "I'll lift you and take you to the old church."

"I'm fine." She felt ill. "The man who was stabbed. Niall. How is he?" She was so tired she wanted to lie down on the spot.

"You don't look well just now. But I'll find out. First I'll carry you to safety. Ready?"

She staggered and he caught her. "Blood spilt on Sionaidh's Day—blood of a poet who makes poems to praise the Ancient One. We will be cursed and doubly cursed."

He lifted her and then all went quiet and dark.

Alasdair lowered Shona to the grass by the enclosure wall, and the old woman from the shore joined them. "I am Morag, the wise woman of Baile Leacan."

"There's a man injured with a knife. A poet."

The old woman drew back, and closed her eyes. "The man has died. Be careful what you say. People are angry and wanting revenge." The luck of the place would change with the blood.

Morag had a small wooden bowl and dipped a cloth into it. She cleaned Shona's face gently as though she were a child. "Nothing more you can do here. Join your men."

He shouted at his clansmen, "To me!"

They filtered out of the crowd, two with arrows fitted to their bows, and others with swords. "No arrows," he said. "Sheath your claymores and batter their knees and heads!" He charged into the fray and struck the knees of a running man, then whirled to face more tattered men who dropped their weapons at the sight of him. "Chicken-hearted men!"

While his men swung their weapons at the ragged men, the Campbells picked up the discarded clubs and staves to help subdue the intruders with fight in them. Soon a score of ragged men sprawled on the sand with Campbells and MacDonalds standing over them.

"Bring the torches closer." Old men brought them, and women with children crept up behind the torchbearers. Alasdair conquered his battle lust—he had a job to finish. He bent over the leader and wrenched his sword from him. He waggled the old blade, then shattered it on a stone. "Steel, you said! Soft as cheese."

A tall Campbell man said, "So you wanted to drink ale from our casks. You would have had your fill if you had asked for hospitality. If we see you again, you'll be thrown into the sea for your drink."

The Lowlanders had no idea what the Campbells were saying, but they knew they were being insulted. They lay still and said nothing .

Another Campbell said, "You wanted bannocks and salmon without asking. You'll get stones from me."

"You were stuffing your bellies before the women finished. Shame!"

"Shame!"

While they berated the grey-coated strangers, the Campbells seemed to accept Alasdair's presence. He asked the Lowland leader, "Who are you? Why are you here? So many of you."

The leader stood up cautiously eyeing him all the while. "Yer the one wha' disna belong, aren't ye? Yer a stranger too. Who are ye?"

A number of Campbells looked at Alasdair and his men.

The tall Campbell said, "We are grateful for your help. Will you tell us who you are?"

"I am Alasdair Ailean MacDòmhnaill from—"

Gasps all round. "MacDonalds! MacDonalds among us."

At that moment Shona reappeared at the gate to the churchyard. The crowd immediately sensed her presence as they had before and they hushed. The top of her *earasaid* had fallen off her shoulders. Her *léine* was darkened with blood. Alasdair couldn't read her face in the growing darkness, but she was weary and ill. "We are very pleased to welcome the MacDonalds," she said, "and very grateful they have come among us. Alasdair Ailean, this is Cailean Liath, our blacksmith."

All the Campbells waited for the old blacksmith's response. The MacDonalds might yet battle the Campbells.

The smith's face worked while he thought. "We are fortunate indeed that you were here with us today."

Shona gave him a quiet smile. "Then let us be rid of these grey-coated devils and return to the feast."

Alasdair grasped the Lowland leader by the front of his shirt, which tore with the strain. He turned the man away from the shore and pushed him along. The man tripped and almost fell. The Campbells and MacDonalds pulled the other Lowlanders to their feet and herded them out of the churchyard.

The leader staggered away while smoothing down the tatters of his shirt. "A MacDonald such as yerself kens wha' dirty work is."

Alasdair ignored the reactions of those around him. "Just what do you know about us?"

"Yer traitors. Ye made a deal wi' the English."

Grumbling behind him told Alasdair he still was not completely accepted as a guest.

"The treaty with the English king? That was nearly two hundred years ago, when our chiefs were kings." *Mac an Donais!* The Lowlander might ruin his chances of a peaceful passage through Campbell lands. "You've not said what *you* are doing in Campbell country."

"Yer the ones shouldna be here. Nae Campbell wad trust ye wi' ony business." Alasdair took a step toward him and the Lowlander backed up.

"I suppose they'd trust you! The quality of your linen suggests that your trustworthy enterprises have not met with success." Alasdair flipped the shirt shreds. Campbells and MacDonalds snorted. "You can't clothe your own men. You can't feed them. What mischief are you up to?"

"No yer business, MacDonald!"

Shona stepped forward. "Enough. You'll get no hospitality in Gleann Muirn. You will leave."

Whatever she felt, she looked every inch a queen. Alasdair prevented himself from staring at her. *Look at her only when she speaks to you.* Otherwise people might notice his interest in this woman.

"We are puir men as ye see. Gi'e us a bite o' food, and we'll go and leave ye a blessing." His voice quavered.

"You've lost the right to any food," said Shona. "Your blessing would be hollow. Go."

The MacDonalds strapped on their sheathed swords and picked up their bows and quivers. Alasdair noticed the skirt of Shona's *earasaid* shaking. He willed her to stand, but readied himself to catch her.

"We are indebted to you for your help," she said to him. Behind her, the Lowland leader evaded his guards and approached her. He pranced about, puckering his lips and kissing the air. The shreds of his linen flapped in the air.

Standing tall, arms at her sides, Shona ordered the two

Campbells to take him away. She was still shaking, but her voice was steady. Not many women would stand up to armed men, however pitiful their weapons. Whatever the meaning of the sea ceremony, her fears were very human, and he found himself wanting to protect this Campbell woman. A novel idea for a MacDonald.

Another woman appeared. Dark-haired, slender and small.

Shona smiled and held out her arm. "This is Una Campbell, my good friend and cousin."

Alasdair bowed to her. Pretty enough, but a brown wren of a woman compared to Shona.

"You must return to the castle." Una pulled Shona's arm in the direction of home.

"I must, truly." To Alasdair she said, "Please stay and eat with our people. Cailean Liath will introduce you and your men."

"Thank you." He tried to speak formally as a guest. He followed her movements like a moth to flames. He had to stop or certainly he'd be burnt.

"You're welcome at Castle Muirn. You and your men will enjoy the best of what we have."

"Your stepmother will find you gone." Una looked toward the castle as if she expected her to appear. "Come!"

He wished Shona had no stepmother. He wished Una would find her own friend for the night, and leave Shona with him. *Dreamer*. He couldn't help it.

"I'm sorry. I must go. I wish you well," said Shona. "Campbells and MacDonalds at peace. A welcome change."

Ruari watched the two women walk up the road. "Won't last."

CHAPTER 3

Shona's room was chilly when she woke. She sat up, confused and unhappy in the darkness of her box-bed. Something had happened. Images of fire and blood had flitted through her dreams like seaware on a wind-blown shore. Perhaps she'd only dreamt of blood and Lowlanders in baggy breeches. *Don't be foolish.* Bloodshed there had been, and she would have to visit the injured that day. Morag had likely seen to their injuries while Shona was as faint as a delicate English lady.

Then she remembered what Morag had said.

When she washed the blood from Shona's face, Morag said she had something important to say. By herself, Shona had thrown the Lowlanders on their backs. She must never raise her hands in anger until she learned control, as the power in her was a deep well. So Morag said.

If she had this power, she should have wiped the blood from her eyes and carried on. Men must do the same in battle. But she could not. Perhaps her weakness had something to do with the Ancient One. She had no idea how to appease him, and neither did Morag.

At least the Lowlanders were gone, thanks to Alasdair MacDonald. She'd think about him and put away gruesome thoughts about blood. She'd think about that black-haired man until thoughts of him danced round her head. Silly fool she was. She hardly knew him. A MacDonald!

So strange to be at the mercy of her clan's traditional enemy. People said the MacDonalds were vengeful and they'd fight any Campbell for their lands. Pitiless they were. But that was not what she felt when Alasdair had carried her over to the church wall. Warm and safe she felt in his arms. She'd trusted him to protect her. She truly did. But that feeling might disappear when she saw him again in the hard light of day.

She closed her eyes, trying to drift off to sleep again behind the sturdy oak walls of her boxbed, putting off the moment when she had to get up. When she had to be a loyal daughter to her house and perform her duties.

That meant dealing with her stepmother. Her father's new wife spoke no Gaelic and was miserable in Gleann Muirn. Once she met a few people and learned a few words of the Highland language, she'd be fine. For her father's sake, Shona was determined to double her efforts to make her stepmother happy in her new home.

The doors creaked open in the adjoining bed, and she heard Catriona, her serving woman, laying a fire in the hearth. She opened Shona's doors. "Good morning, *a ghràidh.*"

As soon as the doors of her bedbox opened, obligation flooded in. For someone unmarried and childless, Shona was weighted with worries, but she tried to match Catriona's smile. Normally her sunny greeting would banish Shona's dark moods, but she had a headache from thinking about the events of the previous day.

"Let's stay abed for a while."

Catriona sat beside her. "I heard about Niall Calum's death. Now it's a feast for a funeral and not a festival. Such a sad time."

Shona was obligated to supervise the preparations for the funeral. Time to get to work.

"Your stepmother didn't ask for you while you were out. She must have gone to bed early and her two servants with her. It was quiet here last night. No weeping and wailing about her fate in the wild Highlands."

"Catriona!" Her serving woman was also her distant cousin and spoke frankly. She always did so.

"I don't know what she says, but it's clear she not happy to live among ourselves. Come on. Might as well dress and face the day."

Catriona gave her a clean *léine* and draped a plaid over her shoulders. "Keep yourself warm and I'll get the foreign clothes for you."

Catriona opened one of two chests in the room, a very grand one with carvings of leaves and tendrils all over it. Her mother's legacy, which her father said had come from Italy. "Come, *a ghràidh*, you don't have to spend forever with her. Right?" Her cousin nudged Shona into a better humour. "Wearing the Lowland clothing when you visit her will improve her mood."

"But not mine. Oh, bring it all here."

"Priscilla." Catriona tasted the name. "Peculiar name. Peculiar clothes." Her stepmother's maids had shown Catriona how to dress Shona in Lowland fashion. "All right. The bum roll, petticoat and kirtle. Then the bodice."

The worst part was the bodice, which stopped the breath in her chest. Catriona began to lace it, and Shona winced. "Not so tight."

"Sorry!" She untied the laces and redid them. "I can't see her wearing the *earasaid*. Can you?"

"Never! Nor can I see her walking out on the moor in this device for torture. With her gentle manners she'll not venture outside the castle keep anyway."

"Now the gown over top." Shona lifted her arms and Catriona slipped it on. "Wearing the gown is easier, rather like putting on a coat and hiding the evil bodice beneath."

"Just you wait. For all your efforts, Priscilla will remind you how barbaric we are."

"I should tell her I'd rather be wicked and comfortable in Castle Muirn."

Shona laughed, but there was no heart in it. "Let's get this over with." Before she left, she kissed Catriona's cheek. "I'll say a charm to keep myself safe."

"From the darts of her tongue."

~

As Shona descended the stone steps of the spiral stair to her stepmother's chamber, only the faint smell of the stables wafted through the lancet window. No odour of roasting and baking for the second feast day rose from the cookhouse outside. She quickly bypassed Priscilla's chamber and entered the hall. No one had laid fires. A dozen boys and old men stood about the hall awaiting orders. The *maor taighe*, the man in charge of the hall, came to her and bowed.

"We'll need the fires lit and trestle tables set up. The linens spread." She spoke as though there was nothing wrong except a late start.

"Your stepmother ... She has no *Gàidhlig*, but she has a

way of making her wishes well known." The *maor* did not meet her eyes.

"You need not worry. I'll speak with her. You're all right to see to things now?"

"Indeed, Shona Iain Glas. It'll take us no time at all." The men jumped to their tasks, happy to do what was necessary.

Shona would deal with the odd woman who was her stepmother later, and take the blame for her displeasure. Normally the Campbells of Gleann Muirn welcomed any strangers, and every other month Shona's father held a holiday feast sometimes lasting a week. There was plenty of food in the castle and the *baile*, enough to feed all the people who expected hospitality at the castle.

Trying not to trip on the long skirt and gown, she carefully descended the outside stair. A young cook came out of the kitchen building. As soon as he saw her, he ran back inside. Shortly all the cooks poured out and gathered round her.

"Listen, men. We must have the feast. We must honour the death of Niall Calum."

"We can't cook." The head cook folded his arms over his chest.

"Priscilla Fleschour won't permit it," said another cook.

"She came into the kitchen house?" The ways of her Lowland stepmother were not easy to comprehend.

"She pulled us away from the hearth and the pots," said a young assistant. "No doubt she wanted us to do nothing."

"Wouldn't let us light the fires." The cook twisted a cloth in his hands. "We did nothing to offend her." He whispered and looked up at the tower.

"She can't hear you with the windows shuttered, and she can't understand you anyway."

They agreed that was so.

"You did nothing wrong at all. She'll change her mind."

Not likely. Not without powerful persuasion. Shona was not good at persuasion, considering the disaster at the shore.

"What will your father say?"

"You told her it's expected?" said the head cook.

"I'll tell her again." The lack of hospitality would shame the Campbells. Did the gentry in Edinburgh not prepare feasts on holidays? "Light the kitchen fires!" She wished her father back soon. "The tables in the hall will soon be ready for you."

"Willingly!" The cooks and their helpers scattered to their tasks.

Now to beard the dragon in her den. With luck and a charm, Shona might survive unscathed.

When she returned to the hall, the tables and benches were set up, and young lads were spreading linen cloths and polishing silver cups and plates. A few smiled a greeting. Now for her stepmother. Whatever jigs her heart and stomach performed, Shona had to appear as serene as a minister. She climbed the spiral stair slowly and wished the castle were higher and the stairs more numerous. In the year or so after her mother died of fever, she'd taken comfort in touching the things she had handled: the table and chairs at the hearth, the thick brocade of the bed curtains, the rich tapestries on the walls. Now a new wife occupied that chamber: Priscilla Fleschour, a merchant's daughter from Edinburgh with two women to serve her. Shona had learned little more since she'd arrived, wet and unhappy, during a heavy rain.

Shona took a deep breath, pushed open the door and stepped up into the room. As though care in walking and opening doors might make Priscilla more pleasant. For her father's sake, she'd be polite and patient. She glanced at the canopied bed dominating the room where her mother had given birth to her. Many a day her family had gathered at the hearth in the evening to hear stories of adventures in strange lands and animals as wise or foolish as humankind. But the warm places of youth were no more. Her step-mother and her maids sat on a window bench opposite a hearth with a tiny fire. The room, cold as a snowy heath, was so gloomy Shona could hardly see the images of unicorns and trees on the tapestries.

"Ye're late. Come ye here," Priscilla said as her two women sat up straight on their stools. Learned men from Ireland had taught Shona the language of southern England, but she had difficulty understanding her step-mother's Inglishe. Her black mood was obvious.

Shona plunged into the matter at hand. "No one has prepared food for the feast. We feed many on the holidays." She regretted it the moment the words were out of her mouth. Too forward. Too bold by half.

"A great waste of food. Let strangers eat in inns when they travel." Without inviting her to sit, Priscilla sat, snatched up her embroidery and studied it. Her strong breathing filled the room.

"Madame, there are no inns here. No need for them when travellers may ask us for food and lodging." Shona had to explain to Priscilla that they were honour bound to offer hospitality. Otherwise people would think the Campbells poor or mean-spirited, and they'd not be offered hospitality away from home.

"No here, they cannae. Nae mair. Ye can go." She held her embroidery to the light. "A darker green for the smaller leaves, I think." Her serving woman put a hand in a wicker basket of yarns.

"I've ordered food prepared."

Her stepmother spoke slowly in a low, menacing voice. "Listen, ma lass. I rule here in yer faither's stead. No welcome dae I give tae thieves and thiggers. Yon beggars can eat cauld brose away frae this castle."

"Most of them belong to our clan. A few from elsewhere. We must show them hospitality and maintain the friendship between the branches of the Clan Campbell." It made no sense to offend people whose help the Campbells of Gleann Muirn might later need. This must be true in the Lowlands as well. Or else Priscilla's family was very different from others. Shona's neck was tense, and she began to shake. She had never faced such a woman before.

She took a deep breath and turned round in her Lowland dress. "I'm wearing yer gift of clothing, madame. I hope it pleases ye."

"Ye look less like a heathen, but ye still think like one."

Be patient. "Madame, generous hospitality is the custom here. It must be done."

Priscilla stood up and her women moments after. "Ye'll nae feed thae beggars! I'll tell yer faither that your behaviour's no seemly."

"Please come to the hall and meet your husband's kin."

"Take yerself aff!" Priscilla turned her back to her.

"You'll be welcome." She heard a quiver in her voice. What would she do if Priscilla came down and started to throw everyone out? She'd already frightened the cooks and the hall servants.

Better if she stayed in her chamber.

Shona quietly closed the door behind her. She wanted to walk down the stair, but she hung onto the doorlatch till her legs found their strength.

The clamour of people arriving in the hall below broke

her spell of weakness. She hurried down as fast as she could. She wanted to change into the *earasaid*, but she had guests to greet.

And perhaps that MacDonald among them. Alasdair.

In the hall, fires burned in the two hearths, making warm shadows in the room. On the high table meant for the chief and his intimates, serving lads placed the precious silver plates, drinking cups and candlesticks that proclaimed a noble house. Others carried platters of cheeses, bread and cold fowl up from the cookhouse to all the trestle tables. On the chief's table, farthest from the entrance, they had also placed strong drink. Only a few, including herself, would sit there that night. Through the crowd in the hall, children rippled like water-smoothed stones in a turbulent stream. One child caught the legs of a friendly woman who embraced her gently, and protected her against the current of people.

Would Shona's father, their chief, shield his people as his family had for generations? Or would the strange ways of the Lowlands come to Castle Muirn, and make the Castle of Delight a place of echoes?

Catriona led in the poet Calum Athairne, a treasure house of stories, enough to entertain the company for days. But he had come for his dead son Niall. Her serving woman had seated him with the harper in chairs by the wide hearth, and they were already sipping hot wine. They would join her at the high table. As they entered Shona welcomed her father's kin, friends and companions.

She signalled Catriona. "Come gossip with me. Talk to me about anything except my stepmother."

"Never mind her for now." Catriona patted her arm. "We kept the poet and the harper in the guardroom out of sight. I told them to stay there till we built a proper fire in the hall.

Your stepmother doesn't know that a poet displeased could rain curses upon the whole of Clan Campbell. You must tell her to behave better."

"I did, and she became angry and was in no humour to listen to anything I had to say. Besides, I doubt he'd curse us."

"Maybe just her." Catriona tittered.

"Be serious. No good cursing her. I think she *is* cursed, poor soul."

"You're right. But walling herself up in that room isn't wise. She's always angry."

"I'm sorely tempted to abandon her there. Maybe it'll be better when my father comes home. Until then I'll try to spend time with her."

Shona held her hands to the fire, which failed to warm them. Then she set to work welcoming guests.

"So the MacDonalds from the shore will be sharing the feast." Catriona studied her. "No doubt the big man with the black, black hair will be among them?"

Shona could feel her cheeks warming at the mention of Alasdair. "I believe so."

"You believe so? You truly hope so." Catriona's eyes widened. "Look at you blushing."

"It's the heat of the fire."

"The heat of the fire. Doubtful! That MacDonald would love to fling you over his horse and carry you off to the west."

CHAPTER 4

Castle Muirn stood out stark against the glassy surface of the sea loch. Not a breath of wind stirred the trees.

Alasdair and his kin passed by the iron yett, left open to admit people to the castle. As they came to the guardhouse, two Campbell men with Lochaber axes came out and stopped them. The thick blades of their long weapons tickled the low ceiling of the entrance.

"*Fàilte dhan a' Chaisteal Mhuirn*. Welcome to Castle Muirn. A great feast awaits you and your clan in the hall."

Not exactly friendly, but not too hostile either.

"*Mòran taing dhuibh*. Many thanks to you."

"We'll keep your claymores, dirks and axes here, if you please."

Not an unusual request, and Alasdair and his men complied. No one would risk a bad reputation by attacking men without proper weapons. Alasdair would have been concerned had they not been asked for them. But of course they kept their small knives for eating.

The largest building in the courtyard had to be the keep.

He and his men headed for the covered stairway hugging its wall. The hall would be at the top of the stair.

Alasdair studied the buildings in the courtyard. "These Campbell men have a grand castle here."

"We saw bigger and better in the Low Countries," said Ruari.

"Our house wasn't as grand. But in good years my father had a proper table with plenty of silver dishes and candlesticks."

"He did that."

"And a good-sized granary."

"Not much is in it now."

"See the stables and barracks?" Alasdair did not point to them. He was aware they could be still considered spies for their clan.

"I do. A dozen horses and a garrison of fifty maybe."

"When they're all here. And they're not, it seems." Alasdair counted three men in the guardhouse and two more stood at the top of the stairs. All older men. There was no light or movement in one of the barracks and, through the open shutters of a window in the other, he saw one light. The Campbells were well off but not well guarded.

"Likely the Lowlanders took advantage of the situation."

"It's unusual for Lowlanders to be so well informed about a Highland castle."

Alasdair led his men to the keep, where they climbed the outside stair.

"So what shall we say to an enemy clan?" asked Ruari. "The topics of conversation are limited." His men murmured their agreement.

"Praise the day and ask they how they are. Be polite," said Alasdair.

Gillesbic's brows and mouth turned down. "Beautiful day and will any of you slide a knife under my ribs?"

"The Campbells know that we saved them on the shore yesterday. No one will tear our hearts out today." Shona had asked them—him—to help her and he had been pleased to do so. Very pleased.

"Tomorrow they'll forget." As always, Gillesbic looked for trouble in every nook. "Your idea sounded better when we were safe at home."

I agree. But their own people had invested in them and they had to go through with the plan. "Keep your eyes on the finish. We make money, we feed our people, we collect cattle for droves next year. We might even be able to buy back our land one day."

"If we live that long," said Gillesbic.

On the threshold to the great room, the crowd quieted and faced the MacDonalds who had appeared at the shore to help them. Shona hoped they remembered that. Alasdair had four men with him, a suitable retinue for a gentleman. His hair hung almost to his shoulders in waves so black they shone blue in the candlelight. His *féileadh* did not hide the breadth of his shoulders nor his shirt the width of his arms. He was nearly two yards high, a figure of strength and menace.

All round him, people stared at the strangers till they passed by and shown to their places by the *maor taighe,* who knew rank and protocol.

They were members of Clan Donald, once rulers of half Scotland, their enemies to the west. Here in the hall at Castle Muirn.

Niall Calum was dead and a few in the room felt the MacDonalds might have something to do with it. Despite the help given them at the shore, the Campbells still thought they were the enemy.

Some gasped. Children hugged their mothers. People moved out of the way as they made their way toward Shona on the dais. Yet Alasdair did not scowl or show discomfort.

Her body warmed.

“The MacDonalds from the shore, no doubt.” Catriona looked at her for confirmation. “Oh, dear. I think their leader quite dangerous. To *you*.”

Shona’s cheeks were burning; she was sure they showed red. She could hide nothing from her cousin and servant. “Alasdair has come for hospitality and entertainment like everyone else.”

“Alasdair, is it? You know his name. And hospitality is all he’s come for?”

“Of course. Nothing to worry about.” He’d visit and he’d leave, except in her dreams, but she couldn’t look Catriona in the eye.

“What will we do with him? Where will the *maor* seat him?”

“He’s a gentleman by his clothes and a hero by his deeds: first seat at the low table close to the dais. Not the high table, but close enough to be honoured.”

The *maor* moved close to the dais.

“There won’t be trouble. They’re MacDonalds. Their ways are our ways. The rules of hospitality will keep them civil. Don’t worry.” She wondered how far the Lowlanders and their terrible leader had travelled. Likely not far. They knew there were few men of fighting age at the castle, and the invaders might return.

Despite a heart sounding like hoofbeats, louder and louder, Shona controlled the impulse to run over and welcome Alasdair and tell him how grateful she was for his help. She stepped off the dais and approached him with what she hoped was a dignified manner—she was having trouble with dignity in the big Lowland dress and sleeves. "Please be welcome. Come by the fire. Hasn't it been damp today?"

"I hardly noticed." A hint of a smile played at the corners of Alasdair's mouth. "But my men are glad to share your feast."

"A warm welcome to you and plenty good food for you ... and your men." Her heart still rumbled in her breast. He must think her silly. She needed a distraction. She said to the head servitor, "Bring the hot dishes." Then, "I am ... we are ... very grateful for your taking our part against the Lowlanders." She had no idea what to say next. *Sorry we took your land long ago?*

"Have you any idea why the Lowlanders were here?"

"None. Here we rarely see the men wearing the baggy breeches from one year to the next." He seemed interested in what she had to say. Maybe he didn't consider her silly. But maybe he was spying for his clan. No, she didn't believe that. His face was open and relaxed. Spies would be nervous, likely. They'd frown. They'd behave more like the thin MacDonald who was always complaining.

"Do you not?"

"Lowlanders came here because my father has married a woman from Edinburgh. They've gone, leaving my stepmother and her maids. My father and uncle have Lowland clothing for visits to the south. We're expecting a nephew of my stepmother's."

"You are obliged to wear Lowland clothing?"

"It's horribly uncomfortable. I'd rather wear the *earasaid*."

"You'd look beautiful in any dress—red tartan or the bleakest colours of the southrons."

"Thank you." That was kind, but he'd likely said it out of politeness. "I'm so glad you came. You and your men." What would he make of that? She opened her arms to the food. "Please, forgive me my chatter and eat." The MacDonalds smiled and started to share the food in front of them.

She hummed a light tune as she returned to the high table. As more people crowded into the hall, the *maor* showed them to benches at the tables. Shona went and greeted Calum Athairne, the *ollamh*, a master poet, and brought him to the high table on the dais. A sympathetic murmur followed the older man. They all knew he was here for his son, who had been killed at the shore. He sat in a tall oak chair with arms, the best in the castle.

"We are sorry for your trouble. There are at least ten people guarding his body day and night. He is washed and wrapped in a new *léine*."

"That is much appreciated."

"A bit more wine?" She signalled for the *maor* and organised drink and food after his journey from his house.

"Come sit by me a bit."

She would do everything she could to please him. He might yet curse her house for causing the loss of his favourite son.

Calum Athairne said in her ear, "Do you have information about my son's death? What might explain the presence of Lowlanders?"

"I have no idea, but I'll send a messenger to you if I learn anything."

"I hear there is unrest in the south. I wonder if it has to do with the fight here. I too will keep you informed."

The candles in the hall seemed dimmer and the laughter less heartfelt.

Shona wanted to talk about what was happening in the Lowlands, but that would be difficult with a castle full of guests. Every corner would be occupied. Even the garden on a cold night. She couldn't go outside the curtain wall, not at night. The guards would object.

"You've shown my son great courtesy and I am in your debt for it. We shall do what we can to protect the countries of our clans."

Shona looked about the hall. Everyone had calmed down. All was as it should be, with a man reciting a poem to the accompaniment of the harp. As she greeted people, she heard whispers about the MacDonalds. Not completely at ease, then.

"How do we know they won't murder us in our beds?"

"Maybe they helped us in daylight and they'll turn on us at night."

"How do we know they are not in league with the Lowland men at the sea?"

The MacDonalds had helped send off the Lowlanders, but now all the bad blood between the two clans flowed back into Campbell minds. "Hush! Be polite!" she whispered in several ears. They quieted, and soon the talking started again. Friendlier chat, she hoped.

And so it was. Conversation ebbed and flowed and laughter broke out now and again. Shona relaxed and returned to the dais for her meal, and conversation with the poet.

Several people faced the spiral stair. Their mouths gaped open. She heard someone say, "Will you look at that?"

"Have you ever seen the like?"

"It's the stepmother."

Shona whirled to observe Priscilla, who slowly entered the hall, followed by her two women. She bobbed along in a black and silver gown from the Lowlands: padded sleeves, a huge stomacher and a skirt puffed up as though she carried bladders of water under it. In her Lowland finery, she was twice as wide as Shona. A starched ruff as big as a millstone framed Priscilla's face, death's-head white. She held a large fan of strange white feathers, which shivered with her movements, a shield between herself and the others in the room.

Shona put a smile on her face and stood. "Our guests have arrived. All are gentry, madame. Quite suitable for our hospitality." Shona stood still, waiting for a response to the file of servants carrying platters heaped with food. She wouldn't tell her stepmother about the people being fed in the courtyard and outside the walls of the castle. All round them the company stared. "Please join me at the high table."

Priscilla didn't move. "A' these vittles—?"

"We must entertain our guests." Shona spoke Inglishe and widened her smile.

"How lang d'ye intend tae feed them?" Priscilla had a way of speaking in a quiet but threatening manner.

Shona hoped no one within earshot could understand her. "We feed them and they feed us when we travel." She prayed her stepmother would be wise and not argue in front of guests. "Three days."

"For naething." Priscilla looked at her maids, whose faces showed their disapproval. "I'll no eat, and I'll no speak tae barbarians."

"Surely you'll want fellowship and news," said Shona. "The old gentleman is Calum Athairne, a poet with fifteen years training in the schools of Ireland. He knows three hundred tales of—" The poet, seated at the other end of the high table, turned to them at the mention of his name. "And he speaks Inglishe."

"A teller of tales and lies!" said Priscilla.

The poet seemed not to understand her, and studied his goblet. Maybe he was too far away to hear.

"You're doubly welcome in our home," said Shona to the poet in Gaelic. He nodded and turned back to his kinsmen, who sat below him on the right side of the hall.

"When you learn Gaelic, you'll—"

"Never will I learn yer heathen tongue!"

Why did Priscilla think Gaelic a heathen language when the Gaels had become Christian over a thousand years before?

Priscilla shook her finger. "Ye've ordered the food cooked, but the remains will be chilled and kept for oor meals. An' ye'll no gainsay ma orders again!"

Anger tightened Shona's throat. If she were quiet and polite, her stepmother might calm down. She smoothed her face and curtseyed with her head down. "Madame, we must—"

"Never again, ye feckless bairn. D' ye hear me?"

As Priscilla's voice rose, Shona looked up. Priscilla's hands were curled into fists and she looked as though she might strike her stepdaughter. The breath left Shona's body. Priscilla could not strike her. She'd never be accepted in the glen. Shona had to stop her stepmother from making a fool of herself.

"Madame!" Shona spoke in her firmest voice.

Priscilla stopped and her meaty hand dropped to her side. Shona heard gasps all round.

"Madame, ye cannot strike a woman of noble blood. It is forbidden."

"Noble! Ye'r nae noble. Ye're jumped-up pretenders. All o' ye! I won't hit ye, but ye'll obey me the noo."

"As you wish, madame." Shona couldn't see Alasdair or any of the MacDonalds. Her jaw tightened. What a position Priscilla had put her in. Alasdair would have a great tale to take home to the MacDonalds of Duacha.

Shona drew deep breaths. She had never in her life seen or heard such a rude person. Yet Priscilla must think she was behaving in a civilised manner. Before that moment Shona had thought her stepmother an unsuitable wife for a Highland chief. Now she realised the woman was utterly ignorant of Highland ways and had no interest in learning anything about her new husband's clan. Why had she married Shona's father?

Her stepmother was livid and breathing hard.

She lifted her head. "Madame, will you require some time to collect your ... thoughts?"

"Now tell them to stop bringing vittles frae the cook house." Priscilla grabbed a heaping dish of salmon from a serving man. "Give me that, ye gowp!"

Her stepmother had gone mad.

She leaned toward Shona and said in a quiet, deadly way, "Tell them!"

Shona spoke to the servers. "My stepmother isn't well. Please continue to serve." Then she turned back to Priscilla and said the words she must say. "Madame, if you speak in such a way, I'll ask the guards to remove you."

Priscilla turned redder and slammed the dish on a table.

"Guards!" Shona called.

"Ye'll regret this. I'll mind it and yer faither will hear of yer wickedness."

Shona fought tears, but she'd not cry in front of Priscilla and their guests. "I can't believe that my father would be pleased to hear you speak thus." She held her shaking hands behind her back and lifted her head. All around she heard comments.

"The new wife is mad!"

"First time I saw her, I wondered about her."

"No wonder she stays walled up in her chamber."

"How does Shona do it?"

Shona did not dare look at the MacDonalds.

"She looks so calm."

Shona was rigid with anger.

Those farthest away began to chat again. They glanced furtively toward the high table and then talked to each other. They must be discussing the disgrace to the Campbells of Gleann Muirn.

Two guards advanced between the two rows of tables and stopped in front of Shona and Priscilla. The guards looked fierce, but they didn't touch Priscilla. In Gaelic they said, "What shall we do, Shona Iain Glas?"

Priscilla looked up at the guards and shrank inside her big dress and gown. She stood a while longer with her maids behind her. "Keep them aff me. I'll sit noo. Ye can serve the food, but dinnae think this is done, ma lass." No doubt about the threat in the last words.

Like a galley in full sail, she filled the space between the tables as she walked; then she stepped up on the dais and approached a sturdy chair. She smacked the cushion several times with her fan. To soften it? Then she sat and filled the chair. She grasped the arms and leaned forward and said to Shona, "Well, I'm stayin' tae eat. They can serve me. Tell them."

Shona bottled her tears and thanked Brìghde, her favourite saint, for calming her stepmother. To those close by she said, "We mustn't be upset. Bring more dishes."

Catriona stood behind her and made soothing noises.

To those about her Shona said, "We have an *ollamh* here. A poet of the highest order. We'd be honoured to hear his poems."

The reciter looked at Shona and nodded to the harper. The instrument supported his recitation of a poem for the lovers Deirdre and Naoise. The harper's fingers plucked and his palms hushed the strings in turn, and the poet's lament stirred some to tears. Finally Shona allowed herself to weep.

When she opened her eyes, Alasdair gazed straight into them. Her throat constricted.

"You enjoyed the music?" Shona asked her stepmother.

"I didnae. Who's yon black-haired man starin' at ye?"

Alasdair. The memory of their first meeting came to her. She didn't want to share anything about him, but she must. "That's the man who saved us at the shore."

"What dae ye mean?"

"The people of the village celebrate the fertility of the land and hope they'll get good crops in the year to come."

"A heathenish rite!"

"Strangers came and ate from the tables during the ceremony. They fought our men."

"Yer menfolk are wild and wicket."

Alasdair said, "Campbell men fought men in grey coats and breeches, madame."

Don't tell her more. Anything might annoy her. "We are pleased to offer our hospitality to the gentlemen of Clan Donald."

"MacDonald gentlemen!" She gave him no time to answer. "Ye have nae land. How can ye call yerself a gentleman?"

Alasdair stiffened and his men looked at him and then

each other. "What did she say?" asked Ruari. "Are we safe here?"

Alasdair said quietly, "We'll speak later. Don't say anything just now."

Shona said, "And this MacDonald rushed in like a lion —so Una said."

Priscilla lifted a fistful of meat to her mouth. "Then he's the only one who's worked for his feed."

Shona spoke in Inglishe. "Sir, this is Priscilla Fleschour, my stepmother. She will be pleased to speak with you, as there are so few here who speak her language."

"I am pleased to meet the chatelaine of this fair castle." Alasdair looked at Shona for guidance.

She nodded. The right approach. "It is difficult to leave one's own folk and travel such a great distance."

"I am Alexander MacDonald, madame," he said in Inglishe. "I'm a cattle drover here to do business with Iain Glas, chief of the Campbells of Gleann Muirn."

"Sir John Campbell tae ye. So ye speak Inglishe. What wickedness dae ye plan?"

A woman of no subtlety. Even if Alasdair were not the most handsome man she'd ever seen, Shona would defend his honour in the face of such rudeness.

He said to Priscilla, "We are not landless, madame. It's true that no MacDonald is Lord of the Isles today, and our chiefs pay rent to the overlords who rule Argyll and the Western Isles. Still, we live and farm the lands of our former lordship. And my father's *birlinn* still rows among the Western Isles."

"So ye thrive as ever? How many warriors dae ye have? How dae we ken we'll be safe in oor beds?"

Shona said in Gaelic, "Please, be not offended. She is a

stranger to the Highlands and doesn't understand our ways."

"We're not offended in the least."

Before she could answer, the Campbells near them spoke up.

"She's difficult."

"Hates living here."

"Always says the wrong thing."

Alasdair smiled. "Don't worry. I'll not jump to my feet and show her a naked blade Not even my little *sgian*."

They laughed. Shona ordered more wine, and soon the whole table was drinking and talking.

Alasdair stood and offered a toast. "The Campbells have given us hospitality. We offer any of them the same should they visit the MacDonalds of Duacha."

The Campbells would be safe among his clan, but Shona doubted he'd offer Priscilla's people the same hospitality.

Shona kept her eyes on Priscilla but noticed the crowd seated near them were wary and watchful. They had become used to the MacDonalds, who were not much different from themselves, but were likely uncomfortable in the Lowland woman's presence. She wasn't happy here and her marriage was not a success. Not unusual for an arranged marriage among the aristocracy. Or between the aristocracy and wealthy burgesses.

"Ye say ye're drovers. I thocht ye were more about lifting other folks' beasts."

Shona's eyes widened and she looked quickly at Alasdair. "Surely those days are long gone. These men are guests."

"Ye don't want tae bring vipers intae oor nest, young Joan."

Alasdair said, "I assure you, our intentions are good. We'll share your hospitality and move off with no Campbell the worse for dealing with us. And that's my oath."

"Deeds speak louder than words, laddie." Priscilla chewed her beef strongly. "Aye, see that ye keep yer word."

Shona looked away. Not a careful thinker, that woman. But she had spent time with the MacDonald. She could tolerate more slights from her stepmother.

Shona met his eyes and smiled. She saw his eyes—blue in the candle flame like the sky in summer at twilight. And he answered her smile with his own.

"Just what are ye thinkin', ma lass?"

Shona straightened and looked her stepmother in the eye. What should she say? What would keep a peaceful conversation going? "I am pleased to see you among our people, madame."

Priscilla studied her and her gaze was not friendly. She leaned toward Shona and said, "Ye watch yerself, Joan Campbell. I aim tae show ye I am mistress in this hoose, and I will bide nae meddling from ye!"

CHAPTER 5

In the days following Saint John's Day, Priscilla spoke sharply to everyone. If anyone who understood Inglishe took offense, they chose not to cause difficulties. Still, the honour of Clan Campbell was threatened. And because she was the daughter of the chief, people complained to Shona. Why did her stepmother stay in her chamber? Should she not be visiting and introducing herself? Why didn't she pay her respects to Niall Calum, who had been killed at the shore? What could Shona have done to provoke her stepmother? These were questions for which Shona had no answer. Normally she eagerly anticipated an evening of songs, harp music and laughter, but dreaded the thought of another feast with Priscilla.

For all her failings, Shona imposed a penance on herself —she embroidered in her stepmother's chamber. As though nothing had happened. As though Priscilla hadn't shouted at her or threatened her.

Shona's eyes streamed tears from a new fire's smoke as she attempted to focus on the framed linen. She made a better fire than her stepmother's maids, but Priscilla said the task was beneath the dignity of a gentlewoman. Priscilla, the burgess's daughter, taught Shona, the descendant of kings, how to be a gentlewoman.

Shona stretched and drew in a large breath. Priscilla sat straight as a mast, her skirts billowing around her.

"Ply yer needle," said Priscilla.

Shona pushed the iron needle through the linen. As though it were alive, it wiggled in her hand and stung her fingers. When she pulled the yarn, the needle made her hand spasm, and her stitches finished tight and tangled.

Until a suitable husband was found for her, Shona would do the right thing—respect her stepmother and live in harmony with her. She'd try. After her marriage, she'd leave Castle Muirn to her stepmother. Too bad Alasdair was a MacDonald. She smiled as she remembered speaking to him on Sionaidh's Day.

"Better ye learn to be a lady," said Priscilla. "Better stay with me than pass yer time with village lasses—and lads."

Shona lifted her head and stared into her stepmother's hard eyes.

"Aye. Best I guide ye. Ye wear heathen blankets like a' thae villagers. Only the lower orders wear them in Edinburgh." The maids bobbed their agreement, then dipped their needles in and out of the cloth with the practised rhythm of oarsmen. "Ye must dress in a civilised way. Yer uncle is bringing mare clothes for ye, and ye'll wear them. Ye'll no shame ony o' ma kin."

Shona did not look forward to that.

Silence as long as time filled the room. A few richly coloured tapestries hid the smooth stone of Castle Muirn. Priscilla had arrived with a little furniture and bed curtains. She spent most of her time embellishing cushions and bed covers for her chamber. She'd said she required Shona's help, but it was merely an excuse to keep Shona penned inside the tower house. The countryside could wash away in flood and storm and her stepmother wouldn't notice, immured in her chamber.

"Ye pass overmuch time with low people," said Priscilla. "Ye spend hours with that witchy woman. Ma Elspeth spies ye when she walks out. Ye'll no dae that ony mair." The servant looked at her with a tight smile.

"Morag's no witch." Shona had to find reasons to escape Priscilla's company for a little time. "I learn herbs and simples from her."

"Mind it's tae care for the folk of the man ye marry. Nae for witchery!" Priscilla snatched Shona's work from her. "Ye're a feckless one. Yer stitches are tight, and see how ye've worried the linen. Pull them oot and start again."

Shona heard shouting in the courtyard. "With your permission, madame?" Thank goodness for the interruption.

"Aye, go see what it is."

She pushed her rebellious needle through the canvas and it finally obeyed, then calmly she walked to the spiral stair. As soon as she closed the door she dashed down, and almost ran into a boy. "Artair!"

"I'm sorry, Shona Iain Glas."

"Why are you out of breath? Calm down."

"The *tànaiste* is back! The regent is here."

"Why is yon mannie shouting?" Priscilla said. "Ye've no idea how tae fashion good servants."

Shona held her finger to her lips to quiet Artair.

"Your father's brother has returned from Edinburgh," he whispered in Gaelic.

She returned to the chamber. "My uncle is here, madame." She couldn't keep the joy out of her voice.

Priscilla sat very straight and said nothing for a time. Shona knew better than to suggest preparations for their guest. She'd ask *his* permission to go to the village more often to see her friends and her embroidery could rot unfinished.

The heavy steps of booted men, their dirk sheaths clunking against the stone wall, echoed in the stair tower. Her uncle, followed by his two clansmen, strode in. They looked foreign in jackets, short capes and baggy breeches. They removed wide black hats and bowed in the Lowland fashion. Although the quality of their cloth was better, they looked like the Lowland thieves at Sionaidh's feast.

"*Fàilte is furan!* Welcome home, Myles," said Shona.

When her uncle and his retinue bowed before her, she felt such relief. Blood of her blood, he would help her deal with Priscilla. He indicated that the two other men should carry a chest to the middle of the room.

"Ye're welcome here, tae be sure." Priscilla embroidered while her black dress rustled like a raven's wings.

"The land looks prosperous, the people happy, always a good sign." Myles gave his hat, cape and gloves to one of Priscilla's maids.

Priscilla studied her embroidery.

"Do ye believe that, madame?" He widened his smile and showed his teeth.

"Dae I believe what?"

Her stepmother would ruin the homecoming with her bad mood.

"If the land is governed properly, there will be prosperity."

Shona wasn't sure Priscilla would take instruction from anyone. But whatever Priscilla did, he could leave her in her dark chamber and go home to Gleann Falach. *Lucky Myles.*

"Uncle, please be seated." Shona brought a chair and placed it by her stepmother. Her uncle sat and Shona was left standing.

"And these are your relations, madame?" The two maids smiled at him.

"Ach, no," Priscilla said. "They're ma maids."

"Then they will stand." The smiles faded.

Priscilla glared at him. He waited until she said, "Stand." They completed their stitches, and put the embroidery frames to one side.

"So what news?" he said while he patted a vacated chair to indicate that Shona should sit. He flashed a wide smile at Priscilla.

"Naething," she said. "It's a' goin' on in Edinburgh."

"You're better off here, madame," said Myles. "Difficult times in Edinburgh."

"As ye say, sir." Priscilla's response was addressed to the hearthfire.

"It's safer to wear Lowland gear in Edinburgh. And I knew it would please yourself if we wore it today."

"Aye."

"I understand there was some trouble here on the eve of Saint John's Feast."

"Some thieves stole ale and cakes," she said. "But wild MacDonalds appeared from nowhere and stopped them. So Joan told me."

"The MacDonalds saved our skins. With only one death —Niall Calum," said Shona. She added in Gaelic, "Bloodshed marred the day."

Her uncle looked at her, his face without expression. He said in Gaelic, "Blood spilt means more blood shed. What did Morag say?"

"Priscilla would prefer that I don't see her."

"While I'm alive, you may do as you please. You have more wisdom than all the young women of Baile Leacan. You won't shame us."

"Thank you, Uncle."

He struck his hands on his knees. "Damn all the plotters in Edinburgh. We're in it whether we want to be or not," he said in Gaelic.

"Ye must speak in Inglishe!" Priscilla faced Myles and Shona for the first time. "It's rude what ye do!"

"We'll speak together again later," Shona's uncle murmured, and squeezed her hand gently. "You are quite right, madame. We forget ourselves. Lovely girl, my niece, well educated. My fault for excluding you," he said.

"I have no set opinion o' that lass's worth."

"Good to be home in my own country." Myles strode to the window and looked down on the din in the courtyard.

"Nae ma country. I endure uncivilised folk, and wild country." She shuddered. "Ye could be murdered in an instant and laid in a bog with nobody the wiser."

Shona had heard that *Edinburgh* was the place for secret murders.

"We have gifts for you, madame. Come, Shona." Myles steered Shona to the chest and whispered in Gaelic, "A sour conniver like the rest of her family. Why your father married this Fleschour woman is beyond me. I fear he's involved in dark matters."

What was her father doing? Why spend time in Edinburgh?

From the carved chest, he drew out a small box. Inside lay a gold ribbon pendant with rose-cut diamonds. "For you, Priscilla."

Eyes wide, she lifted it as tenderly as a child. One of her

maids approached her and fastened the necklace about her neck.

Myles returned to the chest. "No trick to winning over your stepmother. Jewels and money will do," he whispered in Gaelic, but said loudly in Inglishe, "I have gifts for you all the way from Flanders—part of your dowry. Ready for marriage, my pretty one?"

"Aye, she is," said Priscilla. "Her faither's allowed her tae grow wild. Well, she's tae be trimmed the noo."

"She'll have a generous dowry, madame. A harp and a game board, many gowns and kirtles, jewellery, plenty linen, plaids, silver tableware, and two hundred cattle. She'll have her choice of many a man."

"She'll marry according to oor interest. Her faither's and mine."

Myles's voice was as hard as granite. "I am her guardian in my brother's absence."

Priscilla didn't move. Her hands had gone white with gripping her jewel box.

"But surely her happiness and our interest will be in harmony." Myles had slipped a velvet glove over his steel gauntlet.

Once again Shona was glad of his presence. She doubted that her choice of husband would ever agree with her stepmother's.

"So what news from ma loving husband?" Priscilla's fingers caressed the necklace.

"Occupied with the affairs of the great." To Shona Myles brought a gown of sky blue, which shone in the candlelight. "He had an audience with the Privy Council."

Shona fingered the rich fabric. "It's beautiful." The cloth was so fine, it had to be silk and linen.

"For your wedding—to the man of your choice." Then

he proclaimed, "And for visiting your father perhaps, I have more. Clothing for the Highlands and a suit of clothes grand enough for the king's court in Edinburgh: bodice, skirt, shoes and stockings and ... a few other things required by women. That should please you, madame."

"High time she dressed like a Christian and was married," said Priscilla. "Looking proper and behaving proper is the key to a good marriage."

However beautiful the cloth, she would hate wearing the boned bodice.

"Banish that frown, my dear. The new mode is fairly comfortable, so I'm told," said Myles. "And no glittering glass or counterfeit gems for my niece. The earrings and necklace are set with pearls and diamonds."

How many men would value Shona above the glittering jewels? Few. Surely her father would find her a good man, a Campbell gentleman.

Myles reached for another jewel box. "A double rope of pearls with a ruby and diamond pendant for you, madame."

"Let me see." Priscilla took the box and stroked the jewels like a lover. "God has rewarded yer faither in this world for his sanctity and good works."

Shona wondered about the people God rewarded with wealth.

"My brother has considered some suitors," said Myles.

"My own nephew will keep her from mischief. Times are changing. She must be settled before she's abducted for some man's vile purpose. She must marry according to our interests."

"She's safe here for now," said Myles.

"Nests of evil men abound in this country."

"Our families are united, madame, with the union of

yourself and my brother. Strong in Highlands and Lowlands."

"Not strong enough. I agreed to live in this barbaric country and she'll marry the man best suited to our purpose. Ma nephew."

"He may court her, but she may refuse him."

"So ye've a suitor tae see ye soon," said Priscilla. "A fine soldier back fra the Catholic Wars."

Shona gasped. This must be the bad luck brought on by the bloodshed on Sionaidh's Day. This nephew of Priscilla's. "I am ready to marry according to my family's wishes."

But not yours.

Something was afoot, Shona knew not what. From her window she could see the sea loch and the shore. Priscilla was moody, particularly after the banquet, but she had summoned Shona to attend her and embroider cushions. Shona hated the thought of being cooped up for hours. She didn't care that embroidery was the main pursuit of gentlewomen. For her stepmother, it only confirmed Shona's barbaric upbringing. Today Shona had a good excuse to avoid her.

The maid caught her in the spiral stair. "Yer stepmother's expecting ye."

"I'm off to the village. A woman has given birth and requires assistance. Please tell my stepmother I'll be back soon." She backed into the fieldstone wall, smoothed by the passage of many hands. The hard stone comforted her somehow.

Shona could only hope for a speedy marriage and babies for herself, because she had no idea what her position would be at Castle Muirn when her father returned. Priscilla might give him many sons and wield great power. Oh, for a quick marriage to a Campbell gentleman and then she could live a distance away without worrying about Priscilla.

People milled about the hall and the courtyard as she walked quietly among them. No one would miss her greatly. She waved to the guard at the gate and he waved back, smiling. In the gateway she gazed at the houses of the *baile*—she smelled the new thatch and kitchen fires. She made up her mind that, until she married, she would spend most of her time outside the castle.

Nearby pines and oaks still sheltered deer and wild goats. Her ancestors forbade the cutting of the grove, the sacred domain of the People of Peace. Neighbours worked in their gardens and dogs greeted her passage as they had all her life. Nothing had changed for them—only for herself.

Shona made her way down the familiar path to the house of Donnchadh Beag, where she found him repairing his wattle door. Inside, Sorcha, Una's mother, stirred a cauldron hung over the fire in the centre of the kitchen. Shona had spent many days with them. In this house she had learned to bake bannocks for festivals, churn milk into butter, and grind corn. Yet, the proper way to stream the milk from the velvety udder of a cow escaped her. The memory of the powerful scent of fresh milk brought a smile to her lips. The smell of the smoked mutton and beef hanging from the rooftree over the fire meant a winter with food aplenty.

Snuffling sounds came from one of the box-beds. Sorcha brought her to the daughter who lay with her new baby. Sorcha was life and breath to six children, her husband, and widowed mother. And to Shona, the waif from the castle.

Theirs was the *ceilidh* house for the gatherings, and on some winter evenings, people filled the space between the central hearth and the walls. Today mostly women welcomed her to the fire.

"You're welcome in this house as always. Eòghainn, give your stool to the daughter of Iain Glas." And when her young son didn't move fast enough, Sorcha prodded him between his shoulders. "Be polite now. On your feet."

"Is Una about?" Shona had come hundreds of times to this house—why this time was Sorcha treating her like a newcomer?

"Milking the goat—for the new baby. She can't drink Ros Anna's milk. Spits it up. Can't say what's wrong with her." Sorcha indicated the box-bed, one of two on each side of the central hearth. She turned to her son. "Eòghainn, go get Una." The boy ran out without comment.

Shona smiled in the direction of the new mother. Wool plaids, the smell of heather, filled the house. Ros Anna didn't respond.

"Will you look at the baby?" Sorcha rose to fetch it. She placed her hand on Ros Anna's cheek and she turned toward her mother. "You sleeping? It's Shona. She wants to see the child."

Ros Anna had the baby cradled in her left hand, but when she placed her other hand on the infant's belly, she cried out, "Where's her pin? I can't find the pin."

"Don't worry," said Sorcha. "The People of Peace won't put a changeling in her place during the day. We keep her pinned with iron at night."

To protect the baby from the *Sìthichean.* A good thing—unless the baby was one of them. Shona saw the pin in the firelight, and thought it must have come unfastened and fallen off the bed. “Here it is.” She picked it up, but dropped it again. It stung her fingers. *Iron*. Shaking the sting from her hand, she realised she was more sensitive to it than ever. When she was young, she used to get a rash from necklaces or bracelets of the base metal. She should have known.

She herself was one of the People of Peace.

“I have it. Be still, little one.” Sorcha picked it up and carefully fastened it on the front of the baby’s linen. She kissed her grandchild and held her out to Shona. “There you are. Safe as churches.”

Shona crooned to the little one, who hardly filled her arms in her swaddling clothes. She still had the red, wrinkled face of the newborn and huge silver-grey eyes.

Una came in with a pail of milk.

“See if Shona can help her to drink.” Sorcha put the milk in a cow’s horn, tied lambskin over the point to form a teat and handed it to her.

The baby drank a small amount and refused more. A hot stone burnt Shona at her waist. She searched, but there was nothing but the iron pin. She held the infant close, but the burning pained her. “The pin is digging into me. Can you remove it for a moment or two?”

“Of course.” Sorcha took the pin and rolled it in her hand. Shona crooned to the little one and offered her the horn of goat’s milk again. The baby drank the horn dry.

“Haven’t you got a way with children,” said Una. “May you have many of your own and live to a good age.”

Sorcha had a slight frown. Shona thought she should be pleased that the baby had drunk enough to live another day. The infant drank another cup of milk without difficulty. The little one had ancient blood herself, because she was healthier without the iron pin. Sorcha might know already.

Shona would make them gifts of carved wooden and bone dishes.

"You have the gift of healing like Morag," said Una. "The baby's quiet now. She whimpered so much. Nothing loud or annoying, but you could tell something wasn't right."

"She'd have sickened if you hadn't fed her," said Sorcha.

So many babies never lived long enough to be baptised. They all knew it and they didn't name the child or talk about its future for fear of bringing it bad luck.

"I wish you'd become Morag's apprentice," said Una. "Then you'd be here all the time to help us with our babies."

"I'd like that." Shona loved to spend time with them, and hear their stories and laughter, but she had no idea where she'd be next year. She would not be Morag's apprentice.

"You'll be too concerned with the affairs of the great to deal with the likes of us." Una had such worry in her eyes.

"I'll always think about you," said Shona. "When I marry, I'll come and visit and you can all show me your children and I'll show you mine, and we'll all grow fat on bannocks and butter." She laughed and they smiled. This small house was more a home to her than the castle. Many times she prayed that the sun might halt in the sky and the moon hide for eternity. Or at least a week or two so that she could be with people who loved her. Whatever Shona did, she'd protect this family.

"You'll always be welcome in this house." Sorcha threaded the iron pin through her apron.

For the baby's sake Shona hoped she'd not put it back on its linen. Sorcha seemed to realise that her grandchild might be a *sìtheach*. A Fairy.

"I may marry soon," said Shona.

"The way of the world for a woman," said Una.

"I do hope to stay nearby. But Morag sees changes." She

wouldn't spoil the visit by describing the visions. "*An dà shealladh*, the second sight, is a heavy burden."

Sorcha took her by the shoulder and led her to the best chair by the fire. "May I ask a question?"

"Anything."

"Was it Morag who made the sea dance? Or ... was it you?"

In the house, so warm and inviting in childhood, her words chilled the air between them. "It was high waves dashed on the rocks. The winds combined to roil the sea."

"Of course it wasn't Shona." Una held her mother's attention. "It wasn't Shona."

"Well, I've never seen the like. The *baile* has been gossiping about it ever since."

"Do you think Morag is a witch? She's not! Nor am I!" Shona stood.

"Sweet Michael and gentle Bridget preserve us all," said Sorcha.

"We have lived here by the castle for five generations," said her mother. "We hope to stay many—"

"Why wouldn't you?" asked Shona.

"You say we shall stay?"

"Of course. Why wouldn't you?"

"New lords with different ways," said Sorcha. "We hear from chapmen and musicians passing through. Change is coming. War maybe. Hunger."

"You're worried about my stepmother." Shona remembered seeing hungry children after the famine in Ceann Loch, not far away. Did they think that her stepmother was powerful enough to turn them out of their homes? It made no sense to get rid of farmers. "My stepmother doesn't have the right to make any decisions outside the castle. If my father is—incapacitated—then my uncle will rule, and then my nephew when he's old enough. Things will be as they've always been. Why so sad?"

"We saw a long-haired star come crashing through the sky," said Sorcha. "A terrible omen."

They seemed to know more than she about what was happening.

"And we saw a crow on the roof." Ros Anna leaned on her elbow and whispered to them. "Couldn't scare it off."

They heard the caws overhead. "She's back," said Sorcha. "The crow. Something terrible may happen to us. Can you prevent it?" She reached out, but then held her hands in the air between them.

"You will be here for many years if I have any say in it." Sorcha might suspect that Shona was a *sìtheach* too. The family was no longer comfortable with her. She stayed for a time and then, after making her farewells, she left the house of Donnchadh Beag and stood alone, cold in the midsummer sun.

Morag appeared beside her. "You can't escape it. You have a power you can't control. You must learn how to deal with it."

"No, I won't deal with such powers. I want to marry and have children. Make my clan strong."

"So did I. Once." Morag put her hand on the younger woman's shoulder. "You must learn—or your people will be lost. I'll leave you now."

Shona watched her leave. After a time, she knew not how long, she trudged to the castle at the eastern edge of the *baile*.

And remembered the fear in Sorcha's eyes.

CHAPTER 6

Shona couldn't sleep well for nightmares. She woke up weary from the hair of her head to the soles of her feet. Too many sensations for her to cope with. She heard tumbling stone and iron clanging together. Sweat and the copper smell of blood. Darkness and brightness, appearing and disappearing like cloudy moonlight. And more blood, so much blood. What plagued her most was that she didn't understand what she saw.

While Catriona slept in her box-bed, Shona rose and quickly dressed. She waved to the guards, who allowed her to go as they had many times, and walked slowly through the *baile*. She darted up to the outfields as fast as she could —as though she could leave all her difficulties back in the castle. Breathless, she stopped to recover her breath. All about her, nothing looked different. The grasses grew, heather and flowers bloomed, and the skylarks sang their epics. But her world had shattered.

The people of the village thought Morag might be a *ban-sìth,* a fairy woman. Or that her powers came from the fairies. And they suspected Shona herself might be a fairy as well.

A terrible fate.

Sorcha had asked so many questions, as though she suspected Shona had a seer's powers. That was part of being a *sìtheach*. The smells, the sounds, the tastes of her dreams all horrified her. The visions might be sights of a terrible future. She had to do something to protect her people, but there had to be another way to avert the unlucky destiny awaiting Castle Muirn. One that didn't require a fairy woman's powers.

Morag was already on the hill, her basket half full of herbs and flowers. "Welcome, child. Be calm. Rest here a while and tell me what troubles you."

The wise woman seemed to know already, but Shona told her of her visions.

"Violence and war, it seems. I can't see clearly myself. Not anymore."

"You are truly a *sìtheach*? You have the seer's power to see?"

"I am that and more—a *ban-sìth* who warns of death."

Shona stared at Morag. "A banshee! You warn of death in Gleann Muirn!"

"You too are a *sìtheach*. You have the blood of the People of Peace in your veins. You have the power to become a banshee." Morag waited for her understanding. "You know that already."

No! I'll have nothing to do with it. Shona stood. Morag approached her, arms spread as if to prevent her from escaping.

"Listen, I've seen you work the power. You dealt with the Lowland men at the shore at Sionaidh's feast. You pushed them back. You pushed away their weapons. You even kept

Sionaidh's salt water from you. You were dry when everyone else was wet." Morag spoke quickly. "You must be careful when you—"

"No. No. *No.*"

Morag held her arms. "Listen! Be careful when you raise your palms. When you're young, your power leaves your body through your palms."

Shona turned her head away. She refused to listen and pulled away from the wise woman. Crying all the while, she ran down the hillside toward Loch Muirn. She pushed bushes out of the way. She stumbled, fell and rose again. And forced her way through heather and bracken and gorse. Cows and sheep lifted their heads and began to scatter. Nothing stopped her. She came to the cliff's edge and threw herself on the ground.

She wanted to cry but could not. Breathing heavily, she lay in the heather and gave in to her unhappiness. Still no tears.

Bawling cattle brought her to her senses. As she stood up, cattle and sheep had stopped grazing and scattered. When she approached them, they ran off. Something had frightened them. She looked over the cliff and saw a cow, its limbs in spasm. *A recent death.* They were normally sure-footed. What had caused the cow to come so close to the edge and fall over? A family in the *baile* would suffer a great loss. The cow provided calves and milk and cheese to pay their rent. She hoped they had more than one cow.

"Shona! Wait." Morag caught up to her and looked over the cliff. "What do you think has happened?"

A cold hand clutched her heart. Had she had something to do with it? Had the banshee power pushed the cow over the edge? Had *she* brought ruin to a poor family in the *baile*? "I pushed the cow over the cliff?"

"You did."

"I'll compensate the family out of my dowry. I'll go to the assembly and confess."

She'd admit responsibility, but she had no idea whether she could hide the manner of the death. She had no control of a dangerous ability. She'd say nothing about that.

"Be careful what you say to the assembly."

"You'll teach me how to control the power, but I won't become a banshee. I won't."

She'd marry as her family expected, and be welcome among her people. Weddings, babies, and crops would dominate her conversation. She would hide her abilities and lead a normal life. She'd be happy.

Morag spoke gently. "Be sure of this. You cannot escape your *dàn*. Your destiny means you have little time to learn to control your power."

"How long must we sit here?" Priscilla and her maids sat on chairs on a good carpet at the foot of a hill. "I hate thae mountains. Nothing here but bare peaks and jagged cliffs jutting into the sky. Loud rivers crash aboot ma ears. I prefer my chamber under a strong roof."

Shona sat on a stool on one side of the carpet. Not a willing participant either. She preferred to sit with Una and her family. The dead cow would be dealt with today. She had admitted to her uncle that she was responsible.

"Wha's that?" Priscilla peered up at a large, flat rock looming over them at the edge of the field.

"A standing stone. It marks the ancient assembly place of the clan. The village is named for the stone. That's what Baile Leacan means."

But Priscilla had lost interest and stared at gillyflowers growing at the edge of her carpet.

Half a dozen servants set up trestle tables and as many chairs for gentlemen. The tables faced the crowd, who sat in groups on the grass or on rocks in a large hollow in the hill-side. From the slope side the listeners could easily hear the speakers at the bottom.

Myles approached them. "We'll be discussing some local business before we deal with the MacDonald who was at the ritual. A valiant man, it seems."

Myles thinks Alasdair valiant. "What does he want?" She savoured the thought of seeing him again.

"A business venture. I like the look of him—do you?"

Shona avoided his eyes. "It was I who asked him for help at the shore."

"Ah." Myles studied the crowd. "Priscilla, you remember Calum Athairne, the poet? He could interpret for you."

"Ma stepdaughter will dae it."

And that'd keep her pinned on the carpet. Shona would spend a miserable day while others enjoyed the assembly. Servants spread shady tables with damask cloths and laid out pewter plates of apples, pears, dried meats and cheeses. Kegs of ale and whisky waited in the oak grove by the stream. She had no appetite.

At booths nearby customers bargained for ribbons, yarns, cloth, spices and silverware. Village girls laughed with each other, walking among the booths while boys followed them and tried to get their attention. Shona wanted to join them, and search the crowd for the MacDonald. Alasdair.

At last a man came to stand at the foot of the hill and addressed the people above him. They listened quietly and nodded. Then a second man spoke and the crowd had no patience for him.

"What dae they say?" Priscilla pulled her embroidery out of a cloth bag.

"They're disputing an inheritance." She wished they would hurry because she wanted her own affair settled. At day's end she might escape Priscilla and find Alasdair and maybe talk with him.

"Yon MacDonald that was at the feast, what does he want? I ken aboot MacDonalds—bloodthirsty. Ye cannae trust them. We all sleep better in oor beds when they're away." Priscilla spoke as though she assumed those around her agreed with her.

A third man spoke, who was escorted to the assembly by two men. Shona said, "This man murdered his cousin over the ownership of five cows. Drank too much and lost his temper." Her shoulders ached with tension.

"Death tae him," said Priscilla. "He should be hanged."

"Those are members of the murderer's family," said Shona. "They say that he's a good man to his wife and his children. They are offering to pay compensation to the widow and her children." The crowd murmured approval.

"Yon man will get off wi' vile murder?" asked Priscilla. "Hielanders are wicket! Murderers go free. How lang must I listen tae this?"

As long as I. Near the tops of the mountains beyond the assembly hill, Shona could see snow, small spots of white although the longest day of summer had passed. Water crashed through the rocks in a wild descent down the surrounding mountains. She watched eagles floating high above them. *Free.*

"Shona, come now. Your turn to explain the death of the

cow," said Myles. "You've no reason to be nervous. These people are your clan, and they've known you all your life."

After arranging her *earasaid*, she stood and walked to the foot of the hollow. The crowd was quiet. She'd admit her guilt and there would be an end to it. "I frightened a cow and it ran over a cliff on Beinn Mhor. I'll pay compensation —a cow to replace the one lost."

"Whose cow was that?" asked someone.

"She belonged to Cailean Sheumais," said Shona. *No more questions. Get on with it.*

Cailean Sheumais asked, "You wander the hills. You must have often passed by that cow. How did you frighten a cow that knew you? Cows are slow to action."

"I don't know why she ran. I found her dead. That's all."

Someone else said, "Not a good omen. She should pay more for that."

"I offer a cow and her calf. And salt enough to preserve the dead cow."

Several people in the crowd thought the offer generous and their support heartened her.

"Remember the favour shown her by Sionaidh. If we anger the daughter of Iain Glas, we may bring bad luck on ourselves."

"Shionaidh's chosen." The words rippled through the crowd.

If they thought her a wise woman, she'd be feared. If they thought her a fairy of any kind, she'd be barely tolerated. She might be shunned. No friends to support her in disputes, no clan to shield her from enemies. Morag had no kin and never attended assemblies. No one knew her clan or whence she'd come.

Myles asked for quiet, and Cailean Sheumais agreed to

the extra compensation. They agreed the fine would come out of her dowry.

"A cow and her follower then, and salt," Myles said. "You're free to go."

Hoping that payment would stop comment, she quickly sat down. Many of the eyes that followed her showed no warmth. She quieted her ragged breathing.

After half a day, Shona saw Alasdair approach with his men. She sat up straight. He scanned the hillside, turned and saw her. He bowed. She acknowledged him with a modest nod.

"A man like him will flatter ye on tae yer back in the fields." Priscilla grabbed her shoulder and held it hard. "Or have ye lain with him already?"

If Shona said anything, it would make things worse for her.

Her stepmother's eyes narrowed as she studied Shona. "Ye have a good tocher of silver and cattle and ye'll not waste it. Ye'll wait for a man worthy of yer family and mine."

Her stepmother was persistent.

"I await my father's decision or my uncle's." Shona watched her friends flirting with young men.

"Ma nephew wad be the best match for ye."

Never. Not if he's anything like you. "I hope you enjoy his visit." Hiding her anger was a kind of victory over Priscilla. When the man arrived, she'd refuse him. She must ask Myles to find her a Campbell cousin to marry—soon. Then she'd be mistress of her own house. "I shall choose in good time."

"Ye silly whirlygig. Ma Thomas will be good for ye. Ye'll get fine gowns and live in a grand house. Ye'll see the great world."

Shona had no interest in a fine Lowland house or the

great world; she wanted to live close to her beloved Gleann Muirn among her own people. No one would change her mind about that.

Alasdair stood up in front of the crowd on the hillside—a pleasant sight indeed. She straightened to listen.

"Ye'll say his words in Inglishe, if ye don't mind."

Shona obliged. *If only he weren't a MacDonald.*

"They're an evil family," said Priscilla. "They conspired wi' thae Inglishe."

"A long time ago." Shona resented her stepmother's intrusion on her daydreams.

"Nae loyalty tae king and croun. What's he want in Campbell country? How dae ye ken he's no' a spy?"

~

Alasdair deliberately relaxed his stance and tried to appear unconcerned about the fact that he was a man in the midst of his enemies. Two or three groups in the crowd talked together, but others quickly silenced them so that all could hear. "We would like to bring our cattle through Campbell country. That would make our journey at least two weeks shorter and our cattle fatter for the markets in Falkirk."

"Why would we allow that?" asked Myles.

"You would have two pennies for every beast we bring through."

Murmurs of assent passed through the crowd. No work for any and a bit of profit for all.

Another said, "What if you bring an army of MacDonalds to Gleann Muirn?"

Both were questions Alasdair expected them to ask.

He could see that most of the Campbell men were away

from home and those here were old, sick or crippled men. He could indeed bring back MacDonalds and conquer Gleann Muirn. But he said nothing about that. He only pointed out his own weakness. "We will have only six drovers with myself and six herd boys. No danger from us. My word on it."

"He's chancy," said another Campbell.

"Perhaps," said Myles. "But if the MacDonalds have business with us, they'll have no interest in rebellion."

"Rebellion is in their nature."

Alasdair answered, "We have no great love for the Stewart kings, but we know that lawlessness will be dealt with swiftly."

Myles addressed his clansmen. "They want our business as much as we need theirs. They won't dishonour their word. The poet will write it all down on parchment."

"Where you find Campbells at war, look for MacDonalds on the other side," a man shouted at Myles, then stood and strode down the hill toward Alasdair. Three others followed. He stood his ground alone. His own men, who had been seated on the edge of the hollow, rose and started toward him. The Campbell men stared at the MacDonalds, each of whom had left his weapons outside the area of the assembly.

Myles held up his hands and the crowd quieted. He held up one hand to the MacDonalds and they bowed to show their respect.

"We have been two clans at war for nearly two centuries. We've both lost warriors and heroes. Now is the time for a truce." Myles indicated that Alasdair should speak.

Alasdair looked about him. "If you agree, we can take your beasts to market as well. Drovering is not a skill learnt in a day. My clan has been in the business for three generations, and we've driven thousands of cattle to market in the south."

A question from the crowd and others murmured in support of it.

"For the cattle I sell on your behalf in the Lowlands, I'll take ten per cent for my cost. I swear that as long as wind blows and water runs, I will honour the contract with you and MacDonalds of Duacha will not harm any Campbell after contracting with you. May I be buried far from my kin, if I break this oath." He rejoined his men while the people talked among themselves.

"Lies! Trickery!" A large Campbell man waved a thick staff at Alasdair.

Shona stepped off the carpet and headed for Alasdair. They'd had bloodshed on Sionaidh's Day. She'd brook no violence at the assembly site.

"Sit ye doon! Let the men handle it." Priscilla seized her by the arm and sat her down. "Thae MacDonalds should never hae come."

"If the MacDonald is hurt while sharing Campbell food and shelter, we'll be shamed and liable for compensation."

Myles addressed the man in the crowd. "Put down your staff! This is no place for threats. We talk here. Say what you must—without fists and clubs." He looked so strong and yet so calm. Gently he took the staff from his clansman's hands, and spoke to him. "No need to worry. I shall protect the people of this glen in my brother's absence." The man hung his head and sat down.

"We're at your back, Myles!" said one of the Campbells. Many other voices supported him.

Thanks be to Michael and Brìghde—Gleann Muirn was safe under Myles's stewardship.

To Alasdair, Myles said, "Please forgive this man's rash

action. He remembers the past too well and has less concern for the future."

"I'm pleased by your intervention."

"You'll join us at the *sreath*, the circle. We'll discuss things further." When Myles saw Alasdair's hesitation, he added, "You and your clansman will be welcome."

~

Priscilla shook her finger at Shona. "Ye see? I'm no' the only one who kens that MacDonald means no good. I don't like the idea of any dealings with that clan. They'll steal the beasts and plot against this family. And worse, he might abduct ye, who's meant to marry ma nephew. He'll rob us blind and kill us when he's done."

"Alasdair has sworn a powerful oath he won't," murmured Shona.

"How do ye know?" Her stepmother's voice rose.

"It puts his eternal soul in danger, madame." Shona saw eagles still flying above them.

Myles joined the group on Priscilla's carpet and with a curtsey, one of the maids gave up a stool for him. "Madame, the crowd shares your concern, but enough of us are willing to give Alasdair a chance."

"Ye and that fool of a husband that I have! Ye dinnae ken wha's happening." A few curious faces in the crowd turned toward her.

Shona closed her eyes.

"Ye let murderers go free for money!"

"That's the custom." Suddenly Shona wearied of teaching Priscilla the ways of the Gaels.

"Makes no sense tae me. They'll murder us in oor beds. Ye'll see."

CHAPTER 7

Alasdair and Ruari followed Myles to a stone bothy. A white hazel wand lay across the threshold to exclude those not of ancient blood. Myles waved at the two watchmen standing on the heather roof of the stone house. "The guards will keep out intruders so that we may speak privately."

Inside, Alasdair could hear talking and singing with bursts of laughter.

"The last hurdle to the cattle deal is the Campbell gentry. Gentlemen, step over the wand."

The reek of a small peat fire greeted them as they entered. Seated around it on a collection of low chairs and stools were the Campbell gentlemen, their faces reddened by their acquaintance with strong drink. Wooden cups passed from hand to hand. The smell of ale also hung in the air.

The conversation and laughter stopped.

"We've never broken the laws of hospitality." Myles sounded as pleasant as ever.

"We're still alive," said Ruari.

"Come in and have a dram."

Myles named nearly a dozen gentlemen of Clan Campbell. Most of them looked curiously at the MacDonalds. A few wouldn't meet their eyes and a couple glared. Alasdair and Ruari were safe enough, protected by the laws represented by the white wand, and as long as Myles was in charge, no one would dare harm them outside either. His honour and reputation were at stake.

The bothy was for men's business, so women were excluded. He wished Shona were allowed. He'd never tire of feasting his eyes on that magical creature: her wild hair in the wind, her red lips. Her way of walking with such light steps.

Fool! Remember your purpose.

"The gentlemen of Clan Campbell meet here," said Myles. "We can talk without my brother's wife present. She's, eh ... easily upset, as you saw."

"Concerned about the cattle deal, it seems." said Alasdair. She too was a stranger among the Campbells, and Alasdair felt sorry for her. A wee bit.

"Indeed. A business best left to ourselves," said Myles. "Sit down. Your clansman as well."

At the far side of the fire, an oaken table held cheeses, cold pheasant and oatcakes. Apples too. The fruit of a nobleman's garden. Alasdair's family cared for six apple trees that grew behind high walls. They had little land, but they carefully protected these trees from wind and animals.

"Make room for our guests." The Campbell gentlemen pulled their chairs closer together while servers brought new chairs to the *sreath*. When they were seated, a servant brought him a large wooden *cuach,* chased with engraved silver. It brimmed with warm whisky.

"Let's drink." He picked up the *cuach* by its two handles,

and gave a toast to Alasdair. "To the MacDonalds. Peace between our clans." The serving men glanced at the visitors more often than need be, and then cut cheeses and apples, and passed them round on trenchers. "Welcome to you." Myles held Alasdair's eyes and ignored the reactions of his clan. "I think she knows that she wasn't wise at the gathering," Myles went on.

A Campbell gentleman snorted. At least they seemed to agree on the topic of Priscilla. Most of the gentlemen listened intently to what the MacDonalds and Myles had to say.

"Now to business." A servant refilled the *cuach* from a keg and handed it to Alasdair.

"You saw our cattle," said Myles.

"Fine cattle, all of it," said Alasdair. "We'll bring about two hundred of ours."

"Your own?"

"No, about a hundred are ours and the rest belong to MacLeans, MacEacherns and MacIsaacs."

"Families related to Clan Donald," said one gentleman.

"Yes. They have trusted us for many years."

"How much experience have you?" asked a big red-haired man.

"I've been to the Lowlands five times with cattle, and no difficulty."

"You were head drover?" asked the red-haired man.

"No, my father was."

The red-haired man shook his head. "Not wise to go with this MacDonald. Too young."

"You have the Saxon speech?" said an older, fair-haired man.

"I do." Alasdair hoped that Ruari wouldn't be frowning behind him at the insults offered a member of Clan Donald.

"They've no love for Highlanders there," said the fair-haired one.

When everyone started to speak, Alasdair waited for quiet. "Lowlanders love our cattle and I have a certain affection for their coin. So even Campbells are uncertain of their welcome in the Lowlands?"

"Those who can speak the Saxon tongue deal with them. And dress as they do in breeches and jerkins."

Alasdair was surprised. He thought the Lowlanders hated his clan alone, and that the Campbells, great supporters of the king and his law, would be welcome among them.

"My brother said the market for cattle in Edinburgh is particularly good this year," said Myles. "Each gentleman will give you ten cows and share the liability."

"And the profit," said Alasdair.

"The loss of ten cows won't cause devastation and death in my *baile*," said one gentleman.

"I'm not sure I want to lose ten cows to a head drover with so little experience."

"And a MacDonald at that."

"I am Cailean Lachlainn," said another gentleman to Alasdair. "This is certainly a hopeful turn in affairs between our clans. I hope that your enterprise is successful."

The pair of scowlers muttered their disapproval.

"How many men in the *sreath* tonight?" Myles looked at his clansmen. "Ten. How many should there be around this fire? Many more." Myles's voice had an edge to it. "How do you suggest we get the cattle to market? We can't spare the men."

"We don't need to sell them. We'd eat better this winter."

"We need the money, Cailean. You know why. Many men who have gone to Edinburgh will want feeding."

"Do I understand that there will be more people than usual in Edinburgh?" Alasdair asked.

"Soldiers returning from the wars against the Catholic Empire," said Myles.

"Terrible thing," said Ruari. "We fought for the Empire."

"The other side," said Cailean.

"*Bi sàmhach*, quiet, Cailean," said Myles. "We have promised hospitality to the Clan Donald."

"They fight still on the continent?"

"There's a truce and men are returning home." Myles lifted the drinking cup. "*Slàinte*!"

"And thus the need for cattle to feed them and any cloth or hides we may carry to dress them," said Alasdair. "*Slàinte dhuibh uile*." Seal the bargain with a toast and a dram. The Campbell gentlemen weren't really challenging the decision of the assembly or Myles had already dealt with protests. Good enough.

Myles said to Alasdair, "I have another suggestion to entice you. I was thinking that we could lease some land to you—in Islay."

The red-haired man gasped. "Myles, think about what you offer these Clan Donald men."

The Campbells looked at each other. "You want to rent more land to them? Is that wise?"

Their attempts to be polite were wearing thin.

Land. Alasdair's father leased a small farm from the Campbells. Some years they were close to famine. More land meant surer harvests, well-fed women and children. Land was life itself.

"Islay?" The decision to deal with him wasn't unanimous, but Alasdair expected that. He wouldn't question why Myles would offer him land—or risk insulting the Campbell gentlemen.

Cailean leaned forward toward Alasdair. "Formerly the lands of Clan Donald, confiscated by the king and given to ourselves for our loyalty and good service." He folded his arms and sat back.

Like a blow to the stomach, the words opened a laceration still unhealed. The great shame of the MacDonalds who once held half of Scotland—now reduced to renting land from an enemy clan.

The air crackled with expectation. The Campbells watched him to see if his anger would cause a fight. If he'd reduce the house to dust.

He couldn't look at Cailean, who'd referred to the royal confiscation and the Campbells' enrichment. Probably testing him. *Control yourself.* If the king hadn't confiscated the MacDonald Lordship in favour of the Campbells, his father and Ruari would be great landholders. Alasdair took in a breath. They had nearly starved in the wars. Pride was a small thing beside great hunger.

He calmed himself.

Myles interrupted his thoughts. "I could persuade my cousin the earl to lease you land if you do us this service at a fair price." With a look, Myles quelled the comments of those round the fire.

Cailean rose. He started for the door.

"You'll stay where you are. What will our guests think?" Myles spoke in a gentle voice. but there was no doubt he expected obedience.

The man stood for a time. His strong breathing could be heard throughout the bothy. "We'll live to regret our acquaintance with these men. Mark my words." And he sat down.

The Campbell gentlemen concerned themselves with

the progress of the *cuach.* These were Myles's trusted men. Still, loyalty went only so far when land was involved.

"Very enticing," said Alasdair.

Dealing in cattle was the way out of poverty; cattle would return the poets and musicians to their tables, with silver plates piled high with venison and beef. He'd not risk offending the Campbells in any way.

"Not convinced? Other MacDonalds have leased land—" Myles stopped talking as raised voices sounded outside. A woman's voice. Priscilla. "Have her taken back to the castle," he called to those on guard outside. *"A Mhuire Mhàthair!* Mary Mother!"

Her voice abated as she was taken away back to the castle.

Priscilla. Myles's brother must have realised what she was like before he wed her. A political marriage. The Campbells had something else to deal with, and wanted no trouble from the MacDonalds. There might be a connection between the new wife and the offer of land.

Alasdair had no desire to go to war again, and the last thing they needed was eviction. He'd make sure his clansmen did nothing to offend the Campbells. He'd take the land and hold it for as long as he could. The Campbells would get no frantic messages from the west saying the MacDonalds had risen in rebellion again. Not while he drew breath. *Land.*

The *cuach* came round for the fourth time. As Alasdair stared into the deep bowl, he deemed the journey a success. Three hundred cows would bring profits, the first of many trips to Lowland markets. He had a chance to rent and perhaps even buy back land lost to Clan Donald. He took a deep draught of the whisky. Ruari would say he should be more careful, however friendly the Campbell gentlemen.

Alasdair threw caution to the wind. "One other piece of business. There's a golden ewe that would fetch a particularly good price."

Ruari choked on his whisky. Alasdair referred to Shona, but etiquette prevented him from saying so directly.

"Ah well, that one's not for sale. Not yet anyway," said Myles. "She's a valuable animal indeed and we'll not let her go easily."

"What price for her?" asked Alasdair.

"Beyond your means." Myles sat back in his chair.

"Perhaps in the future?" asked Alasdair. *That* was why he'd been invited to the bothy. Myles wanted to tell him that Shona was meant for someone else—a Lowlander with a strong tower and bags of silver.

"No," said Myles. "But I'm pleased to conduct business with you. My hand on it. See that the cattle arrive in good condition." The two men shook hands and Myles signalled a servant and told him to bring more whisky.

"On my honour." Alasdair took the *cuach* and drank a little, then passed it on. He thought of Shona and was determined to have enough wealth in this life to wed such a beautiful woman.

Myles whispered to him, "If you interfere with Shona, you'll never do business with us again."

"Understood."

"And it would be best if you left at dawn tomorrow. I'll say your farewells to my niece."

Alasdair hesitated. Myles's voice was reasonable, his eyes kind. He allowed Alasdair time to think.

So marriage to Shona was out of the question. He hardly knew her, but she was beautiful. *Unearthly*. Still, he had accomplished more than he'd hoped. His clan thought he'd have no chance to make a profit from the Campbells, but he had Myles's word on it. And he trusted the Campbell man. "Agreed."

But the sight of Shona dancing by the sea haunted his dreams. Then it was best he leave as soon as possible. If he saw her again, she might enchant him and he'd forget his business. She was promised to someone else and preparing her wedding.

The next morning he and his men left for the west to collect cattle for the last drive of the year. As he rode away, he looked back for a sight of Shona. Nothing did he see but green hills and Castle Muirn.

~

Shona went to Morag's for the noon meal next day. When they entered, Shona saw Morag and Myles sipping hot whiskies at the fire in the centre of the house. She didn't think that Myles had ever visited before, and certainly, Morag hadn't been inside the castle.

"Is all well?"

"All is well, very well," said her uncle. But the tone in his voice told her it wasn't completely well.

"The MacDonalds have a made a deal with us to take our cattle to market. We have worked out the details and they ... have left to gather together their cattle."

Shona stared at the rushes on Morag's floor.

"Alasdair MacDonald is likeable. But he is a MacDonald and you must marry amongst our clan or our allies. We must be practical."

She said nothing.

"Priscilla's nephew is coming soon to court, but you don't have to accept him. If he's not to your liking, he can return to his estates on the Borders. I understand he's one of the soldiers returning from the Catholic Wars, and he might be a bit rough. See what you think."

She didn't move. She felt nothing. An odd, unsettling cold had seeped into her heart. It surprised her. She liked chatting to Alasdair. That was all.

But apparently that wasn't quite all. She didn't think she'd cared for him that much.

"Please have a seat, Shona." Morag indicated a chair and gave her a hot whisky.

She sipped the drink. "I'm fine. Just fine." The honeyed whisky did help a bit.

"I must away now." As he left, Myles hesitated. "If only they were allies, what I had to say today would have been very different, believe me."

Shona might as well train for a banshee. She had no interest in the world.

In the days that followed, she came to Morag's house often. She knew she couldn't learn in a few months what Morag had gleaned from a lifetime, but the old woman encouraged her to learn till her head ached.

"I should have taught you the incantations when I showed you how to make herbal potions. Say it again."

Morag insisted she repeat the incantations until Shona could say them without hesitation. Almost every day for a month she had come to the little house at the edge of the village. "You must be able to say the incantations whether or not you are in fear of your life—indeed, they may save your life. Repeat."

Awed by the antiquity of Morag's learning, Shona recited dutifully.

Craobh nan ubhal, ubhal airgid,
Chraobh nan ubhal, gu robh Dia leam,

Gu robh Ghealach, gu robh Ghrian leam.
Gu robh Gaoth an Ear 's an Iar leam,
air sgàth maitheis.

Tree of apples, silver apples,
Tree of apples, God protect me,
Moon and sun be with me,
May the East and West Wind be with me,
For goodness sake.

"What do the apples mean?"

"Our power comes from *Abhalainn*, the Land of Apples," said Morag. "Others believe that the fruit is good for eating. We know it has other purposes. These words will help you find your way when you're lost. After you say the words, throw the apple in front of you, and it will show you the way."

The apples had healing and calming powers, and even prevented the loss of teeth. Though that last was a bit hard to believe.

Shona had to respect Morag, but she couldn't think how or why she would use them. Still, she learned the incantations as best she could, though she knew Campbell country well. She'd never need the apple charms.

She busied herself during the day and thought of Alasdair at night.

~

Today she would visit the sick of the *baile* with Morag.

"I'm glad to see you. Did your stepmother miss you?" Morag hugged her apprentice.

"I had no difficulty with that. Catriona helps me and

makes excuses for me. Or pretends she doesn't understand."

"You've done well," said Morag. "Today you meet your first client. Come. We've healing to do. This way." Morag guided Shona to a substantial house of five rooms in the centre of the village. She strode in and greeted those inside —a woman and several wide-eyed children. A red-faced man lay wheezing on a box-bed. "Try the incantation for healing. He has something stuck in his throat."

Shona said the incantation and lifted her hands. The man's breath was ragged as though he were breathing his last. She had no effect whatsoever. She shut her eyes and strained until her sight blurred.

"Gently!" said Morag.

"What am I supposed to do?"

"Keep your eyes open. It is most difficult to use a small amount of power, and easy to overuse." Morag placed her fingertips close to the man's throat and pushed the air a tiny bit. A piece of meat popped out. Immediately the man sucked in vast quantities of air and his colour went from red to normal.

The woman of the house circled around Morag *deiseil*, sunwise, three times to show respect. "Thank you, Wise One."

One of the children said, "What happened, Mammy?" His mother hushed him and produced a live chicken in payment of the service. Neither wife nor husband nor children said anything more when Shona followed Morag out of the house.

"You've made progress learning the incantations," said Morag. "You've learned many, but you must learn three hundred, and how to mix the herbs to go with them. You have to know what causes illness, natural or supernatural, to cure it. The most useful power we have is pushing."

"You pushed that little bit of meat out of that man's throat? I couldn't do that."

"Oh, you will, *a ghràidh*. You'll learn. You *must*."

CHAPTER 8

Head down, deep in thought, Shona wandered on the path near the sea with Una. The quiet beach provided a refuge from her stepmother, who insisted every day that she listen to the advice of a mature woman. Shona didn't care if the suitor was a champion from the king or an angel from God. If Priscilla recommended him, Shona wouldn't marry him.

Myles had told her he'd sent Alasdair away to round up his cattle. She didn't know if Alasdair had tried to see her before he left. She hoped so.

She couldn't ask or appear interested in a member of an enemy clan. But an empty husk was all that was left of her heart. She hardly knew him, but there was something in him that was strong and kind. No one knew she imagined a life with him. She savoured those dreams. Tasted them each night when she was alone in her box-bed.

In the meantime she trained with Morag, not just in herbs and healing, but in how to use her powers.

At the sound of an oar song, Shona scanned the waters

of Loch Muirn, where the Campbell *birlinn* hove into view. Two of the crew lowered the square sail of the galley while the men of Clan Campbell rowed the vessel steadily toward Castle Muirn at the end of the sea loch. Despite the wind or their exertions, the rowers sang at their oars. The vessel shot forward with every stroke, past trees and bare crags, to the sandy shore at the sea loch's end. A dozen people sauntered on the beach waiting for their kinsmen in the galley, who brought news and exotic wares from the south.

Her father might be on board! She pointed out the *birlinn* to Una and shouted, "Come on!"

Her companion trailed behind as Shona bounded through small bushes and bracken to the shore. How much better it would be with both father and uncle at home. She picked her way across the rocks on the western edge of the shore while Una panted behind her.

Shona recognised the voice that shouted over the water —Ailean Lachlainn, a trusted messenger from her father. She heard another man speaking Inglishe, one she didn't know. Excitement filled her like water in a pitcher. She wanted the galley at anchor and her father in sight of her two eyes. Everything would be back as it had been before he left. Fear about what was going on in Edinburgh worried her during the day and gave her nightmares in sleep. Now all that was at an end.

"I've never been sae wet. My skin is raw with sea spray." A weary voice.

"Shut yer gob. Ye'll soon put yer feet on dry land." A hard reply.

"Wait!" Una rushed to catch up. "Why are you so keen to run? We can walk and be there in plenty of time to meet the *birlinn*."

Despite the turbulent water, the galley's crew moved swiftly to perform their chores, never once stumbling over their passengers or cargo. On the heaving deck, a tall, thin man dressed in a buff leather coat and red sash caught Shona's eye. He didn't smile, but stood on the shifting deck with a shorter man in black while half a dozen men in grey coats slumped over the gunwales. Their spew trailed down the side of the ship and disappeared when the prow crashed through the next wave. She'd soon find out who they were. Nothing remained secret in *baile* or castle.

When they were scant yards from shore, the rowers back-oared. A sailor picked up the anchor stone in its wooden cage and threw it into the water, the rope tied to it following after into the sea. Although the galley's draft was shallow, it would be too easily beached if they drew closer to land.

Men jumping overboard gasped as the cold water reached their waists, while others slung large wicker baskets to those already in the sea. The sun glinted off glass bottles of wine as men carried baskets and chests to shore—every time her father returned, he brought more luxuries than a troop of chapmen. The steersman climbed onto the back of one of the sailors. Most of the crew waded to shore, shouting to their wives and children, who slipped out of the crowd to hug and kiss them. The younger ones splashed in the surf in wet tangles of cloth and skin.

Shona searched the rail for her father. Perhaps he was ill. She ran to a sailor. "Where is your chief?"

The rower bowed to her. "He's not with us, daughter of Iain Glas, but he's sent many gifts."

She tried to remember the last time the *birlinn* had brought her father home, and her young brothers had romped on the sand. Since the deaths of her mother and brothers a year ago, she couldn't remember a time of joy.

"Your father's still away." Una put her arm around Shona. "Come stay with us a while."

Not even the promise of a good meal and kindly company could raise Shona's spirits. Her happiness counted for nothing in the great world, but she had her duty. She had to give hospitality to guests at Castle Muirn.

On the heaving deck, the gangling Lowlander folded in half to grip the rail. The rowers noticed his difficulty, but no one laughed.

"Not used to ships, I think." Shona heard no laughing or jokes despite his awkwardness. Had he been a Highlander, they would have teased him and given him a nickname on the first day of his journey.

Three burly oarsmen, dressed only in long shirts and belts, jumped into the water and helped him climb onto the back of one man. The Lowlander folded and unfolded his arms and legs like a heron. On dry land he staggered while the rower steadied him. He had to be aware of how silly he looked.

"Not so fast, ye great Hieland hallion. Gi'e 's the poke." The Lowlander wrenched his bag from another man who had carried it to land.

Suddenly the rower tumbled into the water. He rose up like a dolphin, ready to fight, but others held his arms. He hurled a curse after the stranger. "*Mo mhallachd ort!*"

Had the oarsman been pushed? Surely not. Shona warned the dripping oarsman, "He's a guest in this country, whatever he does." Still, it was a bad start for the newcomers.

The Lowlander snatched his hat from the hands of yet

another rower. Still wet with sea water, he looked around at the crowd of people as if surprised to see them. “Awa’ with ye!” he shouted at them in Inglishe, and waved his his arms at them. They trickled away like an ebb tide soon to flow back.

“They have as much right to be here as yourself,” said Shona. Bad-tempered and no Gaelic in his head. He wouldn’t get along here.

A man wearing a sash about his waist jumped into the waves and started wading to shore. “Come on, the rest o’ ye. Get off the ship.” A quiet but commanding voice. When he reached land, he walked to the man who had pushed his bearer into the sea. “Remember where ye are and behave, ye gowp. Stay for my baggage.”

“Since you’re wet, Rutherford, ye can see tae our miserable men. Make sure they mind their manners!” shouted another tall Lowlander from the *birlinn.*

“Aye, I’ll make them behave.” He began to shout to his men to gather their possessions and stay together on the beach. A large wave caught him and doused him.

“Ye’r a wee bit wet noo, but never mind, ye’ll be your handsome self in no time.” A wide smile lifted his moustache. “See tae the baggage,” he shouted to one of his grey-coated men.

“What are you waiting for?” asked the Lowlander on board. “You want a ride on the back of one of these heathens? Or will ye wade? Move!” The rest of the baggy-breeched men slithered into the water. As the galley bucked and plunged in a fresh wind, the last Lowlander aboard tightened the buckles on his sword. The rowers pointed out a crewman, almost waist deep in seawater, prepared to carry him to land.

“No, thank ye. Stand ma horse—noo!”

The crewman looked at each other without understanding.

Shona could easily hear his voice from shore. "He wants you to allow his horse to stand," she said.

Finally a crewman loosened the ropes that held the horse's head down and allowed the chestnut stallion to rise. Except for shaking his head, the horse moved little on deck while waiting for the crew to disembark him.

The Lowlander shooed the crew away from his horse, then he mounted. The horse was calm. A warhorse.

"Tip the boat."

Shona watched with the crowd. Without understanding his words, they knew what to do. They weren't new at disembarking cattle or horses. But they hadn't seen a mounted man leave the galley. Anything might happen. She could do nothing but watch.

A half dozen men held the galley down on one side so that it listed with the gunwale just above the water. The horse leapt clear and high-stepped his way to shore while his rider held the reins with one hand and placed the other on his hip. His boots were hardly wet when he reached the sand. The crowd shouted their approval at the unexpected entertainment.

The crowd stepped back, then guided Shona to the front.

"You're the one to greet him."

"Your duty, daughter of Iain Glas."

The Lowlander shouted, "Up, Ganymede!" The horse reared, his hooves slicing the air a few feet from her face. The salt spray flying from his legs and flanks spotted the front of her *earasaid* before she had time to step away. She tripped over a foot, but the crowd buoyed her up. His rider removed his plumed hat and waved it in the air while his horse capered and carved deep crescent moons in the sand. Did the fool on horseback not see her? He ensured that every one of his men was drenched at the shore while he pranced around on his horse. *Rogue.*

"Good morning, good people. I am Sir Thomas Connington!" He gave them all a toothy grin and reined the horse backward. "Gentle lady, my pleasure tae see ye." Connington dismounted and tossed the reins to one of his men. "Rutherford, a young and beautiful lass for our eyes to feast upon."

Towering over her and smelling of sea salt and sweat, he thrust his long face straight toward her. A large brown moustache covered his upper lip and muffled his words. Each tip waggled as he spoke.

A great heaviness shrouded her. Her heart fluttered. She tried to breathe deeply, and backed away from him.

"She speaks Inglishe," said Rutherford.

"I am Joan Campbell, the daughter of Sir John Campbell of Gleann Muirn," she managed.

"She's civilised." Connington ogled her. "My pleasure, fair lady. Thomas Connington, nephew of Priscilla Fleschour, wife to Sir John Campbell of Gleann Muirn."

Fear flickered in her belly. So this was Priscilla's nephew —the suitor of suitors. *Pull yourself together.* She curtseyed. "You are a guest of my father, a chief of Clan Campbell."

"I'm known to ye, then." He held his sword hilt with his left hand, removed his broad felt hat with his right, and bowed. A practised manoeuvre. "My lady, it's ma pleasure tae see such beauty bloom in a barren land."

Barren land? His visit would not be pleasant. "My step-mother has mentioned you."

"She is a precious lady tae me, ma aunt." His horse

pranced about, but he controlled the stallion easily as he mounted it once again.

Shona doubted anyone could value Priscilla. He was a flatterer.

"My men require food and a warm fire. They may look like inferior clay, but they have their uses—especially my comrade in arms, Matthew Rutherford." He indicated the other man wearing a sash.

"This way to the great hall." She led the way. "Your aunt awaits you."

"Let's not keep that anxious branch of a mighty tree waiting," said Connington. "Ye'r a queen of a woman. And comely." He kneed the horse so that it stepped toward her.

She turned quickly and obliged him to follow her to the keep. She was glad Una was with her. Two women might be safe from him.

He laughed. "You've put a smokin', burnin' coal in ma heart, lass." Then he shouted, "Come on, ma lads. Follow, follow!" He pretended to dry off one man's face with his sleeve. The man wriggled out of his grasp. "Ye'll dry off soon enough."

Una was laughing at the antics. Could she not see the cruelty in Connington's treatment of his men? Perhaps Shona was making too much of it.

Connington looked handsome on his stallion. Her body tensed as if she readied for a race. She shouldn't fear him after an acquaintance of only a few minutes, but she felt the darkness inside him. Her head told her, *don't be silly,* but her gut said, *beware*.

Connington pulled his man to him. "Please greet Rutherford, my trusting and trustworthy lieutenant. The Lady Joan."

Rutherford removed his dripping hat and attempted to bow.

Connington, his eyes like a wild cat's, drew out his words. "Dear lady, we hunger ... for food. Will ye help us? We're at your mercy."

"Stay with me," she said to Una.

"My pleasure. He's so gallant ... and comical!" Obviously Una felt nothing. No warning.

Shona would have given anything to avoid her obligation to welcome Priscilla's nephew. "Please, come this way."

She led him and his men to the castle, and showed them the stable, where a serving man took the reins of the chestnut stallion. She didn't like Connington—especially the thought of his following her up the stair to the keep. She climbed as quickly as possible. It took forever to climb to the hall.

In the hall, Myles was playing chess while Priscilla sat at the hearth fire. Her face betrayed annoyance. "The villagers are verra noisy." She picked up her embroidery and ignored them all.

Shona addressed her uncle. "Sir Thomas Connington, lately from Edinburgh."

Priscilla's head snapped up and she dropped her frame. Myles left his attendant at the board game. "Grace and peace be unto you, sir."

Connington bowed in the Lowland way. "Indeed, I am glad to meet ye."

"Good news, madame. Your nephew—"

Priscilla leapt up with more spirit than she had ever shown, and ran to welcome him. She was a sight—the skirt of her big Lowland gown bouncing from side to side as she danced around him. Her maids joined her, cooing with delight. "Thomas. Thomas Connington! How have ye fared?

Come! Let me see ye." He obliged and she clutched his hand like a woman drowning. She examined his face and his clothes. "Ye look sae bonnie. How joyful I am."

He smiled without looking at her face and carefully unwound her fingers. "I am well, Aunt."

The man was a soldier from morn till night. No softness or warmth in his greeting to his aunt.

"My lieutenant, Matthew Rutherford, madame."

Rutherford bowed. He kept his eyes down and his mouth shut.

"Yer friends are most welcome, Thomas. What shall I dae? Are we ready for him?" Priscilla looked from her maids to Myles.

"I have a powerful hunger, madame." He smiled with all his yellow teeth at Shona.

Priscilla grabbed her by the wrist and pulled her to Connington. He wasn't unpleasant to look at—strong wavy hair, sun-bronzed skin and lazy eyes. He took her two hands in his. His clothes stank like the sea at low tide. How could everyone else not notice?

He drew her closer. Under his lazy eyelids, she saw a hardness that frightened her.

"We shall become better acquaint." He smiled, but his broken teeth ruined his good looks.

Shona would rather jump off a cliff—or bathe in a pigsty. Probably cleaner.

"Bring food!" Priscilla shouted, and her maid scurried off to the cookhouse. "Speak together with Joan while we prepare for ye." Her stepmother looked heavenward. "Ma prayers are answered. Blessed are they forevermore that restore ma kin tae me."

Connington gripped her hand with bands of iron. Shona

fought to free herself, and scowled at him. He laughed and let her go.

Priscilla's generosity was reserved for her favourite nephew. Shona positioned herself by the oriel window, as far away as possible, where Myles joined her.

"So he's no chance for marriage with you," he said. "You should befriend him at least. If he decides to stay awhile, life will be easier for you."

"I've had enough of him." She rubbed her wrist where Connington had held her. "I'll stay clear of him as much as I can."

Myles's green eyes searched hers. "You need not marry him. Your father is agreeable to your marrying one of our cousins."

He patted her arm, and she was reassured. She remembered the oppression she felt when Connington was near, and couldn't imagine a long life with him. She couldn't have the MacDonald, yet she could imagine a life with him.

"I endure ma exile as best I can." Priscilla pulled Connington to the hearth fire and sat him down.

"Not for long, Aunt." Connington's voice was charming. He chatted with Priscilla while glancing frequently in Shona's direction."Tell me how ye hae passed the time."

"I am imprisoned here." Priscilla's shoulders drooped. "I am assailed at all times by barbarity and cruelty."

Who was cruel to her? Or barbarous? The people of Gleann Muirn had been towers of patience to her. Strange woman. That she did nothing but embroider in her chamber was her choice. At least she could do no harm there.

"Ye work in oor interest. Suffering is a golden garment for which ye shall be rewarded." As he adjusted his sword, he struck her with it. "Forgive me my clumsiness with my weapon, dear aunt."

An accident? He wouldn't have any reason to dislike Priscilla, who made so much of him.

"A small thing. After supper we'll talk." Priscilla glanced at Shona, then held her finger to her lips and giggled. "Ye can tell me the news frae Edinburgh. And what's tae be done here."

CHAPTER 9

Two months later

"You want me to teach you Gaelic." Shona had spent far too much time in Connington's presence of late. "How long do you intend to stay? How shall you make use of the language?"

"I will be required tae tend tae ma own estate, but I'll be pleased tae come tae this country. Tae see my aunt and drink in yer great beauty."

"How charming you are." *At a great distance.* The greater the better.

He said a few words in Gaelic to Catriona, who laughed as she laid fruit and claret on the oaken table, then set out glasses from the sideboard. Shona prevented herself from groaning—he might break her grandfather's most prized possession—Verzelini goblets, brought from London long ago.

"No the right words?"

"Say *mòran taing*, Thomas Connington." Catriona exaggerated the words.

"Moran tank," he said.

She taught him the names of things. He hadn't any lightness of speech, but he managed some phrases, and made his teacher laugh. Connington turned his wolfish face to Shona and smiled.

From the oriel window, she gazed at the wide loch, and ran her hands along the worn stone of the window. The castle had sheltered the Campbells from many a storm. But now the enemy was within—battering down the defences of her faithful kinswoman and servant, Catriona.

"Catriona, a piece of *miel,* if ye please." Connington said the word for honey instead of fruit. Laughing, she went to fetch the fruit bowl. "*Meas*, Thomas Connington. *Meas*."

He had been sitting in the best chair with arms and a cushion—*her father's chair*—but now he rose and leaned on the wall right next to Shona.

"Why are you here?" Shona asked as calmly as she could. Weakness weighted her arms and legs. His sword dangling, he touched her hair. She shivered, and slid along the wall. "What you do is improper and unwelcome."

"Improper?" Laughing, he slithered along the wall behind her. "You're safe in this crowd. Let me see. How many folk about? Four servants, six guards and your woman. And ma dear aunt and her maids."

The servants were used to his presence—he had charmed them all. He made her feel like a child—he kept things from her. Even the way he phrased his words made her wonder if something was wrong in Edinburgh. He ran his hand down her cheek. "And Myles is soon away tae his own house. Then ye must obey *me*."

Shona removed his hand—she'd leave as soon as she could and go to her chamber.

"I am yer stepmother's closest male relative. I am responsible for her and ye, in the absence of your faither." He strolled to the table and poured himself claret wine. Then he lifted the foreign bottle and examined it. "Fine engraved glass—Venetian. Ye want some? No? Alas." He poured himself another drink, drank it at once, and poured a third.

In the quiet of the room, all she heard was Connington. She hated the sound of the liquid in his cheeks before he swallowed.

"Ye'll marry me."

"I think not." She didn't doubt that he was persistent. He didn't fear the power of her father or uncle. Perhaps it was the bluff of a desperate man. He used physical strength because it was all he had. "My uncle says that I need not marry you."

"Ye wull marry me." He carefully set the empty goblet down and strolled over to her, the stench of his unwashed body overpowering. "How safe might ye be withoot me? And yer kinfolk?"

Her body stiffened. Threats? Much easier to give in and marry the man. But living with him would likely be no different. She'd still wage a war of wills with him.

Footsteps sounded on the outside stair. "Nice fresh bannocks," Catriona came through from the cookhouse.

The smell of the baking diffused through a room full of threat. Shona controlled her voice as though her request were nothing unusual. "Catriona, please fetch me a messenger." Her serving woman stood, baking in hand, confusion on her face.

"Any messenger ye send," said Connington sweetly, "might not find his way tae yer faither. Dangerous times."

Anger rose from the pit of Shona's stomach, choking out her fear. "I'm going to request my father's return. Perhaps he should clarify the nature of your stewardship."

"Calm yerself, ma dear." He poured some claret and offered it to her. "Think on it. Rationally." He indicated that Catriona sit. She continued to stand, but didn't fetch the messenger.

"I won't drink." She wouldn't take anything from him if she were starving.

"Is yer faither a stupid man?"

"Of course not!"

"Then he married my aunt and that was a wise decision."

"Why did my father marry Priscilla?" She didn't expect a straightforward answer.

"Why do people marry? Security in these chancy times —when ye don't know who tae trust."

She'd never marry him. Never love him and never trust him. "It sounds like a fine thing. It may not be—"

He slowly traced the pattern of the silk brocade tablecloth up to the engraving on the Venetian glass. And tipped it over spilling the contents over the costly cloth. It rolled to the table's edge. He caught before it fell to the floor. He looked up at her. "Ye marry me and ye will be safe."

"Safe from what? Safe from whom?" *He* presented the worst danger she had ever known.

He set down his empty glass and looked straight into her eyes. "You may learn what you don't want to hear."

What could she possibly find out? Many old families in the district had resented the Campbells since they had acquired land and power. But her clan held no grudges. They rented land to whoever would pay the rent, and give them loyalty and service.

"Ye will marry me."

His words rained down on her, but they did not dilute her will. She returned to the window to look on the green hills to the north of the castle. Why had her father married a Lowland woman? The answer lay in Edinburgh.

"Some pears?" Connington offered her fruit from her castle garden.

In the autumn of the year, Shona walked with two friends on a hill purple with heather above Loch Muirn. She saw people cutting oats and barley, ripe yellow in the sun, in the fields below, and beyond them, Castle Muirn brooded over the dark waters of the loch. She picked up her basket of herbs and patted them down, then stooped to pick more in the marshes that garlanded the Red Stream. She plucked the last flowers of meadowsweet, the strewing herb that would freshen the floors of Castle Muirn in the winter months to come—the normal pursuit of an ordinary person. That's what she intended to be. Ordinary.

She hadn't tried to use the banshee power—she refused to speak of it to Morag. No other animals had died because of her.

Her stepmother allowed her to escape the castle to "supervise" the village girls. Priscilla spoke as though her nephew and Shona were already betrothed, but her uncle Myles protected her. Every month that passed decreased her fear of marriage to Connington.

Ròs Màiri, a girl never worn out with her daily tasks, lay on a smooth stone with only a few herbs in her basket. With her brown skin and black hair, she looked as though she belonged to the earth. "I want to get on with finding a man for myself. I'll lie in the fields with Cailean Bacach during the Feast of Saint Michael. He's got a bad leg, but he works hard enough."

Her friend Una's basket was already filled with the herbs. "Is your stepmother still keen on marrying you to that Connington man?"

"I refuse him daily," said Shona. "Thomas Connington is a danger to us all."

"You might try him out." Ròs Màiri sat up with a dreamy smile. "He might change your mind."

Connington with Ròs Màiri? Surely not! "Have you 'tried' him yourself?" asked Shona.

"A handsome Lowlander with castles and money galore?" said Ròs Màiri. "I haven't, but why not? I could do far worse."

"I think he needs money. That's why he eats our food and drink—and pesters me."

"If I marry him, I may become a titled lady. I'd give him lots of drink and lots of food. And lots of exercise in the fields."

She was reckless for sure.

"He's all yours," said Shona. "Whatever his Lowland title."

"I dub him Sir Belch-a-lot," said Una.

Connington was less frightening when Una ridiculed him. Despite Catriona's teasing, Shona pushed a chest against the door at night to keep him out.

"What about a man whose clan was at feud with ours?" Ròs Màiri looked straight at Shona. "I wouldn't mind lying with a certain MacDonald to test his moving parts."

"A MacDonald," said Una, "is as unsuitable for a Campbell woman as a Barbary pirate."

"Indeed?" Ròs Màiri arched a well-fed eyebrow.

Shona couldn't help smiling as she glanced up *Bealach nam Bò*, the cattle pass where Alasdair MacDonald's herd would come down from the west. Only a lazy eagle floated high above them when she lifted her face to the sun. She said a blessing for the day.

"My grandfather thinks those MacDonalds might be coming through in a week or so," said Una. "They'll be with us for the Feast of Saint Michael."

Ròs Màiri scoffed. "The wild, wicked MacDonalds! Steal your cattle one day and sell them back to you the next!"

"MacPharlans and MacGregors have that reputation, not MacDonalds," said Shona.

"Should I lie with an enemy of Clan Campbell if he were noble?" said Ròs Màiri.

"Your family wouldn't accept the child," said Una.

"They would if he gave her farmland to support her." What if Shona were married to a landless man—trapped by poverty in a Lowland town?

"If you can't find anyone suitable," said Una, "you can fall back on your parents' choice. You can learn to get along with anyone."

No truth in that. None at all.

"Una, meek and mild," mocked Ròs Màiri.

Shona didn't want them snapping at each other. Nothing should mar her day of freedom. "Put a smile on your faces. I haven't much time outside." Shona envied these girls' freedom to choose. She hoped that Alasdair would come soon—she'd see as much of him as possible. She thought him a good man, and he'd shown her what she should expect in a suitable husband.

"Nothing like a loving man to lighten your step." Ròs Màiri skipped ahead.

From high in *Bealach nam Bò*, men's shouts, the bellows of cattle and the barking of dogs rumbled down the slopes toward the women. At first the mountainside seemed to waver. Slowly the shapes of men and beasts emerged from stone and heather.

Alasdair! He had arrived. Shona made up her mind to enjoy the festival of Saint Michael and the company of her friends in Baile Leacan. Visiting, singing and feasting would fill their days while every unmarried woman would look over the selection of available men.

Except for her. She had wanted a marriage with a Campbell gentleman. Now she preferred Alasdair, but she couldn't have him. But she needed to marry soon to stop Connington's pursuit of her.

"Time for me to return home." Shona intended to be in the castle when her uncle welcomed the MacDonalds.

"Keen to meet a certain MacDonald?" said Ròs Màiri.

"Perhaps." She had never shared her daydreams about Alasdair with them, but they had guessed anyway. She turned her face away from them. Betrayed by her own body.

"More than perhaps?" said Una. "You look radiant."

"She's embarrassed." Ròs Màiri shined the pin on her *earasaid*. "I have a new brooch from a chapman. Should attract the eye of a lusty man. Will Alasdair join us tonight? Many a girl would love to be his friend for the night. How will you keep them away?"

"I shall fight them off with cudgels for you." Una put her arm around Shona's waist.

Shona yearned to be with her friends while they lay together in the fields, and chatted the whole night through with all the young men. She wasn't sure how she'd see Alasdair, but she'd have a better chance of spending time with him if she were outside the castle keep, her stepmother's realm.

"Come on! Life awaits." Ròs Màiri lifted the skirt of her *earasaid* to run.

The girls ran down the hill toward the castle and village. The drovers and herd boys settled the cattle in temporary folds on the fields west of the castle. Five riders on ponies, the drovers, detached itself from the herd, and flew over the grass toward the village, their hooves barely touching the earth. They were dressed in trews and shirts in the heat of the day, yelled and waved again. Shona and her friends up on the hill waved in return. Shona saw Alasdair among them.

Her heart thrummed. Her whole body lightened with the thought of him.

What could she say to escape Priscilla during the feast of Saint Michael? She needed a good excuse—an illness among the villagers. She had to help Morag. Not an outright lie. Someone must be sick and she'd visit and bring food gifts. That'd do for several days.

Shona wanted to run over to the riders—to Alasdair—to ask how he had fared in the past three months and where he had been. She wanted to feast her eyes on his smooth skin and study the light of the sun shining on his face and dancing in his eyes. She wanted to reach up and touch his hair, watch his curls spring back, so unlike her own hair, which hung in long waves.

But she couldn't do that. Not any of it. So she'd simply wait for an excuse to be near him.

~

When she returned to Castle Muirn, she found a chapman waiting at the outside stair to the keep, a regular visitor seeking hospitality for the night. "Welcome to you," she said. "Have you had anything to eat?"

The man stood to greet her. "Not yet, daughter of Iain Glas."

"Have you seen my stepmother?"

"She'll see me soon, so they say." The man didn't look her in the eye.

"My stepmother looks forward to your visits."

"Would you like to see my wares?" He pulled his pack from his shoulders. "Lovely ribbons for your hair—red and white. Look—"

Normally she would choose a smooth ribbon or two, but she was in a hurry. "Lovely. Has my stepmother paid you for the silks and canvas she bought last time?"

"I'm sure she'll pay this time." He needed coin, more than a meal or shelter. If her stepmother took all his embroidery silks without paying, the man would never return again, and every village in Argyll would learn she was a genteel thief.

"I'll see to you. Come." She led him up the stair and into the great hall past the curious guards. "Then you'll get a good meal in your belly."

"You'll be a good wife to a great man," he said.

That pleased her. She left him in the great hall, and went upstairs to her stepmother's chamber, where she found her stepmother content as she bent over her needlework in the company of her maids.

"A debt to the chapman has been overlooked," said Shona.

"That man back again." Priscilla eyed her suspiciously, looked at the silk threaded in her needle, and took another stitch or two. "Send him away."

"If he's paid, I'm sure he'll go." Shona hoped to bring this embarrassment to a quick end.

"He charges an awful price. Twice the price that I paid in Edinburgh."

"He has to bring it here on his back."

"Robbery. Give him this." She dug a farthing from the sporran at her waist—not nearly enough.

"You took his stock." She wasn't sure what she'd do if her stepmother refused to pay.

"I needed it." Her stepmother bent to her embroidery again. "I'll hear no more about it."

Shona stood, ignored and wondering what to do next. She had the coin box, a gift from her father. He didn't tell her why she needed coins. From one year to the next, she never handled money. No need. Her father paid for her clothes and jewellery, but he had set aside a little coin for her dowry. And other things, so he said.

After curtseying to her stepmother, she slipped upstairs for the rest of the money to pay the chapman. Her father must know his new wife well.

When Shona gave the chapman his money, he fingered it thoughtfully.

"Have you had enough to eat?"

"Plenty, gracious lady."

Something seemed to trouble him. "What is it?" she asked.

He swallowed with difficulty. "News from the Lowlands."

"What have you seen?"

"Riots against the king—in the street not a stone's throw from Muirn Lodge, where your father stays."

People acting against the king? *Unthinkable*. Her father in danger—at the edge of a whirlpool of great events. "What more can you tell me?"

He seemed concerned for her. "The brawling doesn't last, but that won't be the end of it. The people in Edinburgh are angry about the king's prayer book. He wants them all to use a book in church."

"His prayer book?" Hardly a reason to be angry.

"I don't understand it myself. They won't talk to Highlanders. I buy my stock and supplies and they fall silent when they hear my Highland speech."

"Is my family in danger?"

"No, sensible folk just stayed in their houses. No worries there, Shona Iain Glas."

"You'll stay and rest." She'd have to tell Myles. Her family must return home to the safety of the mountains. Her father home again! Her heart lifted. She left the chapman as he took a stool in the sunshine of the hall, where serving men joined him to hear his news.

From the window behind the dais, she could see a carpet of wild flowers—yellow bedstraw and milkweed—waving freely in the wind by the shore. Shona made her way to the castle garden, a stone enclosure by the curtain wall, where the pear and apple trees sheltered. As she passed through the garden gate, she saw many had already gathered.

"Eleven MacDonalds spotted from the walls, Shona Iain Glas," a guard whispered. "Vipers soon in our midst."

He was joking but half serious. "You'll keep us safe."

"My life is yours," said the guard.

She was more concerned about her father than the danger presented by the MacDonalds. She could only wait—the lot of women. Perhaps the MacDonalds could find out if the Campbell men in Edinburgh were in danger. Without attracting attention, she'd wait for an opportunity to speak to Alasdair alone.

Now, that was something. MacDonalds protecting Campbells.

CHAPTER 10

Shona stood at the garden wall by an old apple tree. Warm from the sun, the fragrance of apples was overpowering. She waited for Alasdair to visit Myles. Her thoughts had dwelt on the MacDonald overmuch and she was bursting to see him. She calmed herself with slow breaths.

Enjoy the garden. Pass the time until he comes.

Myles and his household men sat on chairs and benches in an alcove lined with tapestries while other kin and guests wandered the garden. Birds squabbled and fluttered in the trees as a harper plucked a lively tune on his instrument.

Shona started at the clink of a sword and footfalls. Heavy, blunt steps that she knew well. Connington and Rutherford, his shadow. Connington pulled her beside him with a toothy smile. "Come sit with us, sweet dove." He indicated a bench near Priscilla, who already occupied a good chair in the shade.

He placed his hand on Shona's lower back and forced her in the direction of his aunt. He trapped her hand in his and sat her down. It would all seem so harmless to anyone looking on. She sat up straight so that she needn't touch him.

"Thomas is learning yer heathen tongue," said Priscilla. "Just tae keep ye happy."

"Very nice." She felt ill from his presence—and the iron in his weapons. "Perhaps you could leave your sword with the guard. It's our custom not to carry arms here."

"Tae please ye, ma rose." He ordered a servant to take them away.

The *maor taighe* announced the MacDonalds. Heads high, Alasdair and his men strode into the garden. Along with the rest of the crowd, she stared at him. He appeared confident in a bright new *fèileadh* and a jacket with sleeves slashed to display a generous linen shirt. In the sunlight, gems gleamed on his shoulder brooch. A man who wore such wealth openly must be well able to defend it. With effortless grace, he and his men circled Myles sunwise in the Gaelic manner of showing respect.

Alasdair's smile held all the light of the sun in it. It seemed to be directed at all those in the garden, but then he shone at her. That smile and the light in his eyes brought back the memories of the few times they had spent together. It was a smile that reassured her of his feelings for her. Of her worth. A rare smile indeed.

Connington grunted. She turned to him and was rewarded with a frown.

He stood, legs wide apart and his hand on his belt, and jerked his body toward Alasdair. The two men stared at each other. Connington's eyes narrowed. The two men seemed to recognise something in each other. They were battle ready. Shona closed her eyes—but that didn't make Connington disappear.

Others noticed how still they were, and conversation ceased.

"Welcome back to Gleann Muirn." Myles's commanding voice broke the spell and the two men faced him. "You are most welcome here."

"Ye welcome the enemies of Clan Campbell tae Castle Muirn?"

"We have business with the MacDonalds that we arranged before your arrival."

The world did not wait for Connington's commands. Shona took quiet pleasure in seeing him put in his place.

"In view of the recent news, is it wise tae send off precious cattle intae the unknown?"

Connington's charming yet commanding voice caught the attention of the crowd although most spoke no Inglishe. They had no idea he was arguing with Myles.

"We go as far as Edinburgh and are assured of a good price this year." Alasdair's voice had neither warmth nor chill in it.

Myles said, "It is good—"

"The MacDonalds will steal your cattle tae pay for rebellion," said Connington. "As they have many a time."

Connington should not interrupt Myles. A cloud glided over the sun and greyed the red apples on the trees. Leaves from the fruit trees in the garden fell and drifted at Shona's feet. A swift chill settled on her. Autumn. The dark season would soon be upon them.

"Are you versed in the history of our clans, sir?" Myles voice betrayed annoyance.

"Sae little," said Connington. "I try tae learn what I can. But ye can't think otherwise—the man's hiding evil intent under a cloak of friendship."

"I have made my decision."

"Ye must not give the cattle tae MacDonalds."

"You do not govern here, sir." Myles's voice was low but hard. "I do, in my brother's stead."

For the first time, Shona saw Connington betray an unguarded reaction. Gone completely were the lazy, sleepy eyes. His eyes sparked and flamed. He lowered his head and clenched his hands. When he raised his face again, his eyes were dark. With a tight smile he said, "Rest assured that these hands will be at yer back in any enterprise. I beg ye tae reconsider the decision tae let this man take yer beasts away with him."

"The cattle will go to market and, while the MacDonalds are here, we will offer the hospitality required." Myles gazed about the garden, apparently unaffected by Connington's words. Silence reigned. One could have heard grass growing. "We've heard your opinion and we thank you for your counsel. Now we'll entertain our guests." He turned and gestured to the serving man. "Come, bring the storyteller."

"You are a guest here," Alasdair said to Connington, "but I don't know why. Care to inform me?"

"I am mair than a guest. But that's nane o' yer business." Connington rubbed that part of his coat where his sword normally rested, but the weapon was stored at the castle guardhouse. "Ye still think ye'll get cattle here? Ye never know what might happen. Ye should take yer leave while ye have a whole skin."

"Why should I heed you?"

Alasdair should be careful. Connington did not forget slights or insults.

But Connington's lazy smile was back. "Ye'll be here for the horse race, I think? Ye have a dangerous journey before ye without adding a race to it." Connington sneered at Alasdair. "Maybe ye ha'e no taste for risk."

Alasdair smiled. An indulgent smile. One reserved for children.

Connington tried another gibe. “Ye here for any other reason? Ye want something that belongs tae someone else?”

“Enough.” Myles shifted impatiently on his chair.

“I have first say for—a certain woman,” said Connington.

Connington meant herself, of course, although she had refused him countless times. Arrogant rogue. She saw Alasdair stiffen--he must think that Shona would marry Connington. Never would she marry that repulsive man. Myles had said she had the right to refuse him, and she was grateful she had such as strong man to support her.

“Care for a private wager?” said Connington to Alasdair. “A few silver pennies tae spend in the toun?”

Alasdair’s eyes flashed as he looked over Connington, who wore the same dirty shirt and breeches he’d been wearing since his arrival. “Can you afford a loss?”

“I’ll win. I always win.” He nudged his lieutenant. “Don’t I, Rutherford?”

He had nothing to say.

“We want tae see yer mettle.” said Connington. “We like the idea we’d defeat ye soundly.”

Alasdair glared at him. “I wouldn’t miss it on my hope of salvation.”

“Enough! All here are my guests and my guests will respect each other.” Myles signalled the harper to play louder, then eyed Connington, who bowed.

The contrast between Alasdair and Connington was great. They were both of a height, but Alasdair’s skin was golden and clear and Connington’s burnt brown and wrinkled. Both were broad in the chest, but Connington’s calves were thin, Alasdair’s muscled and strong. Had

Shona to choose between them, there was no difficulty—the Gael in his warm red *fèileadh* would win her. She felt his strength emanating from a distance of six feet and a thrill shot through her body. Never had she felt that before!

Although caught in a whirl of emotion, she'd seen the looks exchanged. Neither man thought well of the other and never would. They were battle ready. If not today, then soon they'd fight. To the death?

"And ye'll be there tae see us strive?" Connington's eyes fastened on Shona's bosom for long moments. She covered her breasts with her *earasaid*. She hated the way he made her feel—like a heifer at a market.

"Will ye join us in this manly test, sir?" Connington addressed her uncle. "Keep us right and gentlemanly."

"No!" Shona couldn't help herself. Not her uncle too. Connington was bent on destroying anyone she cherished.

"I am—honoured by your words, sir," said Myles. "I can't do otherwise."

"Now we're friends," said Connington. "Here's ma hand on it."

Under a grey sky Myles shook hands with him.

Connington's ability to ignore strong feeling against him amazed Shona. The man had courage, no doubt of that, because the race caused broken bones and crippling injuries. Oddly enough, some men finished the race better friends. Not this man. Shona sensed deep treachery in him.

Her uncle seemed blind to it. What could she do? A woman. She couldn't persuade men. She couldn't race. She couldn't fight with a sword. A heavy feeling weighted her shoulders. *Think.*

She took a basket of pears and apples and offered them to the guests until she reached Alasdair. "I need to speak to you—meet me at the big rocks above the Red Stream," she whispered.

~

The implications of her invitation struck her after she hurried out of the garden. Alasdair might think she wanted to be his friend for the night—a tempting thought she put aside. More than anything she wanted Myles safe. If Connington lost the race, so much the better. Myles had a good horse, but he himself wasn't fit, and Connington's warhorse dwarfed Alasdair's pony. But racers often "stole" a better horse and returned it after the event. She'd help Alasdair "steal" her father's horse, the best in the glen, and then he'd keep up with Myles. Or at least distract Connington. The castle guards wouldn't challenge the chief's daughter if she rode out with the horse. When she reached her chamber, Shona told her serving woman what she intended.

"You're going to steal a horse for Alasdair?" asked Catriona. "Everyone will know who the horse belongs to ... and who gave the beast to him."

"Thomas Connington might not find out."

"Not sure about that. He might charm it out of someone. You're sure you want to do this?"

"I know what you're thinking. I'm the youngest in the family and full of peculiar ideas."

"Dangerous ideas. Lots of people are unhappy to see MacDonalds among us. Now you want to see that MacDonald alone?" Catriona heaped more peat in the hearth.

"No one knows except you and your son." Shona trembled, not from cold, but from excitement. "Please help me." She took her cousin's hand. "Will you bring some food for us and a little wine? And find out what my stepmother's doing? Can you go down the stair without her seeing?"

Catriona sighed, but went off and soon returned. "Priscilla is in a passion, walking up and down in her chamber, talking to herself in the Saxon speech. She wouldn't notice the Second Coming." Catriona set a covered basket on a chest. She exhaled and quickly walked toward her and hugged her. Then held her at arm's length. "You're a woman now. And that MacDonald is very much a man."

"A far better man than Thomas Connington. I'll be all right with him."

"Listen, love. He's still a man who will want a woman to bear him children." Catriona brushed a strand of hair from Shona's face and tucked it into her hair ribbon.

"We'll only talk." She didn't want to listen to Catriona's precautions.

"For now," said Catriona.

"He's kind to me. He'd never harm me."

"Women think men are wonderful when they want to lie with us. When they want to give us babies—they're at their most charming. You be careful. If your uncle knew, you'd have no end of difficulty."

"My stepmother says much the same. But I can't sit and do nothing."

"I'd never deny you. But be careful." Catriona shook out a large piece of woollen cloth. "Better wear a thicker *earasaid* to cover your figure. The fewer people who see you leave, the better. You don't want your stepmother looking for you, and a crowd of guilty-looking people all round to make her angrier."

"You have a wonderful capacity for avoiding trouble." Shona hugged her serving woman.

"Get ready."

Shona had a moment of regret at making trouble for Catriona. After Shona married, she'd bring her to the new house. When Shona was dressed, they went to the spiral stair and listened.

"No one coming," said Catriona. "Let's go, *a ghràidh*." They descended the stair, past Priscilla's chamber, to the hall. A few servants spread fresh straw on the floors while others carried trestle tables and benches for the next meal. They hardly glanced over at the two women. But then Priscilla's maid came out of the spiral stair and hurried toward them. Shona's heart leapt like a frighted bird. Her stepmother would appear next and prevent her from leaving.

"Mistress would like some wine and cheese."

Shona spoke with a calm voice of command. "You know the location of the cookhouse."

The maid looked at her closely and frowned. "Young mistress, why are ye wearing that heathenish blanket? Mistress wants ye dressed proper."

"Go about your duties. As I do mine."

She and Catriona waited in the hall to give the maid time to go to the cookhouse.

"Can you keep her in the kitchen until I go to the stable?" asked Shona.

"I'll see what I can do."

"Tell the cooks to pretend not to understand her." Shona looked out at the courtyard.

"Not difficult!" Catriona laughed.

Two of the cook's assistants carried water from the well into the cookhouse. Shona followed Catriona down the steps. She made sure the *earasaid* covered her hair before walking to the stable. Being seen was a certainty; she had only to seem like someone else, a serving woman performing a task.

"While the cooks are harrying the maid, will you get something to feed the horse? And something for us? Maybe some claret?"

"Is it wise to take claret to meet a man?" Catriona shook her head but went off to the cookhouse.

She returned with a few slices of turnip, which Shona tied into a fold of her *earasaid*. "The cooks will hold the maid there. They're offering her all the wrong things, and she has a poor opinion of their intelligence. And this is for you and the MacDonald." She handed Shona a small leather bag.

"I'll be all right with him. Don't worry. I'm off now." Shona hesitated. She could return to the keep and go to her room, collect her embroidery and join her stepmother—the safe thing to do. No, she had to protect her uncle. She promised herself she'd do what she could help Alasdair defeat Connington.

"Away you go, then. I'll go see my son," said Catriona. "I made sure he'd be guarding the main gate."

When Shona slipped through the door to the stable, the odour of horseflesh and clean straw greeted her. Fear Mór, the largest horse, tapped a hoof on the floor of his stall. She offered a bit of turnip on the palm of her hand. "Alasdair is going to ride you and keep Myles safe. May he ride you to victory. The silver pennies will go to him and not to Thomas Connington. You're going to win because you're the best horse and Alasdair the best man. Do you hear me, great one?" She stroked his nose and patted his neck while he whickered his appreciation and lowered his head to search for more tasty treats. "You protect Alasdair and he will protect Myles."

She went to the doorway and saw Catriona and her son talking to the second guard. She should be loyal to her stepmother and Connington for her father's sake, but she resented them for forcing their way into her life. Although she did nothing wrong in lending the horse, she felt guilty and glad at the same time.

She selected a thick blanket for Fear Mór, and threw it over his back. He was the tallest horse she had ever seen, but luckily he wasn't as broad-backed as many of the ponies. The huge Spanish saddle cost more than a score of cows in a country where most people didn't see a single copper penny in a year. She'd ride out to Alasdair. She glanced at the stable door expecting someone to come in, but no one darkened the doorway. Her belly was flip-flopping like a tumbler at a fair.

Normally a stable boy would saddle the horse for her, but not today. She tried to lift the saddle onto the horse, but couldn't. His bridle was tied to a ring set in the stone wall. She swung the saddle over the horse, but her sudden movements startled him and he shied away from the slap of leather. She fell to the floor in a heap of saddle and *earasaid*. She pushed him to the wall, took a deep breath, and threw the saddle up with all her strength. The horse stood with the saddle on top of him. She rearranged her *earasaid* around her waist and over her head, and pinned it. Then she tightened the girth, led him out of the stall, and hauled herself aboard. He tolerated her.

You must ride more often, daughter of Iain Glas.

She was surprised the stallion communicated with her. Many animals chose not to speak with her at all. "I shall, Fear Mòr." They'd get on well.

She dug the heels of her soft shoes into the horse's flanks and he dutifully walked forward, the sound of his hooves clattering on the stone flags. Surely everyone in the castle would be alerted. She bent over to clear the doorway, and spotted the maid coming out of the kitchen. Shona dug in her heels again. The horse shambled along.

Are you sure you want to speed along, daughter of Iain Glas?

"Quite sure, Fear Mòr." Horse and rider trotted toward the gate. Catriona waved. The guard dove into the guard-house as if he were in mortal danger. Very funny. Sitting as straight as possible, Shona rode out of the gate.

"Oh, aren't you wicked!" Catriona laughed behind her.

With the wind whipping out her *earasaid* like a sail, she galloped past the marshes to the sand of the *Traigh Bhàn*, guilt dropping from her as she rode.

She slowed the horse as she turned up the path by the Red Stream, overhanging branches combing her hair. Only a few hundred steps from the beach, ice-smooth rocks made a fortalice, protecting her from the strangers in Castle Muirn. She'd hand over the horse to Alasdair at her little fort. As she rode up the path, she spoke to the birds.

"My special place. And I'm glad you're here to greet me." Here she could talk to the birds, and no one would think her mad or bewitched.

The larks trilled a welcome. *Welcome to you and Fear Mór.*

"I'll visit with you awhile. Say 'Good day', Fear Mór." The horse snorted a greeting.

The man you seek is nowhere in sight. The birds chirped while bobbing up and down.

"He's coming, he is." She lifted her hand to them.

The Crow jumped onto a branch near her head. *Indeed.*

"You don't often visit, Crow."

Merely being sociable. My strong point. The Crow stayed a distance from the other birds.

"There's no harm in Alasdair, you know. None at all. You'll like him," said Shona.

No harm in him, the Crow cawed. *Harm is all round him.*

"We're safe here." Shona dismounted and stroked the horse's withers. "Guide him, please, Crow."

Agreed. But be careful with him. For both your sakes.

Yet another warning, but Shona was sure she could trust him to treat her well.

Crow flew off while Shona loosened the saddle girth. Suddenly she heard the movement of bushes and the splashing of water.

"Damn bird! Give me that back! You little thief!"

The Crow dumped a blue bonnet by Shona. *My part of the bargain fulfilled. Now you mind yourself.*

"All right!"

Alasdair pulled bushes out of his way and the Crow retreated to a higher branch. "I believe that bird brought my bonnet to you."

Shona examined the bonnet and shook off the leaves that had stuck to it. "She did. No harm done." She handed it to him. "Thank you for coming."

She didn't have to imagine him. "So here you are." Her words caught in her throat. He was handsome and he kept walking toward her, his *fèileadh* moving in and out with every stride. Sunlight lit up her little fort.

Her blood sang with his nearness. Her mind was closed to anything but him. He seemed larger than any thing else in the world. She could feel drops of sweat rolling down her back and between her breasts. A warm image of the two of them crept into her mind. She saw herself at his side on his *fèileadh*.

"Are you all right?"

She stuttered as she came to herself. "Fine, fine. I'm glad you came."

He thought she was uncomfortable with him. If only he knew!

Then he smiled in his gentle way. "I must apologise for not saying good-bye on my last visit."

She mustn't seem too eager. "Myles told me he sent you off. I'm pleased you concluded your business successfully." That was stiff and formal enough. Perhaps she should curtsey in the Lowland way. *Time to get down to business.*

"I don't like Thomas Connington."

"I don't care for the man myself." His voice was rich and low.

"He may enter the horse race on Saint Michael's Day. I'd like to see someone else win."

"You'd want a man with connections to your clan to lose?" He must have read the expression in her face. "Right. You have experience of him. Well, he has a Spanish warhorse. Difficult to outride him."

Shona indicated Fear Mór. "This horse may help." The horse shook his head and whinnied. "He's ready for the fray."

"You brought him for me. You'd trust him to me? A MacDonald." The light filtering through the trees danced in his bright eyes. "What's his name?"

"Fear Mòr! Will he be the Great One or the Devil for you?"

"I believe he is great to some and devilish to others. Since you trust me well enough, so will he."

Alasdair stroked the horse's back.

"I believe you're an honourable man." It was difficult to breathe, to think, to speak with this man. This tingling in her nerves, this fluttering in her belly, this speeding heart was a terrible thing.

No. It's wonderful.

"And I believe you to be honourable as well, Shona Iain Glas." He kept a distance from her. Pleasant but cautious—unlike herself. "How lovely you looked riding here. Like a fairy woman, riding the wild wind."

She drew a quick breath. She did not have the courage to ask what he meant. *Does he know I could become a powerful banshee?*

His smile broadened. *A joke*. She must look a mess from her exertions. She looked down, appalled to see her *earasaid* behind her shoulders and her breasts jutting through the thin stuff of her old shift. Head down so he wouldn't see her flush, she pulled her *earasaid* into place. "And in the gloaming you could be *an Donas*, the Devil himself." In the late afternoon sun, his golden skin contrasted with his dark hair.

"But you know my pedigree. I am of sterling character." His eyes sparkled.

"That's not what my serving woman says."

"She's very wise. Come. Will you let me help?" He moved to her side.

"I am capable of removing the saddle."

"So you are."

He didn't assume female weakness. A pleasant change. She picked up the saddle, and the weight of it bowed her like a willow. "It's heavy, right enough. But I managed and brought the horse here." While he held the bridle, she lifted it off, and carried it to a large flat rock. "You should be honoured to ride such a horse." She hardly knew what else to say.

"My backside will be flattered to sit on tooled Spanish

leather."

She liked the idea of his backside on that horse. She must remember her business with this man.

He ran his hand gently over the saddle. "Beautiful. I'll return the horse after the race. I promise."

His words were light, but she believed him. "As long as water runs and wind blows. I know."

Alasdair came to examine the horse. "I'll treat him well as I do all my beasts. He looks fit enough. Still, it's a challenging business, a water race, isn't it?" He stroked the horse's neck. "We've no horses like this one at all. All of our ponies are almost as tall as horses, and broad-backed. But they haven't the long legs and swiftness of this one."

"Fear Mór comes from Spain, part of the ransom of a Spanish gentleman in the Low Countries." She was close enough to catch Alasdair's man-smell, mixed with wind and heather. She retreated two steps.

"Beautiful animal. You'll come and see that we treat him properly?" Alasdair's voice was reassuring.

"You'll train him?" She'd be able to escape the dreariness of the castle.

"He knows you, and you can help him get used to me."

She'd be in the middle of preparations for the race. How often had she stood with great dignity on the edge of fun and sport? Too often. "I should be there to care for my father's property." She sounded like a prig.

"And if I injure the horse of the most powerful man in the district?"

"You must recompense him for his loss." *Prig.*

"My family won't be pleased to pay compensation. I'll lose business and I won't have the pleasure of speaking to a lovely girl ever again." He took two steps toward her.

She held her ground. Something was happening to her,

something that frightened her a little. The sun shone so brightly on the smooth stones of her fortress and she could hear the birds so clearly: *She speaks to a handsome stranger so confidently*. "The worst thing of all."

"There must be crowds of men wanting to be with you. You won't miss me in the least."

"Old men and young boys." She wanted to put her hands around his shoulders, but left them at her sides. "My father's gone off to Edinburgh and left me here."

"He's left you here to deal with Connington." His face hardened.

"I need your help." She forgot to maintain her distance and walked up to him. He towered above her like the standing stone at the assembly place. With the power to crush her. "I'd like to see Connington lose the race. He might show his temper and people would see that he isn't as charming as they think."

"Defeating Connington will be part of the pleasure of racing."

So many ways to die in a water race, but he seemed utterly unafraid. She wouldn't cower behind the doors of her box-bed. But would she race if she were allowed? She wasn't sure how brave she'd be in a dangerous situation. "Let's celebrate Thomas Connington's defeat." She pulled out a pewter flask of claret from a saddle bag and held up a cloth packet of oatcakes and cheese.

"A feast in your fortress. The last meal of the condemned man—with a beautiful woman. Mine is a happy fate."

She held up the flask. "To Fear Mór and victory!"

After drinking a small amount, she passed the flask to him. He swallowed some of the wine.

He was so lighthearted that she followed suit. "No more

talk of the race. Here is a magic place. Forget the world outside. No worries and no enmity."

"No feuding," said Alasdair. "We will be the peacemakers between our two clans." He took her hand in his. The gesture required his sitting closer.

She moved closer to him. "Very noble." She closed her eyes and waited for him to kiss her, imagining the softness of his skin. *May the world be gone from her fortress like people wave-snatched from the shore.*

A bird screeched and she opened her eyes to see Crow on a branch beside her. The bird flitted round Alasdair's head, then back to her shoulder, where she whispered in Shona's ear, *Go now. You are too fond of this man.*

Shona didn't speak to the bird because Alasdair might think her odd. Could she never do what other girls did? The spell was broken. "I do wish I could stay longer, but I must get back. Please take the horse."

Alasdair led the horse from her sanctuary, but she stayed awhile longer in the peace of the old stones. "Don't you say a word," she said to the bird.

I'm as mute as the stones.

She trudged along the shore with the crow following. "You're an awful bird, you know. Awful."

My duty, dear heart.

CHAPTER 11

Next day the two guards greeted Shona as she left the castle. "We'll make sure that no other horses are 'stolen' for the race, else your family will be on foot before long." Catriona's son was smiling—he didn't seem to mind the theft.

"Fear Mór will be back soon."

"That MacDonald had better take care of him." The second guard's lowered brows betrayed his suspicion.

Shona had gone to the shore and returned without comment from her stepmother or Connington. When she did her duty to her stepmother—lots of embroidery, listening to her opinions about the barbaric country where fate had brought her—that was her penance. But Shona imagined a life with the man at the Red Stream. Tomorrow she would slip out to see Alasdair train Fear Mòr.

At the shore Alasdair warmed Fear Mór, while Cailean and Anndru exercised their ponies and Gillesbic looked on.

Alasdair remembered Shona riding Fear Mòr on the *Tràigh Bhàn*. She didn't know it, but he'd watched her the whole way from Castle Muirn to the Red Stream—her yellow hair waving behind her like a banner, her *earasaid* clinging tightly to her body, her voice singing to her horse to inspire greater speed. It was more than he ever hoped to see. He was careful with her. He didn't want to frighten her in her little sanctuary. Now he would see her again. He didn't care if her uncle found out he had passed time with her. He'd savour every moment he had with her, come what may.

With every stroke of his hand on the horse's hide, Alasdair wondered if Shona would come for the training. "We could get a horse for you, Gillesbic." Must be hard not to covet the big Campbell horse.

"I'll get a pony with my share of the cattle profits and not risk it in a foolish race." Gillesbic whipped a willow switch on either side of his legs as though he were mounted.

"I still don't understand how you got the horse. How did you get it out of the castle?" Cailean asked.

"Magic," Alasdair said. The black horse's muscles shook after the rubbing.

"Don't joke about such things." Gillesbic made the sign of the cross.

"Are you wise to take that horse into the water?" said Cailean.

"How do you ready a horse for battle? You surround it with people and shout and wave plaids to accustom it to noise and confusion," said Alasdair.

"War's different," said Cailean. "Fear of the water will make the horse strive for land all the swifter. I won't take my pony to water till we race."

"That old pony won't go any faster no matter what you do," said Gillesbic.

Among the bushes and birches that sheltered the little bay, Alasdair saw spectators watching them train, among them two women, Shona and her friend Una. He recalled the interrupted kiss. Shona's lips curved like young laurel leaves—smooth and soft. "Do as you will, Cailean."

Shona came to the water's edge. She removed her *earasaid*, and kilted up her long shift so that it wouldn't get wet. Alasdair had seen women washing clothes with their shifts tucked up, and their legs red with cold. Never had he seen skin like Shona's, as fair as bog cotton without any flaw. She took off her tiny shoes.

Put your eyes back in your head. Be friendly and carefree.

Alasdair smiled at Shona. "Want to accustom a horse to water with me?"

"Of course."

"He's used to me now. Hold his bridle and I'll splash him." Alasdair showed a bucket of water to the horse, let him inspect it, then he poured the contents over his back. He glanced at Shona, who smiled at him with wide, trusting eyes. "Bring the horse into the sea."

"What does this man want? Don't you wonder?" She patted the horse's neck.

Win the race. Not important to him, said Fear Mòr. *To win you. Important.*

"If only he could, great horse."

She beckoned to her friend who hadn't joined the group. "Come help, Una."

"Don't trouble yourself about me. I'll stay warm and dry here on the sand." Una lifted her face to the sun.

"I have an old plaid to spread out." Cailean shook it out and bowed elaborately to Una. "Alas, I must return to business, beautiful one."

Una smiled shyly and sat down on the blanket.

Alasdair threw buckets of water on the horse. He'd love to drench Shona and see her shift clinging to her legs and slender waist. To wet the top of her shift. Ach no, he really shouldn't do this. He hammered the water hard with a glancing blow, and the horse started.

Give her up. She's not yours. Never will be. Content yourself with that near kiss at the Red Stream.

Alasdair took the bridle and led the horse round the bay, jumping and splashing as much as he could. The women laughed. So they should at the sight of a giant of a man ploughing through the water with a horse. "Right. Let's take him to the stream and clear off the salt."

As twilight came on them, a mournful wail split the air like lightning. A woman's voice lamenting, singing louder, then softer. The muscles of Alasdair's neck and shoulders tightened, and he hunched as if to face an enemy. No enemy there—nothing real. The stallion neighed and danced, but he held Fear Mòr firmly. Shona stopped dead in front of him, and he walked into her. He gasped at her touch on his chest. Without thought, he put an arm round her. So soft and small.

"A banshee is crying for one of us who will journey to the Otherworld." Then Shona recited a prayer of protection.

Una appeared frightened, but Shona stood for a time with the saddest expression on her face. She appeared to be appraising each person's reaction to the banshee.

"We'll see you home," said Alasdair.

The other MacDonalds gathered their gear and horses and prepared to return to their camp.

"What do you think of the banshee's cry?" Alasdair's hands felt twitchy—he gripped his sword pommel just to do something.

"So who will die?" Cailean led his pony with the rest in the direction of the cattle fold as though nothing had happened. "Can't be a warning for one of us."

"No," said Alasdair. "The person to die must be someone who belongs to Gleann Muirn." *Not Shona—may the saints protect her.*

"The Campbells have given us hospitality." Cailean's voice was calm. "We belong here temporarily."

"The priests say it's all nonsense," said Gillesbic. "We are to pay no mind to such beliefs."

"She's powerful." Alasdair reassured the horse with a firm hand, for he seemed as worried as they were. Shona gazed in the direction of the cries as though she expected the banshee to appear.

"She's foolishness." A trace of fear coloured Gillesbic's voice.

"I know a foolish man who found her comb and kept it," said Alasdair. "A cousin of a cousin in Skye."

"He kept it?" said Cailean.

"Wait till I tell you." Alasdair shivered at the memory. "The banshee cried and wailed at his house for days. Finally the wise man of his village told him to give the comb back. The man gave it back to her—on an iron shovel through a crack in the door."

"He lived to tell about it," said Cailean.

"He limps to this very day," said Alasdair. "So my cousin says."

"Why?" Anndru sounded unconvinced.

"When the banshee touched the comb on the shovel, she hurled him across the room with her power." Alasdair believed his cousin—why would he lie?

"Superstition!" said Gillesbic. He wrapped coins in a twist of his *fèileadh*, but had difficulty tying a string around it. The banshee had made him nervous enough to forget his main interest in life.

"What did she look like?" asked Shona. "The banshee your cousin saw."

"She was young and beautiful with golden hair. Like yourself." He saw her flinch. Usually girls accepted compliments well. Not her. He had no idea what to say. "And she wore a green dress."

"When you see her young, she's more powerful," said Ruari. "He's lucky to have survived ."

"How do you know?" Shona spoke quietly.

"Talking to people the length of my life. Taking precautions. Worked, didn't it? You see me old and grey."

Shona must be worried for her people and unhappy, but she was not frightened. She wasn't shaking and she appeared resigned—like people after a funeral when they begin to accept death.

"There's nothing in it. No one will die. I'm for getting some sleep." Gillesbic didn't sound convinced.

"Insulting a banshee," said Ruari. "Not wise, lad."

"She won't be after us," said Gillesbic. "We're strangers. This banshee gave a warning of death for the people here."

"So the whole thing's not nonsense," said Alasdair. "Denying her existence might make her angry." He believed in the power of the banshee, and his experience of life was greater than Gillesbic's.

"You've been very quiet," said Alasdair. A sheltered girl like herself would know nothing about the banshee. Then again, he still wasn't sure about the first time he saw her at the shore—a trick or an accident of nature? Maybe something more.

"We'll be mourning tomorrow night." Her hair glowing amber, Shona stared into the gloaming.

Alasdair thought she sounded ancient—like a wise woman who had knowledge of the Otherworld. She was revealing a new side of herself—there was more to her than he thought.

"Want to race the pack pony, Gillesbic?" asked Cailean.

The animal was over twenty years old. No one laughed at his joke.

"I'm doing nothing of the kind." Gillesbic drew himself up straight and slung his *fèileadh* out of the way of his sword arm.

When they returned to their camp, Alasdair and his men put the Campbell horse and the ponies in the fold, and organised the night watch of men and dogs. While he was walking Shona home, he shivered, although the night wasn't cold. Fear for himself, for those of his blood, and for Shona prevented much sleep that night.

~

Spectators rimmed the shore and a fortunate few viewed the race from the large rocks flanking the shore. As Alasdair urged his borrowed horse through the crowd, he heard comments about the "theft." Ruari stayed close behind on his pony.

"*Hai!* That horse belong to Iain Glas?" A shaggy-haired man, his eyebrows raised, stood in front of Alasdair.

"You've stolen Fear Mòr for the race. No mistaking that big black." A little man searched his clansmen for support.

"And a MacDonald riding him. One of the few times a MacDonald got anything from us." The shaggy one shook his fist at Alasdair.

Before the Campbells built their anger to fighting pitch, Alasdair put his hand on the on his dirk and addressed the shaggy one. "What is your will—race or fight?"

"I've no horse." He didn't mention the second option. "No good luck from us to you." The anger had dissipated from the shaggy man's voice.

"The MacDonalds bring death on us," said the little man. "That's what the banshee's cry means."

"There may be a death in the race." The shaggy-haired one echoed his thought.

"Never happened yet," said the other. "Do you plan such a thing, MacDonald?"

Alasdair stared at him for a long time, then moved the horse forward.

As his bonnet flew off his head, the man skittered out of the way. "I'll be glad to see the back of you."

"Good luck to the bravest man," said the shaggy Campbell. "You're a bold devil."

"That was well done, *a bhalaich*." Ruari waved politely to the Campbells.

The meaning of the banshee's cry had occupied Alasdair. He had no choice—he had to race for his honour. Live or die. And no banshee here to warn him of death.

Here and there, young men and women sang and laughed on the sun-dried sand. Did they not hear the banshee's cry? He scanned the land beyond the shore for Shona, but didn't see her in the groups of women, among the booths and tents set up for the fair. While families shared drinks and oatcakes, and chapmen sold ribbons, ornate boxes, and jewellery, two men near him talked about getting justice at the court after the race. He skimmed over the girls and young women, their hair in filets or ribbbons, their best smiles on their faces.

At noon he joined a dozen racers assembled with their horses and ponies at the shore below the castle. At last he found Shona in the crowd, smiling at him. His breathing sped up. A tide of joy washed over him, a tide so strong it tumbled his thoughts. He forced his mind to turn to the race. He would have to win—for her.

Myles rode his big grey horse on to the sand to join them. Alasdair thought him foolhardy to race at his age. He must be nearly fifty—he should stay on shore with the older men—but he had to demonstrate his courage and strength to his people. At least he had a good horse.

Alasdair spotted the buff-coated Connington prancing his stallion through the crowd, the warhorse scattering people as he rode. Why would Connington risk his neck on this race? The prize was a purse of silver pennies, a fortune for local people, but surely a landowner such as himself wouldn't need such a paltry sum of money. Maybe he did. Lots of unanswered questions concerning that Lowlander.

"That Connington man craves danger," said Ruari.

"We'll make a good show," said Alasdair.

"You'd better—as carefully as you can."

As the sun rose high over the peak of *Beinn Mhór,* each MacDonald removed his *fèileadh* and shirt. They'd ride in trews. Fit and strong from manhandling cattle in all weathers, Alasdair wasn't embarrassed to take off his own shirt. Cailean, Anndru and Donall were shorter than he, but built like bulls. Connington did not remove his coat or shirt. He flashed a wide smile to the crowd.

"The sun on those teeth could blind you." Ruari carried away the Spanish saddle.

Connington's lieutenant also prepared himself for the race. Rutherford didn't remove his coat or saddle either.

The oldest man in Gleann Muirn explained the rules: head into the loch, go around the *birlinn* anchored a hundred yards out, return to shore and race along the water's edge to the church at the far end. Nothing simpler. Alasdair glanced at Connington, who glowered at the water. A squall heaped the waves higher, making the galley bob at anchor.

The old man threw a stone into the water and a dozen racers made a line on the shore. Most had no saddles. They'd hang on to a leather strap tied round the horse's chest, just behind the forelegs, and control their horses with bridle and reins. All but Connington and Rutherford. The water would ruin their saddles. *Peculiar men.* They had something in mind and he needed to watch them.

The old man threw a second stone into the water.

Men and horses soared into the air and plunged into the water like dolphins, terror-struck in seconds by splashing and the shouts of onlookers. Alasdair saw Cailean's horse turn around and head for the shore. He heard his rider shouting and calling on the saints for help. The horse ignored him as though he were a bundle of old clothes tied to his back.

Alasdair heard the shouts and cheers. The racers rode into deeper water until it covered the horses' legs and chests in a high wave and exposed them in a trough. The horses exploded through the crests of the waves, kicking up screens of seawater, hiding the riders from the crowd.

With the reins in his right hand, Alasdair gripped the bellyband with his left. The stallion's head jerked up as the he swallowed water, but his powerful legs propelled them forward. "Keep going, Fear Mór, you wonderful beast!" He counted three men in front of him: Myles, Rutherford and Connington nearing the stern of the *birlinn*. In the galley, men yelled and struck the gunwales to create noise to distract those in front. All part of the game.

The winner would likely be the man who rounded the birlinn's prow first. Connington whipped his horse savagely until he was beside Myles. The rest of the racers hadn't reached the prow of the *birlinn*. Salt water stung Alasdair's eyes and the bellyband ripped into his hand. He focussed his mind and heart on winning. Over the gunwale above him, three rowers screeched like mad kites. But the rough sea made them lose their balance and they disappeared into the *birlinn*.

Fear Mòr surged forward, and Alasdair caught up to Myles, who was closest to the *birlinn* with Connington on his right side. He saw the Lowlander rein his horse into Myles. The grey smashed into the galley with such force that it pitched and rolled away from him and his rider. Above the churning water, Alasdair saw a flash of silver as Connington drove his arm toward Myles's back. Alasdair wasted precious moments recognising what he saw. A knife.

Connington had a knife!

Fear snaked round his belly and seized his heart. Finally he shouted, "*Thugad!*" Myles, look out!" Rutherford tried to pull Alasdair off Fear Mòr, but he held on.

Connington stabbed Myles once more. He sliced sideways with the knife again, and his target was Myles' horse. Blood streamed down the grey's head into the water. Silver flashed again in Connington's hand.

Rutherford hauled on Alasdair's shoulder. "Ye cannae stop him," he shouted. "Get back!"

"What?" Rutherford wasn't as murderous as Connington. No time to think further.

Connington pulled Myles off his horse and pushed him down into the sea. And held him there. Alasdair forced Fear Mòr between Myles and his attacker.

"Out of my way, ye Hieland meddler!"

Connington let go of Myles, and the waves pushed him against the galley. With a fierce amount of splashing and shouting the rest of the racers rounded the prow of the ship. In the seething water, they couldn't have seen or heard anything.

While Alasdair turned toward them, he felt a burning across his ribs. He faced forward as Connington rammed Fear Mór and drove him hard against the *birlinn*'s planking. Again the galley rocked with the force.

The blow to his back winded Alasdair. He gulped air and forced himself to breathe. He was losing his grip, but his hand was caught in the bellyband.

The ship almost keeled over, but it righted itself with a deafening slap. Three rowers flew out overhead. Alasdair's stallion bolted seaward to avoid one of the sailors landing on him. The man splashed into the water.

Alasdair didn't trust the sight of his salt-crusted eyes. Myles had disappeared and Connington had rounded the prow. Only three people bobbed in the sea—the rowers. Alasdair gripped the belly strap while his horse tried to escape the pitching *birlinn* by wading a distance out to sea. Gasping for breath, he tried to master Fear Mór.

Alasdair shook his head to clear it. He was hurt and not sure where.

He wound the reins around his right hand and gripped Fear Mór with his knees. He saw Connington heading for shore. Myles was no where in sight. He urged Fear Mòr beyond the galley's prow. He saw the backs of the other racers and their horses near shore, leaping out of the waves like wolf-crazed sheep. A grey horse followed the other horses ashore. Myles had disappeared.

Alasdair needed more eyes to see what had happened to him. Shouting for help from the rowers, Alasdair forced his horse back round the prow of the *birlinn* to look for the missing man. The crowd hailed someone as the winner.

Alasdair slipped off Fear Mòr and let him go to shore. Then he ducked underwater and searched. Tumbled sand and water prevented him seeing anything. He surfaced, breathed, and submerged again. Nothing and no one could he find.

CHAPTER 12

The tide must have sucked Myles to the bottom of the sea.

Alasdair shouted at the rowers who had fallen into the water to search for Myles. A man still on the *birlinn* shouted for others to come, then he jumped into the water to join the search.

Using the ship's keel as a guide Alasdair ducked underwater and searched the bottom of the hull, slick with seaweed and rough with barnacles. After three futile attempts, Alasdair grasped woollen cloth and leather—a belt. Myles was caught between the keel and rocks. He tugged at the belt, but couldn't shift the body. He couldn't breathe, and rose to the surface.

"He's here!" Alasdair hardly stopped to breathe when a dozen men converged on him. "He's caught under the keel." He gasped. "Need ropes!"

"We'll get him. You've done enough." If they didn't hurry, the sea would carry him off when the tide came in. The water spirits would claim the man and exile his spirit forever. They had to bring Myles to land, and bury him with his own people. From the shore, men waded out to the galley.

His ribs made Alasdair's breathing painful. He hadn't noticed that moments ago. Water battered his body, and he could hardly stand. Pain drummed a beat behind his eyes. He slipped underwater, forced himself to surface and spat out seawater. He tried to wade to shore, but made little headway. He might be the next to die without anyone noticing.

With much difficulty the Campbells freed Myles from under the keel, and lifted him hand to hand into the *birlinn*.

"When the ship heeled over, it might have knocked Myles off his horse."

"Strange his horse didn't head out to sea to get away from it."

"Maybe the horse kicked Myles or something."

"All the racers say they saw nothing."

"But this MacDonald was in the middle of it all."

"Listen," Alasdair croaked. Their faces were blurred. "I saw silver—a knife." He couldn't gauge their answer. Not sure they heard him. His head was spinning.

"Be still." One of them held him up in the water. "Your own people are coming for you."

Alasdair felt hands under his arms. His ribs hurt as Cailean and Ruari hauled him into a small *curach*.

"Listen to me," croaked Alasdair.

"*Bi sàmhach, a bhalaich*. Be quiet and rest, lad." Ruari's voice. "A terrible accident—foretold by the banshee."

When they reached the beach, Alasdair, barely conscious with pain, rolled over the gunwale of the *curach* onto the sand. Ruari helped him to his feet.

Her eyes full of tears, Shona drew near him. Her face

indicated he wasn't a pretty sight at that moment. He had to tell her before other Campbells were too close.

"A bit of warm whisky and I'll be fine." Alasdair wouldn't let this tiny woman see his weakness. "I'm sorry for the loss of your uncle."

"The sea has taken a terrible tax on life this year," she said.

He held her arm and whispered, "Your uncle didn't drown—he was murdered."

She mouthed the word. "Murdered."

Morag appeared suddenly. "She will deal with that later. Now she must prepare for his leaving this world. Come, Shona."

"You worked hard to find him. Thank you." Sadness roughened her voice as she took his hand and pressed it to her breast.

"Come. You have work to do, *a ghraidh*," said Morag.

"The horse. I'll get him to you." Alasdair said to Shona as she backed away from him.

"Look to yourself first," she said.

"A murdered Campbell gentleman and a heap of MacDonalds nearby," said Ruari. "Hurry! Let's get him back to camp."

"And prepare to defend ourselves," said Gillesbic.

White heat flashed in Alasdair's mind. His spirit shook loose from his body. He swirled away toward blackness.

~

While the men searched, Shona had stood at the shore, her breath rasping in her throat, her hands curled into fists. She wanted to plunge into the water and find Myles herself. But she was only a woman. That's what people would say. She could do nothing. They'd say that too. She calmed her breathing and waited.

The men shouted they had found him under the water. Himself had gone over to the next world. The anchor of Clan Campbell, the eagle who protected them. The *tànaiste* was dead.

Her breathing eased and her tears came. *Stop lamenting.* Time for that later. The care of the dead was women's work. She'd not fail her people in that. Myles would be properly mourned. She stretched out her hands and shook them. Ready.

Ruari brought Alasdair to shore. His face was as grey as a November sky and his conversation had not reassured her. But he was with his clan and she had work to do with Morag.

When she saw Alasdair fall, she gulped in air and rushed back to him. The spectators crowded round him. First Myles and now Alasdair. *No more sorrow.* Her knees trembled and threatened to put on her on the sand beside him. She fought her weakness.

Distorted faces and angry voices. She wrapped her arms around herself.

Morag said, "You may help him. Try. See what you can do."

"What can I do?"

Connington surfaced in the crowd like a rock in a stormy-tossed sea. "Verra suspicious, Myles' death. This MacDonald had something to do wi' it. Was he no' close tae Myles in the race?" His men muttered their agreement. "Lift him and take him back tae the castle. We'll find oot wha' happened. This spawn o' the divil will see oor justice!"

His men shouted, "Awa wi' him tae the dungeon!"

"What is this man saying, Shona Iain Glas? We are ready to fight." Ruari's voice was iron-strong.

Shona placed her hand on Ruari's arm and addressed Connington. "You will not take this man to the castle. He needs care in the village."

She stood and walked into the middle of a crowd of Connington's men, Campbells and MacDonalds. To the MacDonalds she said, "They want to put him in prison. They have no concern for hospitality or the protection we have sworn to give you."

Connington swung her around. His sword struck her on the leg. Iron. No strength in her body. She felt the anger growing in her. If she weren't a weak woman, she would march him back to the castle and throw him into the sea from the roof of the keep. She would watch him drown. She wanted to throw every one of Connington's grey-coated men into the sea after him. But wishes were useless. She controlled the redness of anger and slowly she breathed.

She said in the quiet voice her uncle used, "You will regret handling me in this manner."

The MacDonalds tried to rouse Alasdair. He lifted his head, then fell back unmoving.

"Is he deid?" Connington asked. "God Almighty has judged him and sent him tae hell where he'll be met by the Deil himself!"

Her heart flipped in a chest suddenly too small. He might be dead. *Answer Connington.* "Then he is of no further concern to you. Leave and take your men with you."

He looked around in that calculating way he had. The numbers against him were too great for him to do anything to Alasdair. *Coward.*

Campbells joined them. Shona put on Myles's voice of

command. "We are honour-bound to give the Clan Donald hospitality. No harm will come to any of them."

"We are with you, Shona Iain Glas."

"Go and prepare yourselves for the funeral of a great man." They shifted themselves while whispering about the tragedy and how it might affect them all.

Alasdair! Shona bent over him. His eyes were unfocussed, their brilliance gone dark. She bent to listen to his breath. Nothing. *No!* Frustrated, she raised her hands and lowered them. He gasped and coughed. She shouted for Morag to come back. From no where the Crow appeared and settled on Morag's shoulder.

"Give us room." Morag made the crowd move back while she appraised his condition by passing her hand over his chest and head. "There was little I could do."

"He'll die?"

"No. You've done it all." Morag exchanged a glance with the Crow and then said to Shona, "Do you understand what you've done?"

"I did nothing. I didn't touch him."

Crow said, *Speak. There is no one close enough to hear but us three.*

"You lifted your hands over his heart and pushed down. It beat again. You still deny you have the powers of a banshee?"

I am a witness. You expelled death from his body, said the Crow.

Morag was right. Her future would be different. No time to think about that now. They had to deal with his injuries.

The more you use the powers, the stronger you are, but the weaker in the presence of iron. Beware of iron.

"I don't want to hear about—"

"*Bi sàmhach.* Hush!" Morag stopped talking as two

MacDonalds approached. "A sad day for us all."

Ruari and Cailean greeted them. "We can take him back to camp."

Shona said to them, "He needs nursing and tranquility. Take him to Morag's house."

"He'll heal better with me," said Morag.

Anndru held Fear Mór's reins. "The horse is uninjured. We'll see he's all right and return him to the castle."

"Take him then." Shona spoke with a voice that held no warmth or sadness. Crisp. Purposeful. So she hoped.

She would go with Alasdair, and then deal with the funeral of her kinsman. Alasdair had said Myles was murdered. And who wanted that? *Connington.*

The man who pestered her to marry him. Daily. Only Myles stood between her and a forced marriage. And now Connington was blaming Alasdair for his death. Two birds with one stone.

"Take the *tànaiste* to Castle Muirn." The Campbells knew exactly what to do.

A fire of hatred spread out from her belly, filling her heart, burning away the grief. *Tend to the living and put away your hatred just now.* But she would keep the embers warm every waking and every sleeping hour.

The MacDonalds looked at her in a peculiar way, as though she had done something frightening. Or looked dead scary.

Ruari cleared his voice. "We'll care for him."

"He *must* go to Morag's house." She put all her strength in her voice. He hesitated a moment. She gave him no time to argue. "She's trained in ancient healing."

The MacDonalds looked at each other and the old man said, "Let the wise woman care for him."

"Her house is on the north side of the baile. Away from

the castle." She led the way and they bore him behind her. Alasdair groaned. Her chest tightened enough to make her gasp.

"Where's that buff-coated man?" asked Ruari. The others looked blank. "Where's the whole crew of them?"

"Who knows?" said Anndru. "Who cares?"

"We have enough to do," said Cailean.

They passed the shaggy-haired man, who said, "You've killed the chief's brother."

"We are sorry for your loss," said Ruari. "It's no fault of ours."

The Campbell man hadn't seen her, she was sure. Shona stepped forward and he bowed. "Your wounding words make me mourn all the more."

"You should stay with your own," said the man.

"The MacDonalds are guests."

"I apologise, daughter of Iain Glas." He bent his head and said no more. Others might think the same—that the MacDonalds had killed her uncle. Ridiculous. The MacDonalds had no reason to kill him and every reason to wish him well. Connington had done it, as Alasdair said.

They returned to the business at hand. Muttering sympathetic words, people accompanied them from the shore and others emerged from the thatched houses as they passed. Shona led the MacDonalds to the wise woman's house.

Morag prepared a pallet by the hearth fire for the injured man and instructed them to lay him on it. The wise woman shooed out the men, except for Ruari, and told Shona to tear pieces of old linen into strips while she inspected his wounds. After removing his *féileadh* and *léine*, they washed him and were careful not to tear the spoilt muscle of his arm and chest.

Alasdair shivered with cold—he was pitiful to see. Shona told herself to be cautious. She had begun to love him, and could not bear to lose him. Morag had great powers, but there was a limit to them. In one way or another Shona had lost many people she loved. She had no experience of life except for loving people and losing them. Her mother and brothers had died of fever. Her uncle had just been murdered. Perhaps that was why so many women married men they didn't love. It didn't hurt so much to lose them. Still, she hoped for Alasdair's recovery.

"Will you bring in some peats?" Morag asked Ruari. Then she removed Alasdair's *trews* and drawers. He had not come to his senses.

Shona gasped and looked at Morag. Even with a sick man under her hands, a smile threatened to pull back the corners of her lips.

Morag examined him. "His manly parts are of a good size. Good breeding stock, you might say." Morag checked for injuries by wrapping her hands around his lower legs and proceeded along his thighs.

"I wonder what size his rod will be when erect?"

"Morag, what are you about? You sound like a horse dealer at a fair!"

"A very nice comparison."

Shona felt her cheeks flame up like a whisky-fed fire. She'd seen horses and they all had an amazing ability to enlarge and elongate. And, amazingly, the mares were built to accommodate any stallion. *Such thoughts for a virgin.*

"Every virgin has such imaginings."

Shona jumped. "Morag!"

"Watch the left arm. The bone is exposed."

"How can you discuss his ... male parts ... when he is so badly hurt?"

"He'll live. You made sure of that. The shock to the head is his worst injury now. Whatever the state of his brain, at least he can make children."

"Do men suspect that women speculate about their members?"

Morag laughed. "Some do and others never bother to think about it." She felt his head. "Not broken. No splinters of bone in the head injury. Get the silk and bone needle ready for the cuts. Three broken ribs on the left." She carried on with her examination and felt his ribs. "Odd. He has broken ribs on his left side, and a gash on his head. What you'd expect in this race. But he has two long cuts across his ribs. Clean cuts."

Like a knife. No one carried a knife in the race. No place to store it when they raced shirtless without saddles. No need for it. Alasdair had said he saw a knife and he might not have been raving.

Connington. She thought that he'd worn a shirt to cover his chest out of ignorance and used a saddle from cowardice. No one questioned the peculiarities of a stranger, especially a Lowlander.

"Hold his shoulders down if I touch something tender," said Morag.

Shona held him and stole glances at him while Morag worked. Shona felt a heavy sadness for her uncle, but if Alasdair's heart stopped again, so might hers.

Morag was the wisest woman in the whole of Argyll. Alasdair might yet be whole. The old woman felt his chest on the left and Alasdair jerked. He squirmed and turned to his other side. Shona quieted him with a murmuring charm as if he were an infant. He relaxed and they rolled him flat again.

"We must deal with the arm and the chest cuts first. The

abrasions we tend last." His chest was turning blue with bruising. "The head bleeds freely, but the skull is least injured of all. Can't say about the brain inside."

Morag glanced up when Ruari came in with the peats. "Hold him." She showed Ruari how to hold Alasdair's shoulder and upper arm while Shona pulled on his wrist. "Pull and don't let go till I tell you." As they stretched out the bones, Alasdair woke and screamed, then fainted again.

Tears welled in Shona's eyes. *Fight them. Don't let them fall.*

She pulled until the exposed bone slipped back under his skin. Morag ran her hands down his arm to make sure the bone was truly in position. "The arm should heal without fault—if you hold it till it's splinted."

She wrapped more bog moss and healing herbs in a poultice and placed it on the wound, then wrapped it all in linen strips. Then she wrapped staves of wood round the arm to hold the bone in place while it healed. Morag exposed abraded flesh on his chest that seeped blood. "Pass me the linen." She spread a poultice for the wound and then wrapped his chest in linen.

She wrapped his head to stop the bleeding. Lastly she placed *alla bhuidhe* under his left arm. "You remember the healing plant is placed here, where it's closest to the heart. Now let sleep heal him."

Shona prepared a hot drink of herbs for all of them. "I'm giving up thoughts of living with a man I love, and listening instead to the opinions of people older and wiser than I."

"Your stepmother? Older, yes, but wiser? Hah! I can't tell you what to do—only advise you. Trust in your power to know."

Ruari added three peats to the fire.

Alasdair moaned and moaned again.

"Let's check his ribs again." Blood had seeped through the bandages. "Lift him while I add bandages to his chest." The old man slipped his arms carefully under Alasdair's chest and held him like a beloved child. Morag and Shona passed the bandages around his broken ribs.

"Mind you tell him to be careful of the ribs. One could pierce his heart and bleed fiercely inside. I've seen it happen," said Morag.

Ruari said, "As have I."

The old woman sewed the cut in Alasdair's forehead. "The cut will heal with little scarring. It's the mind that causes the difficulties. It draws away courage."

"Can you fetch him a plaid and another shirt?" asked Morag. Ruari nodded and left for the MacDonald camp.

"*Eisd, a ghràidh*, listen love, Crow and I have discussed this. We've decided we must tell you."

"Tell me what? What?"

"Myles's death changes what will be. I searched with the eyestone and this is your man. He will be a strength and a weakness for you."

"My man? But ... you didn't want me to spend time with him or be friendly. You wanted me to become a banshee to follow after you and practise the secret arts."

Morag winced. "Yes. But both things are possible. Especially for you."

After weeks of skirting the edges of that dangerous thing called love, she could let herself love him. But really, what might Alasdair say? He was friendly to a lonely lass as he passed through her country. Alasdair might not agree with the vision in the eyestone.

"You and Alasdair will lie together ... if you both live through your tribulations."

"He is kind and gentle. Yet I won't. Loving is too painful for me."

Morag's old face softened before she snapped back to her role as healer. "Enough chatter. We'll nurse and heal him. You'll have time to think."

They covered him and sat with him at the fire until Ruari returned with the shirt and plaid. They dressed and covered him again, then allowed him to sleep. His clansman prepared a pallet for himself at the fire.

"That Connington man will bring great misery." Ruari lay on top of his bedding.

"He has already! I live with his words and deeds every day."

Morag shook her head. "He will bring a withering on this glen."

Shona felt weak, as though her bones had no substance and would not hold her up should she attempt to stand. Were her banshee powers of no use? "Can nothing be done? Is Connington too strong?" Her uncle might not be avenged.

Ruari snored gently and Morag put a plaid overtop him.

"Battle him with all your strength and power. Connington will never know or understand love. But you won't last long without it. This man under our care will love you."

"But I've seen too much death. I don't want to lose anyone else."

"You will see more unless my sight fails me." Morag put one arm around Shona's shoulders. "Seek what joy you can in this life." Then Morag spoke with the voice of prophecy, her words coming slowly at first, but then the rhythm increased with the passion of their meaning. "When I dream of Connington, I see dead children and sorrowing women. You'll never know joy again if you go with that Connington man. Defeat him and crush his evil." She took Shona's two hands in her own. "You must do all you can to learn about your powers."

Shona couldn't answer. Her chest jerked with short breaths.

"Change will come, *a ghràidh*," said Morag. "You become Connington's toy ... or a powerful banshee."

Shona knew that. Her mind knew. She needed to discipline her heart. It didn't make walking into tomorrow any easier.

"You'll train in fighting Connington."

Fighting Connington. That was all she needed to know. "I agree."

"We'll go now and see to your uncle. We will mourn a great man."

After the mourning women left the great hall to rest, old people stayed the remainder of the day to guard his corpse from the evil beings who might steal his spirit and soul. Shona took her turn watching the body with her clan through the second night. They told stories about the *tànaiste* she hadn't heard, and she cried, and they laughed at the good times. They knew his spirit was near listening to them. They assured Shona that he'd enjoyed the telling of them, although he was unable to reply.

Shona wanted to say a few words to the corpse, but couldn't in front of the others. Myles had died, leaving a widow and young children. It meant deep sorrow for them, but was hard for her, too. He had defended her right to choose her husband. Now who would fend off Connington? Only her father.

A bad winter was coming, so the farmers said. It would be doubly difficult inside Castle Muirn.

No matter if Priscilla shouted and waved her arms about, Shona told the servants to prepare food for the mourners. And they must bring up all the ale, wine and whisky from the cellar below the great hall. Myles had been a gentleman, the scion of an ancient house, and his funeral would show the magnitude of his loss. His widow had arrived from Gleann Falach in the west, and she would share the solar chamber with Priscilla and sleep in the other bed. It was the grandest room in the house, as befitted the widow of the chief's brother. Shona must confront Priscilla about that this evening and tell her that she would be sharing her chamber.

The servants offered a large *cuach* of whisky to everyone who came through the door. Everyone took a sip and passed it to another guest. A piper played small pipes at one end of the great hall and at the other a *seanchaidh* narrated the adventures of Fionn MacCumhaill and Diarmaid Donn, their ancestor.

More Lowlanders with baggy breeches entered the great hall with the mourners. Menacing. Where had they come from? Were they different men or were they the ones from the shore? Shona couldn't say, but she had to offer them hospitality. She saw her stepmother and Connington come into the great hall with their servants, and take up positions in the best chairs by the south-facing window. Shona started trembling.

Shona saw Priscilla scrutinise what she called the *heathenish blanket*.

"This house has been touched again by the cold hand of death," said Priscilla. "Ye'r not lucky."

"She has no worry about her next meal or a good roof over her head," said Connington.

"Ye have much tae be grateful for," said Priscilla. "Look at ye—yer face ruined with weeping. Ye've no idea what great sorrow is. Ye'r too young. The widow with children has the right tae weep."

Shona did not remind her of her mother's early death.

Three women, sitting in the window seats, laughed at something in their shared conversation.

"Look at them. Have they no respect?" asked Priscilla.

How respectful was murder? Constantly thinking about the murder had dulled her anger. She had no difficulty controlling it. She smoothed the folds of her *earasaid*. "They've remembered something about my uncle."

"A sad funeral can be a long and dreary affair, dear auntie," said Connington.

There was no feeling in the man. Shona suspected he was wanting something.

The piper moved to the middle of the room and played a lively tune. The widow danced, still weeping, while others stood up and joined her.

"Can we stop that caterwauling?" asked Priscilla. "Weeping and dancing. And all that singing. Never heard the like."

"It's our custom," said Shona.

"When can we bury the man and send them away, Thomas?"

"Tomorrow," said Connington.

Shona gasped. "He's a great man in this country. He must be mourned for five days at least." People had to be shown that the clan was still strong, with the ability to feed and protect their people.

"We can't afford that," said Priscilla."A' thae food they've stuffed in their bellies."

"The lass is concerned for the reputation of the Campbells," said Connington.

"The food and drink in this room would feed a gentle family for a year," said Priscilla. "Who will pay for it?"

"My family *is* paying for it!" In her father's absence, Shona had to fight for her dead uncle's rights. Her nightmare was relentless.

"Yer family is represented by your stepmother and she says that she won't pay," said Connington.

"You must give my father time to come home." Things weren't right in the world.

"Yer father is concerned with oor interests in Edinburgh."

"What could be more important than his brother's funeral?"

"Not yer affair. That flock of hungry gannets goes away tomorrow so that we may give your uncle a *decent* funeral," said Priscilla.

"A decent funeral?"

"The household alone. Thomas has a minister coming tae marry ye. And if he fails tae come, Thomas can say a few words over the body like he did in the wars against the Catholic empire."

Connington bowed. "Alas, I have much experience with death."

"And he can recite great verses o' the Bible."

"Behold the amazing gift o' love the Faither hath bestowed on us, the sinful sons o' men, tae call us sons o' God."

He paraphrased the Bible to support his lies. How impressive. Maybe he'd killed some of those poor bodies himself. "What must I do?" Shona asked.

"Ye must accept ma proposal of marriage."

How could she put him off? She chewed her bottom lip.

Despite the fires in the hall, she was chilled her to the bone. "Accept you?"

"Ye hae two weeks tae prepare and then we marry."

Stall him. "You must send a messenger to my father and ask his permission." A message *had* to arrive in time.

"Ye're the weed that's grown wild," said her stepmother. "Ye'll be a fair flower in Thomas' garden."

"My greatest pleasure. Trimming." His eyes raked her up and down, polluting her.

"If I agree, you'll let them bury my uncle according to our customs?"

"Of course," said Thomas. "Ye hae ma word."

"And I have two weeks to prepare?"

"A fortnight."

Shona joined the crowd dancing to the piper. The mourners would think that her tears were for her uncle, but some were for her own fate. If her uncle was to be treated with respect, then it seemed she had to agree to a unwanted union. Her life would be easier if she gave up and married Thomas Connington without a fuss. But he had trapped her, and she resented that.

She'd already sent a messenger to her father's town-house in Edinburgh asking him for permission to marry whomever she pleased, and begging him to return.

Connington allowed the funeral to go on for three more days, and Shona spent her time avoiding him. After tending Alasdair with Morag during the day, she passed the nights in the hall with the other mourners. She had to tolerate Connington's presence for now.

She had time to plan.

CHAPTER 13

At the castle, Shona arranged the details of the funeral. She organised food, greeted mourners, and filled her mind with her tasks. In unguarded moments, vivid images of water and blood surfaced from the dark corners of her memory. Then she returned to Morag's house, and stayed up to tend to Alasdair. Morag told Ruari what do for the sick man while she and Shona went to the funeral. Morag looked haggard. The wise woman left her hair free of its linen cap, so it hung down in long grey and black tendrils to her waist. She wrapped a black and white *earasaid* over her shift, and went out barefoot into the autumn wind and rain.

People were milling around the main gate when they arrived. Four mourning women, *mnathan tuiream*, dressed as wildly as Morag, joined them, then they all passed easily through a multitude awed by their appearance, and entered the castle.

The light of a bleak day and four large candlesticks illuminated Myles on his bier in the hall. No fire burned in the hearth. Heart-stopping grief seeped into her from the hidden places it had lived since her mother died. Shona wanted to spend as much time as she could with her uncle, but at the same time she wanted the funeral over. How was it possible to hurt so much? The throng outside filtered into the hall while Shona stood with twenty others who guarded the corpse, and sang the lament.

Shiubhail thu, shiubhail thu!
Shiubhail is cha d'fhuirich thu!
Chan fhaic sinn tuilleadh thu,
A Mhaoileis Mhòr nan Tùr.

You are gone, you are gone!
You have gone and not stayed!
We'll never see you again,
Great Myles of the Towers.

Morag put a wooden plate on his chest, another mourning woman placed salt on it and a third, earth. "Salt is the spirit and soul, and earth the corruptible body." Then the six of them stood around his head and at his sides to proclaim the grief of his widow and three children, who sat close by the bier.

The source of their protection and strength was laid low.
Who will bring them corn?
Fish from the stream and deer from the hill?
Who will keep the roof over their heads in the long winters to come?

Who indeed. Who would keep them all from harm?

What if it were Alasdair's body lying on the staves? Shona was relieved that he lived, even while her murdered clansman lay in front of her. The physical sensations she experienced in tending Alasdair swelled in her and made her squirm. In the presence of death, she wanted to make love. She imagined dashing out of the hall, down the stair and through the *baile* to Morag's house where he lay. She quashed the impulse. *Foolish woman.* The man to whom she wanted to make love was still unconscious. *Foolish, selfish woman.*

At the end of the funeral, Shona caught Connington's eye and looked away. He looked as serene as a minister, surrounded by four grey-coated men. If he had murdered Myles, as Alasdair said, she should rain curses on him from all the mountain tops, but she couldn't bring herself to do it. Curses let loose might go where they weren't deserved. None of the Campbells had done anything evil. Yet she was cursed with Connington. But one thing she decided—she wouldn't live in a house with her uncle's murderer.

She went up the stair to Priscilla's chamber to pay her respects.

Her stepmother read her psalter at the hearth. "Ye'r overlong comin' tae see me," she said without looking up.

"I helped prepare my uncle. And nurse the MacDonald."

"Yer uncle must be respected, but not that MacDonald." She turned a page. "Ye must mind the company ye keep."

Shona already followed that advice. She avoided Connington as much as she could. "Isn't healing part of a woman's duty?"

"Ye saw tae the wrong man. His soldiers brought in ma nephew."

Shona imagined an injured Connington and herself ministering to him. His care would be wanting. "I saw him. He appeared uninjured."

Priscilla frowned. "Fortunately, he's hale and hearty. Ye can give him yer good wishes at supper—in ma chamber.

The body of yer uncle and every other body between here and Perth has plugged the hall."

"I don't feel hungry in the least."

"Sir Thomas is oor guest and ye'r expected tae sup wi' him."

Priscilla might have known about the murder. Maybe not.

"Ye say 'no' tae any man who comes by, but ma Thomas is a patient man."

Her stepmother's prattling irritated her like gnats at twilight—always there, always plaguing her. Alasdair was lying injured at Morag's house. She wanted to see him, to make sure that his chest rose and fell and a pulse beat in his neck. To minister to him. She crossed her arms to keep herself in her chair, to prevent herself from bolting for the door.

"He's a good man, weel mostly—and ye need a good man tae stand by ye." Priscilla stabbed her finger in Shona's direction to emphasise her point. "And remember, yer family has the infirmity of being Hielanders. No civilised person trusts ye. Ye cannae be difficult in oor time of troubles."

A good man? In any way? Doubtful. "Troubles?" The troubles might be the reason for Connington's presence at Castle Muirn. Shona wanted to ask her if her father and the fighting men of Clan Campbell were in the middle of unrest. In prison? Injured? She had thought that troubles in Edinburgh wouldn't affect the people of Gleann Muirn. The world was an unsafe place, where people died too soon.

Priscilla was about to reply, but pressed her lips firmly together, and returned to her reading.

Perhaps she regretted telling Shona anything. "Is my

father in danger? I heard about a riot in Edinburgh—against the king's prayer book." *Not another death.*

"Tae many taxes and imposts," said Priscilla. "And he's pushing his Inglishe ways on us."

"But the king is anointed by God. Has he not—"

"Enough! I'll have my Thomas talk sense tae ye."

"Did Thomas have a hand in the riot?"

"Thomas will tell ye what ye need tae know."

Was there a connection between the riot in Edinburgh and Connington's arrival?

She had barely finished the thought when Connington himself entered the chamber.

"Ye'r wanted doon the stair. Dae something wi' the gannets diving intae oor food and drink."

"Sit ye doon, Thomas, ma dearie."

Connington made a dismissive gesture with his hand. "Joan, get doon the stair and sort the food!"

"Please stay a while yourself, Thomas my dear." Priscilla indicated the most comfortable chair in the room.

Shona didn't need to be told to leave twice. She stepped out into the stair, but stopped outside the chamber to listen and learn.

"Ye dae naething tae help ma cause. Ye're sae stupid—ye've the brain of a butterfly. Ye can't see what's happening. Ye've no idea why ye're here."

Priscilla snuffled and began to weep. A chair scraped the floor and Shona heard her footsteps coming toward the spiral stair. Shona descended a few steps. How could Connington be angry at the aunt who fawned on him?

"Sit doon! I'm no finished wi' ye. I need that Campbell woman's dowry." He breathed heavily. Shona crept back up.

"I need more than that. I want the Campbell treasury.

What did ye think aboot that? I'm no closer tae wedding or silver than when I came."

Shona was wanted for her dowry. And whatever wealth the Campbells had. She had suspected as much.

"I've a new plan and ye'r not needed."

The weeping stopped. "I can return tae Edinburgh."

"No, ye can't. Yer husband won't have ye."

The weeping began anew.

"Fer God's sake, woman, stop yer bubblin' afore I batter ye. Ye stay in yer chamber, ye useless auld fool."

For the first time, Shona truly pitied her stepmother. The Lowland woman had to live among strangers and now her own nephew had insulted her. Shona wanted to stay with Priscilla and comfort her, but likely an offer of sympathy wouldn't be welcome.

Besides, she had to tend Alasdair.

When she entered Morag's house, she saw the old woman looked tired. It was more than the fatigue of a day's work—or even a week. It was a lifetime's hoard of fatigue. "Morag, sleep. I'll see to him."

The old woman went to her box-bed and crawled in with hardly a word. "The poultice on his arm. See to that." She closed her doors.

That Morag trusted her with nursing a man so seriously injured pleased her. She slowly pulled the poultice from his broken arm. His eyes remained closed and he did not move. After inspecting it to see that it had been thoroughly cleaned, and smelling it for decay, she checked his face. His eyes were still closed; the poppy flower held him in sleep. She placed a new cloth with a goodly amount of the all-healing and the king's plant on his arm, and slowly lifted the arm and wrapped it in clean linen. She lifted his head enough to remove his bandages. His stitches held and the wounds were closed. Good. His chest bandage she left for now until she'd someone to help lift him into a sitting position. He looked as placid as an angel, his face smoothed of all care.

She wondered at the feeling that coursed through her—a fierce sdetermination to protect him from his enemies. She bent over his chest and kissed his forehead. She gathered his soiled dressings and when she returned, she found his quiet blue eyes gazing at her.

Neither said a word. They just stared at each other. Perhaps he couldn't speak. Or worse.

She placed her hand on his uninjured arm. "You're all right. You're at Morag's house." She waited for a response. He moved his head and sighed. He was still alive. "Would you like a drink? Watered whisky. The best thing to get you moving again."

"You kissed me?"

"I did. I'm sorry." What must he think? Morag would think her too bold by half.

His words were slow and formed with great care. "I feel safe here ... want to stay here forever ... with you."

"I'll get a little whisky for you."

"Am I dreaming? Are you a *sìtheach*? A fairy queen. First time I saw you that's what I thought."

She drew in a breath and held it, hoping that would slow the pounding of her heart. She couldn't answer him—he was too close to the truth. She rose stiffly and filled a horn cup with warm water and whisky, and brought it to him. Her breathing was nearly normal.

"Don't talk. Save your strength." *And don't ask any more*

questions. She lifted his head and poured just a little into his mouth. His lips gave way to the pressure of her hand. For a hard warrior, he had such soft skin.

"Thank you. Enough."

She busied herself with checking the *crùisgean* lamps and banking the fire.

"Shona." He said her name.

A flood of longing seized her. A flood so powerful and elemental it threatened to shrink the whole world into this little house where only two people and their love existed—the only currency in this world—the highest value was on insistent, demanding love.

"Please come to me."

She knelt beside his pallet. Obedient. Connington and his aunt would have paid a fortune in silver for such compliance. He reached for her face and drew her toward him.

Her breath stopped. No air descended into her chest.

He said, "I never thought to hold you so close to me. I thought I'd be in my grave today."

Then his soft lips pressed on hers. His heat and scent warmed her. And he pushed her back gently and looked into her eyes. "Are those tears? I should not have kissed you."

"No, no! Not tears of sadness. Tears of joy. I'm glad you are still alive. Very glad."

"Never better." He sighed and closed his eyes. "The sweetest kisses I ever had. My mother included."

He pulled her to him and kissed her again. Like striking steel on flint, her blood carried the sparks and her skin flamed. She could not draw breath fast enough. Neither could he and he was injured. She had to stop. She might kill him with her enthusiasm.

Still breathing quickly, she sat up. "Are you all right?"

His friendly smile was back. He might be well on the road to recovery.

"You should sleep, Alasdair." Was he truly himself again? Would he remember these kisses?

"Will you sit with me? Will you sing?"

Why not? The rest were away for a while. She sat beside him and sang a lullaby and he fell asleep. She lay down beside him and nestled into his chest. She'd rest for just a moment.

Something, someone shook her shoulder. She woke up. Morag. Alasdair's face sheened with sweat, he was restless and murmuring.

"He has a fever."

Alasdair awoke from a nightmare of water and horses' hooves. He reached for his claymore. Not there. The light of bright day filtered down the smoke hole and lit up a creepie stool near his pallet. For a short time he had no idea where he was. He inspected the room and saw but a few chairs, two chests and a box-bed. He recalled the Shona's sweet scent and cool hands. Shona, the *sìtheach*, the fairy who had brought him to the Land of Apples for healing. Where one hour counted as one day. Where kisses were sweeter than honeyed apples. He closed his eyes. Would he return to a people who didn't know him?

He tried to remember what happened. His fairy woman and an old woman had bathed him and wrapped his head and chest in the bandages. Ruari and the others had carried him to shore. Thinking hurt his head. He banished the world from his mind.

When he awoke again, the *crùisgean* lamps cast a gentle light on the old woman. *Morag.* Her name came back to him.

"I see you're back with us." Ruari hove into view.

He was still in the right world and little time had passed. He breathed a long sigh.

"You'll take some broth now you're awake. Best thing for you." Morag gave Ruari a small clay vial of liquid. "And this."

Ruari smelled it and grimaced. "I'll make sure he takes it."

"Your clansman rarely left your side," Morag told Alasdair. "I told him you're on the mend, but he wouldn't leave. Most of the time. So he's made himself useful."

"I mended a few things. Wove heather rope, and built up the dry stone wall that protected the herb garden."

"Good man." Alasdair dropped off.

One day Alasdair's eyes stayed open for a long time. recognised the fairy queen who had fluttered in and out of his dreams. *Shona of the sweet kisses.*

She smiled. "You're still feverish. Do you remember me?"

He'd never forget her for all eternity. "You're beautiful." He followed her movements. She had no idea she was so lovely.

Morag came to him, unwrapped his bandage and examined his ribcage. "The wound in your side won't heal quickly. See that you keep it wrapped."

"How is he keeping?" asked Ruari. "When can we leave?"

"Did you give him the medicine in the vial?"

"Of course."

"He'll mend just fine. Just a few more days and he'll be able to ride."

Shona brought him more broth. "You must drink." She propped him up with more pillows and spoon-fed him.

He wished for a hundred years in her arms. "You're a fairy woman," he said.

Both women paused and looked at each other. Alasdair said nothing more, and they resumed what they were doing.

"This is a magical place," Alasdair turned his head from side to side. "Magical."

"You're still mad with fever," said Shona.

"You have the most wondrous hair," he said. "Like new gold. " His tongue was thick in his mouth. He spoke as though he were drunk. Must be the medicine that Ruari had given him.

"We're off," said Shona. "You must rest."

"Falling in love with your nurse, are you?" asked Ruari when the women left the house.

"What day is it?"

"Three days after Saint Michael's Feast."

Alasdair scrutinised the neat house and knew it well now. "The race?"

"You lost."

Ruari's wooden face hid something. "What else?" Disturbing images flashed through his mind. *Silver. A large dirk.*

"You were hurt."

Not funny. Alasdair tried to rise and couldn't. "Evidently. Will you help me?" When Ruari brought him to a sitting position, the pain in his ribs stopped his breath for a few moments.

"I'll put you back down."

"No, let me be." Alasdair's responsibilities returned to him. "The cattle?"

"Fine. All fine. We're safe, but there was a death," said Ruari.

"I remember. Myles Campbell, who was drowned." He could make no sense of the jumbled pictures in his mind. Connington's horse screaming. The water surrounding him like a waterfall. Tumbling riders and horses. Yelling. "Did he fall from his horse?"

"I believe he did, but he had help leaving this world. His *léine* is stained with traces of blood. His face is all right. He'll look good at his funeral."

"I was pushed into the side of the *birlinn.* That's all I remember." Then he remembered the knife.

"We must leave as soon as you're able. The women haven't said anything to you, but the Campbells think you murdered Myles."

"Me! Why would I do such a thing? I have a deal with them."

"So enough Campbell gentlemen say. And Shona Campbell herself. That's why you're not lying in a pit in Castle Muirn."

"I'll answer any accusation they have." Only one person benefited from Myles's death. The one who had wielded a knife in the sea.

"Best we leave soon."

"I'm sure Connington is joyful that I was unwell and unable to answer to anyone's accusations. Has Myles been buried?"

"Today."

"Then we'll go and witness it."

"Are you strong enough? Cailean and Donall can represent us."

"I'll go," Alasdair said.

The old man opened his mouth and closed it, then brought him his *fèileadh* and belt.

"Help me dress." He had fallen in love with Shona, and blurted out his thoughts in his sillier moments. Her uncle's death changed nothing for him. He was a MacDonald, the ancient enemy. He wondered if they would still do business with the Campbells, and take their cattle to market. He was supposed to avoid any impropriety with Shona. Well, that fence was broken, and he was glad. He could fill his eyes with the sight of her and kiss her.

How much time would he have with her before she was stolen from him?

CHAPTER 14

The mourners had gathered outside the castle when Alasdair and the old man joined them. Myles's shrouded body was carried out on a bier of staves by the strongest men in the district. Morag and the other women, who'd lead the lamenting, followed, their feet naked, their hair long and dishevelled.

Alasdair saw Shona with Connington, arm in arm. He had a powerful urge to go and tear her away, but he restrained himself. He and Ruari joined them.

Connington put his hand on his sword and sneered at Alasdair as he passed by. Alasdair quickened his pace to catch up to Connington before the funeral processed to the church. Ruari kept up with him.

"Are you well enough to walk this fast?" said Ruari. "Besides, it's not polite."

Alasdair ignored him. Ruari grabbed his arm and stopped him. "What are you about, young fool?" Then Alasdair saw hostility in the faces of those in the procession. "Enough of them think that *you* killed Myles."

"I'm sorry." He'd have to tolerate Connington, holding

Shona close to his side. The Lowlander stopped and pulled her to him. He crushed her against his chest and studied Alasdair.

AHe didn't know what to do—Connington had murdered her uncle, and now he was free to court Shona. The Lowlander planted a kiss on the top of Shona's head and she wrenched her body away. She had no liking for him. That was clear to Alasdair, but to all the world it looked like Connington was comforting the bereaved. Even at a distance Alasdair saw her face had gone white and her eyes were wide. She saw Alasdair. She opened her mouth, but no words came out. Connington pulled her to him. Her face darkened.

No grief there, it's anger.

"You still have the fever." Ruari pulled him aside and sat him on a large stone.

Alasdair looked up at the old man.

"Whatever mad thing you want to do, you can forget," said Ruari.

He was old, but he had been a soldier and he was still strong as Fionn the hero. Alasdair sat and watched the mourners pass by.

"He's not well, this man," said Ruari to the curious in the procession and they nodded politely. And glanced back at Alasdair after they passed. He smiled weakly, reminding himself where he was. Alasdair stood and joined the procession far behind Connington and Shona, his captive.

His clan approved of him wanting to deal in cattle, not marry a Campbell. Right, then. He wasn't going to marry her, but he had to make sure she was all right. Had to know she would not be forced to marry against her will. And he had to make sure the Campbells knew that Connington was a murderer.

The wind unfurled the dark mantles of the mourning women against the grey stone of Castle Muirn. Morag raised her voice to sing, low and quiet at first, but slowly rising to a great volume as they walked toward the church. The rest of the women joined her song. At the end of every phrase, they struck their palms together like drums. Their voices, their claps echoed among the black rocks on the bleached shore of the loch. As the women reached the churchyard, pipers began to play and the voices of the mourning women soared above them.

In the churchyard the whole procession travelled *deiseil* around the church three times. The funeral was held outside in the churchyard, as the church was too small for the number of mourners.

Alasdair screwed his eyes shut. His mind filled with images of Shona with the Lowlander. He banished them to the bottom of his mind, in that dark place where lay the horrors of the war. After he made sure she would be allowed to make her own decisions, he'd gather his men and they'd drive the cattle eastward, where he could make his profit. After that he could look for a suitable bride, though he had no desire for anyone but her.

A sharp pain ripped through his head behind his eyes. *No more. Don't think any more.* He placed his hands over his ears and bent down to recover.

He felt a hand on his shoulder.

"Rest easy, *a bhalaich*. You're still not well."

Alasdair waited for the pain to ebb. Finally he lowered his hands and lifted his head. He breathed normally. "Thank you for watching my back. Again."

"My duty. Look at the Lowlander. A minister of the Reformed Church saying part of the service."

"I haven't seen any of them here before."

"All in grey or black. They haven't much in the way of coloured coats, it seems."

"Why would a Lowlander say the service in Inglishe? So few of us speak it."

"It'll be Connington's doing. Well, everyone is polite, at least."

The minister in the long black gown and thick white collars of the Lowlands began his service for the dead. Why did a Lowlander offer prayers at a Highland funeral? At the end a piper struck his bag, took a deep breath and piped the return to village and castle.

Some village women chatted on the way.

"They don't look happy."

"It's a funeral. Why would they?"

"Thomas Connington has his arm about her."

"I hear they'll marry soon."

That wounded Alasdair once more. He wanted to put his hands to his ears. However, that might not be her choice if it were true. He'd find out.

Ruari put his hand on Alasdair's shoulder. "That Connington man looks right cocky. She has the face of mourning on her."

"Because her uncle's dead."

"I wonder," said Ruari. "Have you noticed the numbers of Lowland men about?"

There were many men with the baggy breeches of the Lowlands outside the castle. Many more than there had been even yesterday. Too many.

With a grip of iron, Connington guided Shona away from the church. She had no strength to push him away--he wore his big iron sword and dirk. Morag was right —Shona was a banshee and here once again was the proof.

At the edge of the crowd, Shona saw one of the Lowlanders cut a branch from a rowan tree and lay it across the door to the church where Myles Campbell's body awaited interment in the family's tomb. Obviously he was afraid that Myles's spirit might rise from the grave and haunt him. And he was fearful because the murder might start a bloodfeud between the Campbells and his family. A bloodfeud caused by someone connected to him. *Connington.* But he had to belong to the Highlands if he knew about the rowan.

The funeral party slowly returned to the castle and prepared for the last feast before returning to their homes. Cooks roasted fowl and beef at a bonfire as high as a horse. After people helped themselves at the tables, they sat down to eat in family groups on a field that rippled with plaids: soft reds, leafy greens, earthy browns. A living quilt of Gleann Muirn people and their loved ones.

She longed to be among them.

Her suitor strutted like a raven among pigeons, with her arm trapped under his. She heard people say, "A wonderful funeral."

"He'll have a good journey to the next world." They looked content, while she felt like throwing herself into an open grave. They must not know about the murder. She saw Una and Ròs Màiri.

Shona smiled as sweetly as she could manage, and withdrew her hand from under his arm. "I will greet my friends."

A short distance away her friends smiled at her, but the

smiles faded when Connington came close. His eyes could wither oak trees.

"A blessing on the day to you," they replied, but as they approached to speak further, Connington steered Shona's shoulder to the edge of the crowd. "Dear lady, ye're fatigued."

"No, Sir Thomas."

"Pray set a moment and rest yerself." He tried to take her hand while she pretended not to see the gesture.

"No need, sir."

He waved the unwanted hand in the direction of the quiet loch. "A very peaceful place. You've had no dealings with the dangers of the world."

"My father says many a Lowlander will not come to the Highlands without making a will. Have you made one?"

"Yer faither jests. No one in the Hielands is a danger tae me." When he leant toward her, he smelled like rancid butter.

"Why do you wish to wed me still?"

"These are troubled times. We seek our friends where we may." He paused as if to remind himself of the purpose of marriage. "I've had no time tae take a wife. I was too lang a soldier."

"And my dowry is considerable." She walked ahead and didn't look at him.

"Are ye afraid?" he asked.

"Of what?"

"Wifely duties: bairns, servants, the sick. Are ye fearful of the married state?"

"I will do my duty to a loving and respectful husband." *Not you.*

"Ye answered me, ma little fledgling. Be sure I'll guard ye well." She tried to walk away and he held her arm tighter.

"You hurt me." She shook his hand loose. "Sir, if we marry, you cannot treat me so."

He pulled her close to his chest like a lover.

"Ye agreed." He grabbed her arm and swung her around, his sword caught between them. Her knees wobbled with weakness.

"I will do my duty to whomever becomes my husband."

He gripped her right arm painfully. "So ye will. But ye're a young lass, ignorant. "

"Not so ignorant I can't recognise unseemly haste."

"Ye do what I say or I'll make ye mind. Tomorrow ye ride wi' me tae see the MacPharlans."

The next day, Shona rode out with Catriona and three Gleann Muirn men, followed by Connington and a dozen of his. Clouds dulled the beauty of Loch Muirn into a hard floor of glass. She'd discover why Connington was in the Highlands, and if he planned another murder and whose it would be. She wondered once again how her family had come to form an alliance with his.

"How many tenants has yer faither?"

The question ended her speculations about his motives. "Three hundred on the rent roll and another hundred cottars, I believe. Why do you want to know that? You won't live here. If we married, you'd get my dowry, and you'd take me to the Lowlands."

"What extent are yer father's lands?"

"I don't know."

"Any difficulties with neighbours?"

"Sometimes." She didn't understand why he wanted to know about Gleann Muirn.

When he rode closer, she flinched. "Yer family may need ma especial help. Speak."

When she said nothing, he pulled her pony's bridle. The animal snorted in fear and jerked its neck, ready to rear. She hung onto the saddle while murmuring to it and stroking its neck. She calmed the beast by whispering quietly so that only it could hear.

Anger strengthened her voice. "You've mishandled me twice. I am noble and you shall not strike me. My people won't follow your orders if you don't respect me."

The Gleann Muirn men glowered at him.

"Then answer me when I question ye. I'll brook no games." His voice was gentle with threat, but the men relaxed. "Truce then?"

She'd didn't trust him, but welcomed a period of calm before the next storm. "Truce. Our neighbours are MacPharlans and Combanaich. The Combanaich have a charter for their land and the MacPharlans don't. They must make a living however to pay the rental of the land."

"How? Stealing."

"They reive cattle according to ancient custom. They only take a portion of a wealthy person's stock to live on, not enough to impoverish them."

"The Hielands harbour packs of thieves. Who else lives hard by?"

"MacDonalds—an ancient clan in the districts to the northwest." She surveyed the land in that direction in case he saw her sympathy.

"The cattle drovers."

"Yes."

He sneered and licked his lips.

The sun stole into the sky and lightened the green in the trees and the blue in the loch. Connington and his men said nothing for the rest of the journey. He had tried to scare her and she had made him stop. She considered the exchange a small victory.

Before she saw the house, she heard a rhythmic thudding and smiled.

"It sounds like drums and shouting. A fight," said Connington.

The compelling rhythm of women singing a labour song, interspersed with yells, filled the air. "No, they are women." She enjoyed his discomfort, and urged her pony to trot closer for the singing.

A dozen women sat on the ground in front of wattles, pounding wool cloth with their feet and singing. Connington's eyes widened and his mouth dropped. "They're mad."

"They're happy—it's a *luadhadh*. They are waulking cloth and fulling it. Everyone in their *baile*—"

"Enough. They're a' daft!"

He frowned and jerked his horse away from the group as though the women were wild wolves who threatened him. Connington seemed nervous about something. Perhaps he didn't like being amongst so many women. A weakness.

The MacPharlan longhouse coursed with people. Besides the women waulking the cloth, four men rethatched the roof while two women stamped clothes in a washtub and several others tended a kailyard. As the tune finished, another woman began to sing and the rest joined in the chorus.

Baile Leacan used to be like this—before Connington and his strangers came.

Beyond the workers, she saw Lowlanders. No mistaking their baggy breeches and dull colours. Highlanders they weren't. She thought she saw a few of the ragged men who fought at the shore on Sionaidh's Day.

"So this chief appears well served."

His comment brought her attention back to him. "He has done what he can to survive."

"He thieves."

"How did you survive the wars against the Catholic empire?" She knew he'd stolen food, but also gold and jewellery. She wasn't sure how she knew, but she had images in her mind of his thefts. A banshee power?

"Mark my words, I've known hunger. The world is changing, and I intend to survive—in comfort."

She saw an image of him starving and searching for food. Impossible to feel sorry for him. Her whirling thoughts overwhelmed her, and she saw no more. He had a way of lulling her, making her forget his evil. She'd have to watch that.

"Help her, Rutherford!" he shouted. "Dear lady, ye must forgive ma poor servant his manners."

Connington's lieutenant slid from his mount and offered his hand to her. He said nothing as he knelt and she stepped onto his cupped hands. She thought him kind, the wrong sort to be among Connington's soldiers. She thanked him and he nodded quickly. She could tell he appreciated the comment. Must be hard to work with Connington. Why did he stay on with such a harsh man?

They made for the room with the fire, at the middle of a long, narrow house.

Stately as a king, the chief of the MacPharlans, a man with a white beard flowing to his chest, emerged from his house. When she introduced Connington, she saw that the old man only bowed—Connington thought the custom of bowing and circling *deiseil* was ridiculous. The MacPharlan knew how to behave among Lowlanders. He'd had dealings with them before.

The old chief indicated the door with a flourish of his arm, and they entered the house at its middle. Inside the chief's wife stirred stew in a large bronze cauldron hung on a chain over the central fire. Her two daughters baked bannocks on a wide hearthstone.

"Ye speak Inglishe, d'ye?" said Connington to the chief.

"Just a bit."

"Your work. A dangerous business." Connington faced Shona. "Translate that for him."

Shona recognised the impatience in Connington's voice, and did so.

MacPharlan continued unhurried. "The way of the world. I arrange the return of beasts lifted by desperate men. But you're wanting a bite to eat. We'll talk in the chamber. This way. Many of the unfortunate men, bereft of their cattle, are Lowlanders, and they don't think much of me."

"And they trust ye, do they?"

"Sir, I am a gentleman." MacPharlan answered mildly despite the insult.

Shona told him what the old man said.

In the chamber the chief rubbed his hands over a brasier as he spoke. He sat on a low chair with carved arms and back, but jumped up again. "The *cuach*! I'm a poor host if I can't offer you a drink." He looked at Shona and waited for her to translate.

His wife heard the comments and fetched a large wooden drinking cup with chased silver on the rim.

"We have matters to discuss." Connington smiled in his most charming way. "Make sure ye get this right," he said to Shona. He pulled her toward the chamber.

She wanted to overturn the cauldron on his head. *Patience.* "I'll translate for you." Perhaps she'd find out what he planned. She followed him and MacPharlan into the best room. Connington changed with the wind, from choleric to charming. She had to think of a way to defeat him, but her head emptied of ideas.

"Here's what I need done," Connington murmured as he and the chief settled in the best room. "Ye wull keep another fifty of ma men in addition to the fifty who now live on yer lands."

MacPharlan would billet one hundred Lowland soldiers! And the Lowlanders from the shore were here. They were Connington's men. No surprise.

"Our resources will be truly exhausted by one hundred warriors. It will require much more silver."

"Ye wull have one silver penny for every twelve soldiers, as before."

"We require one silver penny and one copper for shelter and food for every twelve soldiers. Tell him that."

The MacPharlans would do almost anything for silver.

"Hieland rogue! He gets the same as he got before. Tell him that."

"Why do you keep these men here?"

"No yer business. Tell him he gets what he got before and his son will guide us tae Edinburgh in a month's time."

Alasdair was taking his cattle to Edinburgh. The MacDonalds knew that soldiers were heading for the burgh after fighting against the Catholic Empire, and Highland cattle would be used to feed soldiers like Connington's. But why? What drew soldiers to Edinburgh?

A short time later the barking of dogs and neighing of ponies startled her. She recognised one voice amid shouts and laughter. *Alasdair*. She followed the women who rushed out to greet him. The sun lit his face like a saint's image. He should be abed—not on a horse.

"Welcome, Alasdair Dubh," said the chief's wife.

Birdsong was not as sweet as his voice.

~

Alasdair gave his horse into the care of a young MacPharlan boy. "*Tapadh leat, a bhalaich.* Thanks, boy." To MacPharlan's wife he said, "A while since I've seen yourself and MacPharlan."

"Welcome to you, welcome at any time." said MacPharlan's wife. "You'll want to see my man." She looked back into the house, then said in a low voice, "He's got a Lowlander and Shona Campbell with him. Up to no good. But my man won't believe any bad opinion of him. He's got his eyes on the silver. But look at you."

"I've not been well."

"Poor man! Come in! Come in! Take a seat on the bench by the fire while I butter oatcakes for you. You have men outside who need to be fed?" She led him back inside her house.

MacPharlan's wife sent her two daughters out with food for his men. How pretty they looked as they went out. All seemed as it should be.

The sun and moon of his life appeared at the threshold of the best room.

"You're much better, I see," said Shona. "I'm here to get more drink for the negotiators: Connington and MacPharlan."

"Much. I'm glad to see you in good health." The sight of her gave him a lift.

He looked around to see who was listening, but the chief's wife had returned to the fire and was clattering a large wooden spoon on the edge of the cauldron.

"Why are you here? Connington doesn't know how

much time I spent with you—when you were ill. I don't think your status as a guest would protect you if he knew."

"I'm here now. Please join me." He patted a spot on the bench. "Oatcakes will be ready soon."

She sat beside him. He wanted to touch her, but he kept his hands in his lap. Studying the softness of her skin was all right for now. A few months ago he'd thought that all he needed in this life was money from selling cattle to make a decent life for his clan. Buy back a bit of land. Gain the respect of neighbouring clans. But now it wasn't enough. He had a hole, a huge gap in his heart, and only she could fill it.

A young girl brought Alasdair cakes fresh from the griddle, covered in new butter, then took a trencher full to the best room.

"Why are you here? You should keep to your bed."

"I needed air and exercise." He hesitated. "Besides, Morag was concerned about you."

"She could have sent a village boy. Though you look much better." She raised her hands as though she wanted to touch him.

"She could have, indeed," said Alasdair. "But she had a dream about Connington. No good omens concerning that man."

"How did you find us?" Shona stood in the sunlight pouring through the door.

"Not difficult to find that black-coated man in this bright land." Alasdair nibbled the oatcake. "Wonderfully good. Morag said that he wants to marry you. And she wants you for her apprentice." Laughter broke through from the chamber.

"I don't care to be her apprentice, and I refuse to marry Connington. Never will I change my mind about him. I do want to marry, to be of service to my people. But things have gone down a different road than I expected."

"I appreciate your ability heal and will recommend you to all."

"I do enjoy learning about plants and the earth, and the stars from Morag. And herbs. And how to nurse the sick back to health— including you."

And for that he was profoundly grateful. But he wanted more than that. He wanted Shona, a life with her. He had to make sure that she would agree. Clan loyalty might yet prevent her from loving him enough to live with him.

"Connington isn't pleased about that." She smiled and leaned over till their shoulders touched. When she heard the chief's wife returning, she quickly sat up straight.

"Are you ready to join the other gentlemen?" Her brows were furrowed and her mouth moved as if she wanted to say something more. "This way."

"Indeed I am." Before Shona rose to go, he whispered to her, "Be careful. If you have trouble with him, I'm here to help." She didn't look reassured. More frightened, if anything. He held her back. "What is it? You can trust me."

Shona whispered, "Can you send a messenger to my father and tell him Connington is conspiring against the king? Can't say any more just now."

Conspiracy against the king! He had underestimated Connington. "Right. I will." He wanted to reassure her by taking her into his arms, but did not. Too many people moving about. He followed them to the chamber.

Connington, the MacPharlan chief, and Duncan MacPharlan, his eldest son, studied him as he joined them.

"Welcome to the house," said the MacPharlan chief to Alasdair. "We don't see much of you."

"You have so few cattle for us to take to market." Alasdair

spoke to the MacPharlan, but looked at Connington. The man sat calmly as a saint without sin or stain.

"Not just now. Perhaps soon," said the MacPharlan.

"Ye'r well, it seems," said Connington. "I was inquiring after ye in yer camp, but couldn't find ye at all."

"Here I am. Safe and well." Alasdair opened his arms wide. He saw an odd reaction on Connington's face—he was surprised to see him whole.

"I may want to relieve ye of some of yer cattle."

"Buy some?" asked Alasdair. "Most of them are promised to cattle dealers at Crieff."

"The Campbell beasts are mine to dispose of," said Connington.

Shona said, "They're not!" Brave woman. "My uncle gave permission to the MacDonalds to take them to market. His word stands."

Connington glared at her. Somehow that Lowlander would make her pay for her defiance. But not here. No one moved.

The MacPharlan chief came to life. "Am I not a poor host!" And he called to his wife for drams and she brought a leather jug of whisky to them. The MacPharlan poured a generous amount into the *cuach*, his only possession of worth in sight. He lifted it with shaky hands and hesitated. He seemed undecided about who should drink first as the more honoured guest. He gave it to Alasdair, who accepted it and lifted it, his eyes looking right at Shona by the fire. He saluted her and drank.

He turned to Connington and said, "I understand you're to be married."

Connington ignored him.

"To beauty and love." Alasdair drank again before giving the *cuach* back to MacPharlan, who gulped a drowning amount before passing it to Connington, who also drank deeply, his eyes narrow above the cup. "Ye'r dead curious about ma business."

"Curiously alive," said Alasdair.

"A wise man tends tae his own business and stays safe."

"You are quite certain of your position in this glen." There was no answer.

MacPharlan's hands shook as he took his next dram.

"Looking for a safe haven from the difficulties in the south?" Alasdair cheerfully ignored Connington's silence and said in Gàidhlig, "And Duncan here. What have you been up to?"

"Nothing. A bit of cattle breeding here and there." Duncan looked at his father and then Connington for answers, but none came.

"Any of your men or boys need employment?" asked Alasdair.

The MacPharlan shifted in his chair. "Not just now, thank you."

Not now. Connington must have hired them. Alasdair's little excursion had paid off. He knew whom he couldn't trust.

Connington's grip on the *cuach* tightened almost imperceptibly. He said no more.

When they drained the cup dry in successive rounds, Connington made his farewells and indicated with a movement of his head that Shona should follow him out.

Her eyes pleaded with Alasdair to come with them. Her hostess and her daughters had no smiles for Connington as they left. Alasdair thought they'd be happy to see the backs of guests who insulted each other without their understanding.

Alasdair pulled aside one of the MacPharlan sons. He

had no clear idea what business Connington had with the MacPharlan chief, but it was nothing good. “Listen, Ailean. Warn your father that Connington man means you harm. He will stop at nothing to get what he wants. He killed—”

The young man took Alasdair’s hand off his arm. “My father must keep a large family alive and he knows best how to do that.”

“You may regret your words.”

Alasdair went to say farewell to his hostess and warn her.

“*A ghràidh*, surely you are imagining things. You had a bad blow to the head, did you?”

No one would listen. The MacPharlans may have billeted some of the soldiers who ruined the feast at the shore. But he doubted the clan had anything to do with Myles’s death. They didn’t think themselves in any danger. Perhaps they planned to reive MacDonald cattle? The MacDonalds would have to be doubly watchful.

Connington was weaving a wide web which might catch too many people Alasdair cared about.

CHAPTER 15

"Time we were returning." Connington seized Shona's other arm and turned her round to the west, the direction of Castle Muirn. Her new prison. "Now ye behave or ye get hard treatment."

The rough handling must look like lovers' play to the MacPharlans. The sun blinded her, but she started to walk as Connington held her arm behind her, regulating their pace to appear unhurried and happy. He released her as their horses were brought round.

"I and my bride tae be offer thanks tae ye for yer hospitality." He bowed deeply to the MacPharlans in the Lowland way. The MacPharlan folded over in response. No one circled him *deiseil* in the Gaelic manner.

Shona resisted the desire to rub her sore arms and mounted up with the help of one of the MacPharlan sons. She galloped off. He didn't overtake her, but worried her heels like a vicious dog.

At Castle Muirn, Shona ran past the guardroom. A guard hung his head out the door, but she rushed for the spiral stair like a hare for its burrow, hoping the guards would stop the hunter. She ran up the steps into the hall. She could stay with the mourners or go up to her chamber. She couldn't face them. She headed for the stair at the other side of the hall. She had to find Catriona. She couldn't see well in the darkness, lit only by the fading light of a loop window round the next turn of the stair.

Suddenly she could smell his damp clothes and rotten teeth. He caught her by the waist and swung her around. She thought she would fall and break her back on the stone stair, but he caught her easily and as she fell against him, he laughed harshly. He threw her against the outer wall, where her head cracked on the stones. She was so weak, she couldn't stand.

"Ye drive me mad. I've had enough of waiting."

When she opened her eyes, she could barely see him in the fading light. His face was completely dark; his hat jutted out like the maw of a wild beast. He held her against the wall with his forearm pressed against her throat while he pinned her right arm with his body. He controlled her movement by twisting her right arm in his left. They were as close as mating dogs as he began to rub himself against her. Under his clothes, she felt him grow hard.

"A taste of what's to come."

She tried to scream, but he lifted his arm and snapped her jaw shut. She uttered a squawk. Her back pained her as he pushed her up and down against the wall and the hilt of his sword scraped her side. Footsteps thudded across the hall.

"Ye do as I say or I start murderin' yer folk."

The floor seem to fall out from under her.

"Stand still, ye silly woman."

A voice from below asked, "*Dé tha dol?* What's going on?"

"Answer him, ye—!"

“I won’t.”

“Ye’ll no refuse me.” Connington let go of Shona’s hand. He descended a few steps stamping his feet and groaning like a drunk. Then stopped as if he had tripped. “Goddamn.”

The man below spoke no Inglishe, but he recognised the curse and laughed.

Connington tried to catch up to her again, but suddenly she had the speed of a deer in her legs. She sprinted up the steps.

But the stair seemed to darken and shrink in size. She looked up, took a deep breath and fought the narrowing space. Terror rushed like a river from the skin of her head and back and chest. A taste of metal filled her mouth. She must use the power of the banshee.

But her mind filled with bog cotton. Dizzy. She must stand. Must not fall. She told herself that the stones in the wall and under foot, the air and the sky above were hers to command. She repeated the words again and again.

She’d face him—calmly and quietly. She pressed herself against the wall and took strength from their roughness. The smooth stone of the stair calmed her. She willed the terror which filled every particle of her body to rise up far above her into the sky. Her arms warmed and her hands tingled. She lifted them into the air.

Connington roared as he thundered up the steps, his face dark with the blood of anger, his naked sword in his hand. Fear was his ally, filling the space all round him, pushing upward to surround her, threatening to smother her once again. She had to repel him before his iron sword was too close.

As he appeared on the stair, she *pushed*, and lights—small flames of fire—lit the stair. Around her came a light sound of singing. As if a wall of earth and stone had struck him, he tumbled backwards down the stairs. He expelled breath as he hit the stair or the wall and he cursed. The falling went on forever. Finally she heard him tearing great breaths from the air. Her heart flipped in its cage. *Still alive.* She wasn't sure if she was relieved or disappointed.

"Ye'll sorely regret the trouble ye caused me. Ye won't get clear of me."

She was safe for the moment.

"Yer folk won't either!"

She was shaking again.What could she do about his menace? *Sort that later.*

"Catriona!" she shouted.

The door of Priscilla's chamber opened and her step-mother appeared. She stepped back into her chamber and said nothing.

Shona ran past her up the stair. Connington cursed loudly below as she ran into her own chamber.

~

Catriona slammed the door shut behind her while concern for her nurseling filled her eyes. She barred the door. Shaking, Shona told her what had happened.

Catriona gasped. "I can't believe it. I never thought badly of him till now."

"I was lucky to escape him."

"If that Connington man woos every woman like that, small wonder no one will have him," said Catriona. "He'll not get you while I live. You're safe now."

Catriona could do little if he tried.

Catriona fetched a plaid from a chest and wrapped it

about her, yet she felt faint and couldn't stop shivering. "I'll get you something hot to drink."

"Please, don't leave yet. Not yet. He is still dangerous." She held onto Catriona's hand. She wanted Campbells around her all the time. Next time he caught her alone, he might rape her. If she and Connington were betrothed, people would give them privacy to let them discover more about each other—which was the last thing she wanted. She could do nothing to prevent it ... unless she trained and became stronger in wielding her banshee powers. She groaned at the thought.

Her bruised arms and neck pained her. Shona was the child of a gentleman. A chief. No one was allowed to lift a hand to her. She had never been mistreated in her life except by this man. She couldn't depend on anyone else for protection. They depended on her. She'd not weep, she'd not weep at all. She'd think and make a plan to deal with Connington.

"There must be a way I can escape Connington."

Catriona's eyes widened and she shook her head. "Even your stepmother can't deny he's done a terrible thing. But she'd do little to help you, so blinded by his charms is she."

Someone tapped at the door. Shona and Catriona looked at each other.

"Surely it won't be Connington. He'd ram the door to splinters." Shona stood to meet the threat.

Shona heard a plaintive female voice. Priscilla's. She went to the door, but Catriona rushed to her back and put her hands on her shoulders to hold her back. "Don't open the door. No, it's a trick."

Shona heard sadness and regret in the voice. Not betrayal. She unbarred the door, and found Priscilla there alone. Even her dark Lowland dress seemed less starchy and full.

"Come in quickly!" When Priscilla was inside, Shona looked up and down the stair. No one. No cursing. Only quiet.

"Where are her maids, is my question," said Catriona.

"Your maids?" said Shona in Inglishe.

Priscilla stood in the middle of the floor. "I cannae trust them. I cannae stay long, but I ha'e something tae say tae ye."

"Please sit, Priscilla. Stay as long as you like."

Catriona brought each a chair and set it close to the hearth. As she passed by Shona, she looked up and shook her head. Her pursed lips told Shona that she distrusted Priscilla. But Shona felt sadness in the older woman—a profound well existed inside her without joy, without love.

"I ken what Thomas is. He'll charm ye an ye dae what he says. If ye dinnae, he insult ye and even batter ye. Like he did in the stair. I know a' that. I kent it many a year ago. I just coudna admit it."

Catriona looked at Shona, alarm in her wide eyes. "What's she saying?"

"She knows Connington is evil." Shona understood her stepmother so much better. She was a stranger in exile, without friends or allies.

Shona made the decision that had been in her mind for days. She had to refuse Thomas to her father's face, and she had to tell him about the plot against the king. "I must leave."

Catriona drew a quick breath. "You can't tell your plans. She'll betray you—she's a blood relative of that vile beast."

Priscilla considered Catriona. "She disnae trust me, your

woman. Aye, I know. But I willnae betray ye. I'll help ye. I'll dae anything."

Shona studied Priscilla and placed a calming hand on Catriona's shoulder. "I believe her."

Catriona wept. "Her people mean us no good."

"You may be right about most of them. But not about Priscilla."

"I'm leaving as soon as I can, Priscilla."

Priscilla worried a cambric handkerchief. "I can mislead Thomas. Tell him ye've gone where ye havenae."

"If he finds out, he may harm you."

"I deserve a beating."

"You don't. No woman does."

"I'll tak' what comes tae me."

Shona asked her stepmother, "Will you come with me? Do you want to return to Edinburgh?"

"I wadna be sure of ma welcome," Priscilla said. "Yer faither willnae listen tae me. I have no say in Edinburgh."

"Are you sure? We'll travel as lightly as possible. No more than what our horses can carry. Four plaids, four changes of linen, silver plate and a bag of coins. I'll bring my uncle's gift of silk *lèine* and *earasaid.*"

"I'll stay. I dinnae ken how long I'll be here, but I'll keep yer secret."

To Catriona's unspoken question, Shona answered, "I invited her to go to Edinburgh with us."

"The better to betray us. This woman is up to no good." Catriona shook her head. "And that Connington man has so many soldiers here. They'd catch us up and drag us back."

"I'll say I'm leaving to visit my uncle's widow."

"Maybe that'd work."

Priscilla quietly studied the tiles on the floor, then spoke to Shona. "I'll try tae make him blyth and merry again. Then ye can come down and get what ye need."

"If you won't go to Edinburgh, I'll tell Morag and she'll help you if you need anything. If—if you're in any danger."

"Morag will have trouble enough protecting the rest of us." Catriona's voice was still unfriendly.

"I'd best go downstairs noo." Priscilla went out her Lowland dress trailing behind her.

"Let's pack up. Come on, I need to do this and I need your advice."

Catriona slowly went to Shona's chests and opened them.

Shona bundled up a sheepskin mantle to keep her warm at night. Essential. She'd get some herbs and ointments from Morag for insect bites and abrasions. She chose some linen shifts and two plaids with which she could make an *earasaid*. She'd have her linens washed somewhere on the way.

"Will you ask the cooks to set aside some cheese and oatmeal? And some whisky. I'll barter it for milk and apples."

Catriona wept.

Shona stopped and embraced her serving woman.

"I see what I can bring back." Catriona wiped her cheek and went to arrange what she could.

Shona barred the door behind her and pushed a chest against it. Her shoulders fell with the weight of dread on them. She would have to confront him again. Not quite by herself. She had a new ally in Priscilla.

When Catriona returned, she chewed her lip. "You won't get by him, my dear. He has ears like a wild cat. He is very suspicious of me. How wrong I was not to trust you."

Shona knew she was right about Connington when

everyone thought he was handsome and charming. But she couldn't say why. Banshee power? And she knew that Priscilla would not betray them. "I have to see Alasdair. I have an idea that will keep us safe ... safer."

Catriona grasped her two hands and looked in her eyes. "Whatever you decide, you can count on my help."

~

Shona descended the spiral stair behind Priscilla. Connington sprawled in her father's chair in front of the hearth, chatting with his soldiers, his words followed by their comments. They filled the hall, two at the windows, two by the entrance and the rest seated at a trestle table round Connington. *Try not to look right or left. Head high. Look unapproachable and perhaps none of them will.*

Connington looked far too comfortable in her father's chair. She lifted her head to the portrait of her father, painted after he'd become a knight. At the time he said everyone would know he was powerful. No one would dare offend the Campbells of Gleann Muirn.

Heart fluttering like a caged bird, she crossed the room. Morag's cottage, her refuge, was a few minutes away.

"Our lovely lass favours us with her presence." Connington flashed his best smile.

As though he had never touched her in the stair. Her shoulders rose with anger. She drew herself up straight as a queen.

"Come here, ma dearie." He curled his finger at her.

She'd rather gut rotten fish.

"Noo wha' must I dae tae make ye mind?" He sat in the best chair with arms and a cushion while twirling one of the finest goblets in the house. It almost spun out of his hand.

Shona spread her arms as if to catch it. He watched her, not the precious glass, and sneered. He looked significantly at his soldiers and said, “Your faither’s bed is verra comfortable. Aye, a fine bed in a fine hoose. Meant for a fine purpose.” He smiled with pressed lips and then licked them. The soldiers laughed in harsh tones all round him.

His words seemed harmless to them. Part of a normal courtship where they came from?

“The minister’s agreed tae stay and marry us. No need for any heathenish ceremony.” His gaze freely roamed her body. The tip of his tongue stuck out from his mouth. Such a small thing—it disgusted her.

“My father will return for the wedding?” If her father returned, she could beg him to turn out Connington. Her father wouldn’t force her to marry such a man if he knew about his evil ways.

“Too dangerous. If yer father leaves Edinburgh, the Tables will believe he’s a Royalist spy.”

“Tables?”

“The name of the new government. Different classes of folk sit at different tables in the assembly. Yer faither knows about ma courting ye. He’s not against it. Ye doubt me? Ye’ve no choice. Ye may as well accept what will be.”

She said nothing, But she would fight him in whatever way she could. She would feign compliance. She curtseyed as Priscilla had taught her and walked away.

“Come back, Mistress Campbell.”

She stood still with her back to him. Her breathing quickened. He could do nothing to her in front of the household.

In an instant, he strode to her and crushed her arm in his fist, still smiling. “Sit, if ye please. Where I may see ye.”

After forcing her down, he said to Priscilla, “Dear aunt, I wull have speech with ma future bride.”

“But surely I must—” Priscilla’s face showed her concern. She and her maids shuffled away to the far end of the hall, gawking at Shona, and then discussing the quality of a tapestry.

And yet, she knew what he had tried to do in the spiral stair. *She too fears her nephew.* Still, the truce with Priscilla might help her deal with Connington.

“We’ll journey tae the borders, tae my own country. Ye’ll bide there safe while I’m awa’ in England. Ye bring any trouble tae me and ye never see yer folk again. D’ye understand?” He increased the pressure on her wrist.

She nodded, caught like a canary in a golden cage, the door open for the cat. She stepped toward him, the smell of unclean flesh assailing her nostrils. *Think.* “England? You’ll leave me for England?”

He released her and she rubbed her arm.

“Aye, we go tae war against the king, an ungodly ruler in God’s eyes.”

“Against the king.” He hadn’t always been a good king, according to her father, because he ignored Scotland. But God’s anointed king wasn’t evil. Surely not. “You’ll be hanged for sure.”

Wrong thing to say.

“Though that wad please ye, it’s King Charles may come tae an untimely end.” One hand chopped through the air onto the other.

She flinched. *Treason.* What he said was unthinkable. Like killing a saint or an angel. Perhaps he was mad. The rebellion couldn’t be widespread. Though maybe it was … the chapman had spoken of riots in Edinburgh. Perhaps her father and brothers were in great danger among such men.

She had to learn more of the great world beyond Gleann Muirn.

Priscilla completed another round of the hall, chatting with her maids, then halted in front of Connington.

"Aye, ye can sit. Ma bride and I understand each other. "

"She'll need my company in yer hoose." Priscilla stood behind him and gently put her hands on his shoulders.

He turned around rapidly and shook them off. "What are ye doin', woman?"

Her face was a mask without expression, her eyes without life.

God only knew how Connington would use the MacPharlans. They had no interest in the king or his battles. More likely, they'd welcome a chance to lift someone's cattle. Alasdair's. But they had little idea of Connington's ruthlessness. Shona had to get more information. She ate the evening meal beside her intended husband and Priscilla.

"And I shall never go home to Edinburgh. There will be no end to my exile," said her stepmother.

"Yer husband may see ye well provided for." Connington chewed on a massive leg of ham.

Priscilla lowered her head and stuck out her lower lip.

Connington cleared his throat and smiled at Shona. "Dear lady, a light labour and a pleasure for ye tae preserve yer husband's patrimony."

Priscilla did not looked pleased. And so the evening passed. Shona heard no more about the conspiracy.

Before she left for her chamber, Connington said, "We marry at Martinmas. As I told ye, ye've two weeks to arrange yer affairs."

At *Samhainn* she'd be among strangers unless she acted

soon. She couldn't live in his house. She couldn't live with this brutish man.

She swore she would not.

Shona opened the chests in her room to decide what to take with her. Her recent conversations with Priscilla explained a great deal. She wouldn't leave with them. If Priscilla stayed, she'd surely be safe with Connington.

"Would you like to go out walking with Catriona and me?"

"I don't fancy walking out on thae moors."

"You attended the assembly."

"I found it difficult ... I hated it, truth tae tell. Nae hooses, nae streets. I don't want ever tae go oot again."

Priscilla was afraid of being outside.

Astonishing. To Shona, the fields and hills of Gleann Muirn were as much a part of her as the flesh and bones of her body. The smell of the pines and the scent of wild flowers filled her with joy and renewed her. Without them she would be an empty husk without purpose or meaning.

"Will you come with me to the parapet walk, then? We'll be on top of the world. Good fresh air up there." She covered one of Priscilla's hands with her own, but did not presume to touch her too long.

Priscilla hesitated. Then she nodded indicating the maids. "They need fresh air as weel."

Shona smiled at the maids. Up they climbed to the top of the keep, much to the surprise of the four Lowland guards who bowed to them.

"We won't be long."

"May I tak' yer arm?" Priscilla walked on the inside, and

Shona set off *deiseil*, the lucky direction of the sun. Every few feet Priscilla touched the hard slate of the roof as if she might fall off the tower at any instant. They circled round the tower followed by the faithful maids.

"I hae mair tae tell ye."

What could Priscilla add to the list of Connington's sins? "What is it?"

"I'm no sure. Couldnae hear well. But his evil grows. Ma heart is riven and split. I dinnae ken wha' will become of us and I grieve for us a'." Her face had gone white and her eyes were too big for her skull. "He plans murder in Edinburgh."

CHAPTER 16

At Morag's hearthfire, Alasdair adjusted his *fèileadh* at the front while Ruari saw to the folds at the back. The wattle door of the house opened and Shona stepped through, framed by brilliant light. He stared at her. He shouldn't tantalise himself—he'd only cause more trouble. He knew that he couldn't have this Campbell woman, that he'd find a woman when he had a bit of land to support a wife. And he'd get that land by dealing in cattle, and he'd deal in Campbell cattle if he kept his hands to himself.

When he saw her slender figure shaped by light in the door, all his admonitions and warnings for himself went up like smoke into the thatch. He forced himself to speak. "Morag isn't here. Someone came for her to minister to a sick man."

"I came to see you," she said.

A dangerous thing indeed.

Ruari stopped arranging folds in the plaid to look at her, and then, his eyes suspicious, he looked at Alasdair.

"We're almost ready to go," Alasdair told her. "Can you bring my pony, Ruari?" He grasped the old man's shoulder to reassure him, and his tutor left. *Perhaps that wasn't wise.* They were alone, completely alone for the first time—and healthy. "I'll sleep in our camp tonight."

She looked up at him and took a breath. He wrapped his arms about her and kissed her on the forehead. He cradled her and waited for her to collect herself.

"Your father's horse is safe and sound?" He waited for her to tell him what was on her mind.

"Yes, there was no injury to him at all." She worried a fold in her *earasaid.*

"I'm sorry for your tribulation." Many of her family had died in the last year and now she was dealing with that Lowland blackguard. She had great courage and he felt joy in her presence. Not difficult it was, with her to gladden his eyes. "I'm thankful for your care."

"Can you sit for a while?" she said.

He sat down a distance from her, on a creepie stool at the hearth. Shona and he had talked endlessly when he was ill, but now she said nothing while he watched the peat fire's flames.

Finally she said, "I'm going to Edinburgh."

"With that Lowland man? Thomas Connington?" His jaws tightened. His anger surprised him.

"No." She turned to face him; she was lovely with the fire making her eyes as wide and deep as Loch Muirn. "I asked you to send a message to my father in Edinburgh."

"I'll do that willingly."

"But I've decided to take it myself. I want to go with you."

The words struck him like another blow to his head. The dangers were too great for a gentlewoman. And yet ... he wanted her to go with him. "What will you do about Connington?"

"I won't stay any longer with him here."

Her clan would say he'd stolen the daughter of a chief of the Campells for a ransom. But while she had nursed him after he was injured, he saw that she was truly a good woman, a woman he wanted. Full of love. But they had to deal with her family. "Your stepmother thinks she's made a fine choice for you."

"My belly turns at the thought of him." She took his right hand like a supplicant. He could smell her fresh skin. "Rank and wealth don't matter to me. I want a good man. *You*."

"And I want you. I want to spend whatever time I have in this world with you. We must make peace between our two families. Convince them we are suitable for each other and for our clans."

"My father wouldn't make me marry against my will. He'd allow me some choice." She looked at him in the light of the cruisie lamp. "And I choose you."

He drew her close and covered her with his *fèileadh* while he stroked her back to comfort her.

"My father would welcome me. I'm sure of it." She looked up and begged him with her eyes. "Only Catriona would go with me. We'd take nothing but what is absolutely necessary. A single pack horse."

He held her at arm's length. "We can't take you and attendants. With a serving woman, chests, furniture and ponies, it would be obvious you are a gentlewoman. Connington would easily determine *which* gentlewoman." He let her think about that. "We are a dozen men and boys. Connington has over a hundred men. He would walk up right behind you, throw you over a pony and carry you back to Castle Muirn." He tried to speak lightly, but she wouldn't have it. She twisted away from him and he heard her sob. "With those numbers we must try to trick him."

"I don't need the ponies and chests," she said. "Catriona doesn't need much."

"She can't hide her womanly figure. She would still stand out. And Connington would know that, where she is, you'll be close by. She can't go."

"I'm going to Edinburgh if I have to travel alone."

She was so innocent, so unknowing. "The road is rough and if you survive the journey, we still have to face your father. You still want to come on the drove?"

"Yes. If I have to walk barefoot dressed only in a *léine*."

"We sleep rough outside."

"I've slept outside."

"Not at this season. Not where we're going." He looked at her closely.

"I'm leaving one way or another."

"What about our reception in Edinburgh? Will you survive the scandal? Tongues will be wagging like bell-clappers. Your father may be furious with you."

"I'll survive."

He didn't know any other gentlewoman who would go against her family's wishes. "Rare is the woman who can survive without a dowry and marriage. Except women like Morag."

Shona raised her eyes and looked at him with an expression he hadn't ever seen before. he didn't know what to think of it. As if he had happened on some sort of secret.

He shook his head. "Iain Glas may not welcome his daughter with no female dress, no attendants and no guards but MacDonalds."

He watched her face change, could see disappointment build into anger and fade into sadness. She lowered her head, wrapped her arms around herself, and told him what Connington had done in the stairwell. How he had held her against the tower wall with his body. How he hit her and she'd managed to escape. How she spent her days trying to hide from him.

A chilling image captured his mind. Herself, beaten and bloody, crouched at the foot of the spiral stair. Anger flowed like molten silver throughout the veins of his body, shutting out thought and reason. He'd take her with him. No more discussion.

Alasdair saw her shiver in the heat of the fire. She seemed to fear Connington even when he was nowhere in sight. Alasdair put his arms around her and they sat together.

"I have to escape that man."

"I know." If that scarecrow were in the room at that moment, he'd be flat on the earthen floor and dead with Alasdair's dirk in his belly.

"Marriage with him would be my coffin." Despair thickened her voice. He had no doubt she would walk barefoot to Edinburgh. "If he found me and took me back, I'd leave again. He has recruited men from the district like the MacPharlans." Tears welled in her eyes, but she banished them with her fists and laughed bitterly. "I need to go to my father and ask him if he approves of his crowd of allies. Thomas Connington says that war and rebellion are war coming. I need to go there to warn my father."

"What could you do? A woman?" She huffed at him and ran to the door. He staggered to his feet. "Wait." She put her hand to the wattle door. "Wait, please wait."

"Will you take me?"

"Please, come back. Sit down." He would be mad, clean mad, to take her. But Alasdair couldn't help himself. He had made up his mind to keep her safe.

"You can't travel as a gentlewoman."

"I'd travel as a tinker's woman if I had to."

"You'll travel as a boy. Then, at a distance, you'll fool anyone who sees us pass." Up close he was sure she'd have the scent of a woman. As she did now.

"Agreed," she said.

"You'd have to work as a herd boy."

"Agreed."

"So you say now. *A ghràidh*, I hope your spirit and strength will see you through."

On the journey she wouldn't be hard to look at, even disguised. If she were discovered too soon, he'd fight to keep her. "I'll find you a boy's *lèine* and plaid. Don't take anything with you but—"

"I have some boy's clothes and a bonnet, but I'll need the clothes that gentlewomen wear in Edinburgh. For my arrival."

"You've dressed as a boy before!"

"No, but I've thought about it. The clothes belonged to my brother, who died over a year ago."

"We leave in two days at sunrise. We may not be able to spend a lot of time together on the drove."

"In two days then. At your camp. Whatever happens."

The journey could turn out badly. Especially with her along. But something in the back of his mind told him he was doing the right thing. His heart lightened at the thought of her close presence in the days to come.

And with luck, for a lifetime.

~

With her *earasaid* pulled over her hair, Shona slipped out of the keep. Connington's man stopped her at the guardhouse.

"I'm going to minister to a sick man in the village. Captain Connington knows what I'm doing." The mention of his captain's name made the guard shrink back. "I shall report the nature of the illness to him." He stepped aside and Shona hurried down the path through the *baile*.

Morag's house, an island of green fertility, had no appearance of rebellion against Connington and his soldiers. Her vegetables were ready to be culled and her herbs to be plucked.

Morag herself rose from her kail beds and greeted her calmly. "You'll be leaving now." She handed Shona a basket of kail, enough to serve soup to the whole village. "Follow me."

Shona went into the house with her, straight to the hearth room. "Your father won't know what to do with you." How did she know? The eyestone wasn't that accurate. Morag pulled down herbs, drying on the rafters over the fire, placed them into a bowl and crushed them to powder with a smooth stone. "You'll be needing these. Make sure you keep them dry or they'll rot."

Shona knew that.

The wise woman folded them into a strip of linen. She selected another and repeated the exercise. "Do you likewise with the *alla bhuidhe*." The all-healing herb was the best to take on a journey. She hoped she'd have the strength to finish the journey.

"I want to hear from his own lips that my father accepts Connington."

"Hard it is sometimes, to understand your family." Morag's eyes had a faraway look. Did she see past or future? And then she was back. "Not worried about being killed?"

"Why would I be killed? I'll be a herd boy, a person of little interest to anyone."

"Don't be silly. That Connington man will go to the ends of the earth to get what he wants. You keep your eyes open. Think of me when you need to."

What does that mean?

"When you are in danger, listen to the Crow."

Morag was short with her. She seemed to expect Shona to have some idea of what she was talking about, but there was no point in asking the old woman to explain. She did things in her own way in her own time.

"How would he find out? You and Alasdair are the only ones who know where I'm going."

"If you and the cattle disappear at the same time, it won't be difficult to figure out where you might be. No, I think you'd best fall ill. I'll send word to Catriona and she can tell your stepmother. You tell her what the Inglishe words are." Morag thought a bit longer. "I'll have you die in a few days. You'll have to drown. You ran into the loch in your fever and drowned. We won't recover your body."

"My spirit will spend eternity with the seal people."

Morag turned sharply to her. "Don't even say it. *Mi-fhortanach*—it's unlucky."

"Thank you for your help." She was difficult to know, but Shona could trust her life to her.

"No one will hear from me. I know how to keep secrets." The wise woman took her by her two hands. She said nothing for a time. "You don't want to be a banshee, but you may be forced to use the power. Use it wisely."

"I can't control it. If I kill someone, I'll be as evil as Connington."

"I'll guide you."

"How?"

The Crow, who had been sleeping on the meal chest, shook her wings and cawed.

"That bird is my messenger. Pay attention to her and you might survive." The Crow waggled her head up and down.

Morag rolled more herbs into linen strips. "And fire-starter." She handed over the cloth and a little wooden box of dry moss and flints, which Shona placed in her leather bag. "And these." She held out eight copper and six silver coins.

Shona took the largest and examined it: a sword and crown on one side; she turned it over and saw a shield with a lion on it with another crown above it.

"The Lowlanders call it a dollar. The silver pennies are worth more than the copper ones."

Morag had money—another wonder.

"Food is not for the asking in the Lowlands. You must use the coins to get it. If you need to buy a bit of food, use one of the small pieces. If you need to feed a great many, use the silver dollar."

"How did you—"

"It will buy you food or whatever you need to save life." Shona had a few coins left in her coinbox. She had almost forgotten about it—she never had any use for it. Neither had anyone else in the village. But she knew her father had a great deal of money, and took bags of it to the Lowlands with him.

"I'll never leave this place," Morag replied as if she had spoken. "But I thought you might. I'll send to Catriona for the other things you'll need. You stay here tonight."

Shona had spent many nights with Morag. No one would think anything of it.

"One more thing. Connington may come to see you if he learns you're ill."

"To convince him, I should be really ill."

Morag untied more herbs from the rafters. "I'll give you

a potion." She took the herbs to her kitchen chest to mix them.

"How long will it last?"

"You'll have a fever for a day. You'll be able to walk after the second night." Morag ground the mixture to a powder and put it into a horn cup with water. She offered the cup to Shona, who drank the liquid.

They heard voices outside Morag's house. Inglishe. *Priscilla?*

"Morag. I need tae see Morag. Where does she stay? I need tae see Morag."

Priscilla, who never left the castle. For whom even the parapet walk was a trial. Something compelling had brought her out to the *baile*.

Morag stepped out to meet her.

"Would ye dae me the honour of a visit wi' ye?"

Morag replied, "Honour is ours. Come."

Priscilla had a shawl over her head. When she removed it, Shona saw that her face was red with weeping. "What is wrong?"

"I know ma Thomas murdered yer uncle. He boasts o' it. I hae been sae blind."

"Come. Sit." Morag took her to a little chair and told Shona to make the calming Spanish tea for her. When she'd had a sup or two of the tea, she began to speak.

"The Catholic wars hae ruined Thomas. Destroyed him. But I thought there was still good in him. But he's gey impatient tae savour the best in life—fine food, houses fu' o' polished furniture, gardens of flowers and the company of the powerful."

Connington needed gold for his conspiracy. He intended to become wealthy and powerful.

"So beautiful things are like a potion that revives him. Such as the Venetian glasses we have in the hall cupboard."

He could forget the war in possessing and caressing them. That made sense.

"And yerself. Ye'r a beautiful woman."

A possession. Shona understood him better, but had no desire to belong to Thomas Connington. But why was Priscilla sitting here in Morag's little house?

Priscilla turned to her and took her hand gently. "Ye are a great beauty and ye might hae healed ma Thomas."

"I cannot."

"I wished ye'd marry him." Priscilla bowed her head. She looked so frail in the light of the peat fire. "But I ken he's evil."

There was no point in saying anything further. Shona couldn't say he was evil incarnate, but nor did she tell the other woman about his attempt to molest her. Priscilla had had enough shocks.

"Ye love someone else?"

"I do."

"I haven't been happy in this marriage wi' yer faither. I dinnae understand why I had tae dae it. Nae body told me why. They said women must keep their nebs oot o' the affairs o' men." Priscilla's voice was touched with anger. "Thomas called me a *besom*. I dinnae ken what he's aboot, but it's no good." She had never said a harsh word about Thomas before.

Morag told Shona to tell her she might come and stay at any time.

"You showed great courage coming here. You are welcome anytime."

Priscilla nodded and sat quietly for a few moments. "I ken ye'r leavin'. What can I dae tae help?"

Next day Shona woke up in a fever and Morag sent for Catriona, who brought some clothes: two short plaids, two man's shirts, and two pairs of drawers and a pair of short trews. She also brought Lowland dresses, including the green gown, Myles's gift, and some silver dishes. They hid it in Morag's chest and waited for Connington and one of his men to come and inquire after her health.

Catriona put her hand to Shona's forehead and studied her face. "You feel hot."

"Hot but well."

"She'll look like death's handmaiden when the strangers come," said Morag. "I'll concoct a sick smell."

When the mixture was made, Shona drank that as well.

They heard Connington and his men coming through the *baile*.

Morag peeked out her door. "He's opening the door of every house and looking in. Not very polite in his manner either. My neighbours are pointing in this direction." Morag closed the door and went to the central fire to stir the cauldron. "No time for any other charms."

If the stench-charm sickened Shona, it'd convince the Lowlander for sure.

Shona lay back and pulled blankets around her. Connington opened the door with such strength that he tore off one of its old leather hinges. He stuck his big nose into the house and pulled back, assaulted by the foul odour. He took a deep breath and entered, hunched over to avoid the drying herbs and strips of beef that hung above. At the fire he stood up and glanced around. On the other side of the fire Shona hunched up on her side on a pallet, closed her eyes, and moaned.

"Is not good," said Morag in Inglishe.

"I can see that. I'm not blind." Connington went over to Shona and pulled her onto her back. She moaned again and then started to cough. He jumped back quickly. "Ye make sure she gets well, ye auld besom."

Connington didn't dawdle. From her place by the fire, Shona could hear him talking to one of his men outside, and then their footsteps faded away.

"Smell works wonders—in love and war," said Morag.

~

Shona lay awake for hours. Soon she'd leave her home. A few short months ago, she thought she'd have another year here in Gleann Muirn and then she'd marry the son of a gentleman in the next glen or across the loch. But now the home of her childhood was a cold heap of stones, with strangers living where crowds of people had once sung and told stories. At last she fell asleep.

In the half darkness of early dawn, Morag placed her finger on Shona's lips and woke her. "Hush!" She rose quickly and washed herself in a bowl of hot water. "Get your things together while I look about outside." Morag took a water pail and went out. She replaced the torn door upright at the threshold to hide Shona while she changed into the boy's clothing. In minutes Morag returned. "Looks like he's left only one man. He must truly believe you're ill with something dreadful."

"Clever Morag!" Shona put on her *léine*, drawers and short trews.

"One more thing. You must cut your hair." Morag picked up a fine strand of it. "You'll never pass for a boy with hair to your waist."

In her other hand she held the shears.

Suddenly Shona realised the enormity of what she was doing. She had no breath as though someone had sat on her chest and poured terrible images into her mind: the race, the drowning, Alasdair bloodied and Connington's sneering face above it all.

Morag sat her down gently as though she were a nervous horse. She slowly cut off a strand and waited. Then she cut more until Shona's hair reached her shoulders and little more. She was a boy to all the world.

"Move yourself! The fingers of dawn spread quickly."

With Morag's help Shona wrapped her *fèileadh* around her body and put a large belt around her middle and a bone pin to hold the top on her left shoulder. Then the old woman placed a large wool bonnet on her head. "That'll keep the rain off you."

Shona placed her coins in her *sporan*, and packed her clothing, food, and herbs in a large leather pouch. Morag stirred the cauldron and loudly sang a ditty that insulted their guard's ancestry. "Your singing should keep him away from the door."

Morag pretended to frown, then sang to the finish.

Shona picked up her pouch and went to the old woman and hugged her. She could feel the tears on Morag's cheeks. She hummed and pointed to the roof where the thatch was loose; in case of fire, the inhabitants could escape out the door or out the lower edge of the roof. Morag had a great respect for fire and had long ago told Shona what was to be done in an emergency.

"You'll say good-bye to my friends for me?"

"You know that I can't."

"I know."

Shona removed the thatch, then picked up her pouch

and crawled out over the wall into the darkness. Connington's guard was silhouetted in the growing light of the eastern sky. She straightened her back and walked westward to the camp of the MacDonalds.

Shona hadn't ever visited the MacDonald camp, although they had been in the district for two weeks. She walked past the cattle and a herd boy called to her. He wore a *léine* and thin *fèileadh* of a few yards of cloth.

"What do you want?" He stood between her and the cattle, a wooden staff across his body to fend off wolves and Campbells. He might be fourteen years old.

"I have no weapons but this knife," she said. "I mean you no harm."

"You should carry them." He looked her up and down. Not very polite. Not very friendly.

Shona prevented herself from smiling. She was sure that he thought her another boy.

"*Cò leis sibh?* Who are you with?" asked a smaller boy as he approached. "I'm Finlay. Finlay Beag because I'm so small. Just you wait, I'll grow bigger than any of the rest."

She almost smiled. "I am a Campbell," she said. "I have urgent business with Alasdair Dubh."

"Listen to him! As if he were a person of some importance," said the first boy.

"Look at him, Uisdean. He has shoes and a bonnet," said the small one, who likely had no such things even when the snow hag threw her cloak on the land. "And lots of yardage in his *fèileadh*."

"You are wearing trews. Only the drovers can afford to pay a tailor for the tight trousers."

Obviously she had impressed them, she lifted her head proudly. "Take me to him now. You'll regret it if you don't."

The two herd boys studied her and then the little one said, "I'll take him to the tents."

The older herd boy remained on guard while Shona and her escort walked around the cattle fold.

"What's your business?" He sounded curious and friendly. "What have you in your bag?"

"A second plaid and shirt. A few other things for the journey."

"You have wealth indeed," he said. "You're coming with us?"

"That's for Alasdair Dubh to know." That silenced the boy. Shona felt she was a little hard on him. But she couldn't say she was a girl who wanted to go with a large number of cattle and a dozen men and boys, enemies of her clan, on a long journey to Edinburgh.

The tents were only three wool plaids strung between trees to keep heavy rain off the drovers and herd boys as they slept. Two men extinguished the small fire at the edge of each tent. Other men spoke quietly as each put on his *fèileadh* and packed his gear. The breaking dawn revealed more herd boys who folded the tenting.

Shona couldn't see Alasdair, but she saw Ruari and walked right up to him. "If you please, can you tell me where I may find Alasdair Dubh?" she said in her strongest voice. She was certain she chirped like a titmouse.

"Who are—" The man stopped talking and looked hard at her. "It's *you*! Yours is a bad business, young—" He looked around and indicated that she should follow him to the last tent next to the cattle herd.

"Alasdair told some of you?" asked Shona.

"Only me. Don't want the young lads to be spooked. We want them looking carefree as they leave."

"Very wise," she said.

"Not wise for us to take you away." Ruari seemed less friendly than he had been in earlier days.

"Fortunately for me, Alasdair disagrees with you."

Two young boys came up to Ruari. "Away with you. I'll talk to you later." The old man glared at them and they scuttled away.

"He told me something of what that Connington man did. Saw his like in the Wars of Flanders. Come." Ruari shook his mane of white hair, but he led her to Alasdair, who slept despite the bustle around him.

"We're packing up as quietly as we can. Then we'll wake him."

"He's had a potion?"

"Indeed. We could all sing in chorus and not rouse him."

"Shall I stay with him?"

"You shall not. You're a herd boy now and you'll be expected to work with the others." He beckoned to a tall, thin young man. "That's Gillesbic, our oldest herd boy. He could be a drover at his age, but he has neither horse nor cattle to invest in the enterprise. So a herd boy he remains." The old man called to the younger, "Gillesbic, a new herd boy for you to train up in the knowledge of the cattle trade."

"Where would you find a new herd boy?" Gillesbic looked closely at her. "He's a Campbell! He looks like them! Why are we—"

"Not quite sure. The—lad—has lost a parent. He has family in the Lowlands who'll take him."

"I know how that goes. But a Campbell?"

"Alasdair has promised he will protect him."

"Not my obligation."

"It's Alasdair's obligation, it's *our* duty," said Ruari. "We'll get him where he's going and there's an end to it."

"And will he work?"

Nasty voice. The journey looked impossibly long. "Of course."

"Come, you little rogue." Gillesbic walked toward the cattle without checking whether Shona followed.

Shona consoled herself with the thought that the drove would be better than staying home and basking in Connington's attentions. Had to be. And Alasdair would tell Gillesbic to treat her with respect.

The oldest herd boy showed her how to take down the ropes and temporary heather enclosure that kept the herd together. "The fences don't do much. The dogs make them mind."

Shona set about her task and watched everything and everyone to learn what she could. When everything was packed but Alasdair's tent, Ruari and two drovers woke him up. He rose to his feet slowly. Ruari helped him dress and when he left the tent he looked around for her. He spoke briefly to a young herd boy, who came to her.

"You're to see Alasdair. Now!" And off he went to attend to his own tasks. Shona walked slowly over to Alasdair while his possessions were packed onto a pony. A shaggy grey dog sat up as she approached. Alasdair looked weary and her heart softened in her chest.

"So you've come," he said. His voice was grave. The shaggy hound plopped down beside him.

"And Ruari put me to work."

"Rightly so. You'll stay hidden longer if you work and convince anyone looking on that you are indeed a herd boy." His voice banished her misgivings. "No one knows but Ruari, but they may find out eventually. When you don't act like a man—or boy—should. We'll face that when we come to it. But no one here will betray you."

"My name is Seathan," said Shona.

"Seathan it is then. Listen carefully." He dropped his head close to hers. "Drovers such as myself go on horseback, and you, a herd boy, go on foot. We don't carry any gear for you. One pack pony carries a cauldron, some rope, a few extra plaids and the tents; the other two carry hides and hawks for trade. It's unchancy to make this drove so close to *Samhainn* and the dark season, but we need the money and the Lowlanders want the beef. If a stranger comes near, stand with the herd boys. They'll protect you."

"I understand."

"Still want to go with us? You could take a galley to Glasgow and go overland. I'll take you to whomever you wish."

Her heart sank to her heels. "I need to go to my father in Edinburgh. I don't know who else to trust."

"I'm pleased you want to come. You can trust me. I swear as long as wind blows and water runs, I'll protect you with my life. All right—what have you got in that big bag? You weren't supposed to bring half the castle!" He pulled her possessions out of her pouch onto a plaid and laughed. "What's all this?"

"Two plaids, spare shirts and trews. Two day gowns for Edinburgh, stockings, shoes."

"You don't need all that. One extra *fèileadh* and one *léine*. What are these?"

"Trencher, bowl and cup, spoon and knife. And a few pieces of silver plate."

"*Iosa is Muire Mhàthair,* Jesus and Mary Mother! Carry that much with you and people will think you're a chapman. The horn cup and spoon you can take." He rummaged in the heap of her goods. "The coins as well." He pulled out a small bundle of linen. "What's this?"

"Herbs. They might be useful if someone is sick or hurt." She tried to match his tone, but could hear a little quiver of fear in her voice.

If he heard, he gave no sign. "All right. They take up little room."

"I've some waxed cloth to keep them dry as well as your oatmeal and peas." Was this the same man who had laughed with her? Was this the same man who had been so ill in her care a short time ago? Perhaps this was difficult for him. He was trying to think of her as a herd boy, not as a woman.

"Here, you'll need a good knife." He gave her a sheathed knife about eight inches long. "Tie it to your belt like this." He showed her his own dirk.

"I have a horn knife inset with obsidian." She searched her goods and found it.

"This one is better."

"I can't wear it."

"Why?"

"Morag says I can't. It's a *geas*—forbidden to me." Was that a dart of fear shooting through his eyes?

He picked up a bundle of cloth knotted at the top. "What's this?"

"My gown and skirt and jewels—the best I have. My uncle brought it from Edinburgh. I must look like a gentlewoman when I arrive."

"Show me." She undid the knot and opened the four corners of the bundle and the silk gown spilled out like water. His eyes widened at the sight of it. She held it up to her body. He closed his eyes and opened them. "You'll carry this yourself. I'll give you some waterproof cloth to wrap it in." He placed the bag over her shoulder. His touch was as gentle and soft as down feathers. "Now that bag won't will make you stand out. You can only take a very few things."

She settled it on her hip.

"Now it lies flat on you. And you can cover it when you bring the *féileadh* over your head and shoulders." He bundled up what he considered unnecessary. "I'll send these back to Morag."

Occasionally his hound looked at him. When she spoke strongly, the dog stopped wagging its tail, jumped to its feet and faced her, ready to spring on command.

Alasdair said, "That's Luath. The dogs save us a lot of work."

She recoiled from the dog. There had been few dogs in the castle since her brothers died and her father had gone to Edinburgh.

"Be firm in your voice with him and when you stroke him. He knows that I like you and he likes whomever I like. And I do like you, *a ghràidh*. And I would like to kiss you. But with all the coming and going, it's not wise."

She stroked the dog firmly and patted his sides. "Aren't you pretty!"

"How I wish I were that dog."

Alasdair went to get his pony, which was held by a herd boy out of earshot. Alasdair chatted to the boy and gave him her things. He didn't even look her way, but trotted back to the village with her bundle. By the time Alasdair was back, Shona and the dog were comfortable with each other. The dog rubbed up against her legs with complete acceptance.

"He'll howl unless he's with someone he likes."

"We managed."

When the dog started to follow his master, Alasdair turned and told him to stay and he did—right beside her.

"He accepts you. He'll guard you with his life. You're one of us now."

"Do you want to introduce Gillesbic to me in the same manner?"

"What—"

"Not so friendly," she said.

"He'll thaw," said Alasdair. "So will they all."

She looked into his eyes and she saw the truth in them. "I know."

"It'll be different on the road. We'll make time to be together. Be strong." He gripped her arm. "Cut yourself a switch for encouraging the stray cattle to return to the herd. Ruari will show you what position to take at the back of the herd with the other boys."

She was ready. She'd be strong. Stronger than he expected. She'd face whatever was in front of her. Alasdair went out and she followed. They would travel together and warn her father in Edinburgh. All would be well. She'd be safe with him. She'd always be safe with him.

After stuffing her second *fèileadh* into a leather bag attached to his saddle, he put on his blue bonnet and mounted the broad back of his pony. He made a signal with his hand and the drovers and herd boys shouted at the cattle. Suddenly the campsite filled with noise. The dogs barked and the cattle bellowed; the hawks screeched and the horses snorted—and the whole mass moved forward down the road eastward.

CHAPTER 17

On the day the MacDonalds left, Rutherford smelled the herd before he saw it. The air was rank with animal odours mixed with the scent of earth in a land not raided or burnt. The shouts of men and barking dogs made him deaf to the birdsong he usually heard in the morning. He went to the wall of the castle and studied the spectacle. Connington and a half dozen of their men joined him.

Two drovers led the herd on the road out in front, looking for the best route—they signalled the other drovers by hand movements. Behind them plodded the herd, strung out in a long, winding line. Although most of the cattle were calm, a few in the rear wandered off, but barefoot boys ran to retrieve them. The strays were probably local cattle trying to return home. The village people stood in groups at the edge of the village as the cattle shambled by.

Two drovers on ponies and four herd boys controlled the flanks and one more drover and four herd boys at the rear pushed the stragglers forward. The MacDonalds seemed to know their business. Rutherford had some experience of cattle in Wishaw, where his family had a farm.

“I think it’s time we relieved those beggars of the care and worry of that herd,” said Connington.

“To serve our high purpose.” Rutherford knew all of Connington’s rhetoric. He wanted the cattle to feed an army of rebels. Rutherford wanted no part of theft and murder, yet he might get a share of cattle to sell for profit—and then he’d be closer to going home.

“Indeed.”

They’d had a setback because Shona had proved resistant to Connington’s charms, but not to fever. Bad stock. *Ye have to be careful choosing women and cattle.* Connington's wisdom.

He saw the village witch with some fleece under one arm. As she stood watching the cattle leave, her hands shaped the wool into yarn, which she wound onto a wooden spindle dangling above her right ankle. The old hag turned toward him as though she knew what was in his mind, and tugged on the yarn. Rutherford swallowed hard.

“A nuisance, that auld woman,” said Connington. “It’s superstition. She can’t end yer life by cutting that yarn.”

“The witch has overlooked us with her evil eye!” Rutherford ducked below the level of the wall. The witch might send out killing rays from her eyes.

Connington looked down on him, cowering at his feet. “Are ye well, Matthew? If I hadn’t seen ye fight so well against the Catholic Empire, I’d wonder about yer courage. Stand up, man. I’ll protect ye.” He drew his lieutenant to his feet and dusted him off. “She wouldn’t grow a year older where I had influence. I’d make sure she was tried as a witch.”

“She should be drowned. Or burnt.” After several minutes, Rutherford felt no different. The witch’s evil eye hadn’t touched him, yet he was unsettled still. He remembered her performance at the funeral for Myles Campbell. "She's a danger tae us. She'll bring us doon."

"We'd best see tae that. We'll speak tae the MacPharlans. They ken people who have the wisdom tae defeat spells, whatever the auld woman's power. Gather four men. We're going tae pay the witch a visit."

"Hadn't ye better first speak tae the MacPharlan?" Rutherford hesitated. "How d'ye ken what tae do with her?"

Connington gazed at him from under lowered lids and didn't answer. He was in an indulgent mood, for which Rutherford thanked heaven.

"We control the village; we control the witch. She doesn't want any harm tae come tae her neighbours, I'm certain."

The villagers were still returning to their houses when Connington and his men marched out of the castle. As he passed through the village, children scattered out of his way despite his determined effort to smile. People went inside or disappeared behind houses. Doors closed before they passed by.

"The witch has poisoned their minds," said Connington.

His right hand on his dirk, Rutherford studied the houses on both sides of the path, expecting an ambush. They walked to the other side of the village to Morag's house. No one spoke to them.

When they were a few feet from her door, Morag appeared on the threshold. She drew herself up to her full height, her brindled hair hanging down her back, uncovered and thick as a young woman's. Rutherford thought her uncouth as ever in a blanket of black and white, wrapped round her like that of an ancient queen.

"I'll see Mistress Campbell." He stepped closer.

"She has the fever." She didn't back away.

The old woman had power. Connington never showed

fear in the face of danger—he must have some occult power himself, but Rutherford had no clue about its nature.

"Yer Inglishe has improved."

"I benefit from the salutary presence of yourself and your men."

"We don't fear ye."

"No?" she said.

Rutherford drew himself up and slammed his sword in its sheath. He doubted he'd scare the old witch.

Their men, standing by the wall of a house nearby, avoided looking at her.

"I can't curse anyone with the evil eye. I have no power to do that at all. Your men may look at me without fear."

"Let me pass." Connington advanced toward her. To his men he said, "Stay here and watch the hag."

"You may seek your death," said Morag, but she stepped aside.

Rutherford swallowed with difficulty.

"Come in with me," said Connington.

After his eyes adjusted to the dimness inside, Rutherford saw her yellow hair, dishevelled and dirty, and then her face, red and swollen beyond recognition. She moaned without opening her eyes and turned over. Stunned, Rutherford ran into his captain, who had stopped in front of him. Connington studied the sick woman for a few moments and then turned and walked out the door. The old witch went outside with them.

"Ye've done a poor job of nursing her. Ye make sure she recovers. She dies and—" Connington made the sign of cutting a throat with his thumb.

"And you lose the chance of a rich dowry."

"We understand each other."

"I understand you." Morag showed him her back and closed the door on him.

"That woman needs a lesson in manners," said Connington.

~

Morag met Catriona on a path in the village. "Let's walk." Catriona started to march toward the far side of the village. "Take it easy." Morag tucked Catriona's arm under her own and patted it. "Remember, you have no cares but the care of the chief's daughter. Her stepmother knows where she is. She's out of Connington's hands."

"So I believe. Ròs Màiri performed well?"

"She did her part in helping Shona escape. Though a little of my artistry has ruined her beauty for now."

"I hope we haven't to put up with that man much longer."

Morag willed Catriona the strength to carry out her part. "We won't," she said. "One way or another—and that's a prophecy."

Catriona looked like she wanted to speak, but was overwhelmed.

"We must leave," said Morag. "Nothing else to be done. We'll go to the caves."

"How can we leave just like that?"

"Put your eyes back in their sockets, my dear, and listen," said the wise woman. "Bring all the food you can out of the castle. Every time one of our people leaves the castle, have them bring out food." Morag told her where to take the food, then she reached under her *earasaid* and pulled out a small linen packet. "Put this in the strangers' food—a strong tasting dish like spiced meat."

"Will it kill them?"

"You know what I believe." She and Catriona were of an age, but a chasm remained between them. "You've known me for decades."

Catriona studied the ground ahead.

"They'll have a nice nap and we'll carry off what we want and leave."

"Why don't you pretend that Shona has walked into the sea, as you planned?"

"Not a man to accept the evidence of his eyes. Connington would stretch a few backs and wring a few necks to confirm it." Morag shook her head. "Lies, burnings, evil deeds. That's what I see in him."

Rutherford stretched and yawned on his pallet. Connington, his captain, still lay abed snoring. The lieutenant frowned at the memory of the MacDonalds' herd heading east. The drovers waved at village people as they passed, but the herd boys who glanced in Connington's direction looked away quickly. As if he could curse them on the spot like the witch.

Many a time in the Wars against the Catholic empire even a single cow had been a rare treasure. Rutherford still marvelled at the sight of several hundred fat cows. He had developed a taste for dogs and rats in the wasted lands of conflict—anything to keep body and soul together. Connington said that the fires of purification would burn throughout the island kingdoms, with no kings and no prelates left to rule. Rutherford had no interest in such matters. His focus was food—a hungry man made a poor fighter.

He could hear people moving about downstairs in the hall, but he didn't smell any cook fires. He leaped out of bed and gently shook Connington awake.

"Go look, ye fool!"

Rutherford hauled on his breeches and belted his sword around his middle.

A corporal met him in the stairwell. "I can't find a soul who belongs to the castle. They're all gone!"

"Choose ten men to stay in the castle and ten to come with me. I'll tell the captain." Rutherford wasn't sure what his captain would do, but he'd be in a better humour on a full belly. "Assign two men to the kitchen. Make us something hot."

"There's nothing left in the kitchen or storerooms, sir. Nothing—not so much as an onion!"

"Cursed witch. She has something to do with this."

The corporal made a sign with his fingers to avert the evil eye.

"Come with me." The two ran back up the stair to Connington's chamber. He was awake and had already dressed.

"All the people are gone, sir," said Rutherford. "Shall we search the village?"

Connington glared at him. "We'll have something to eat first."

"There's—"

His captain finished putting on his coat. "Spit it out, man!"

"No food left. No servants."

Connington grabbed his sword belt and went down to the hall to collect the men who slept there. Rutherford followed as fast as he could and shook the laggards awake. Not a single curse or complaint came from them. They ran out of the hall and down the steps. No one in sight. No sound from the barracks or guardhouse.

"We'll search the village." Connington left ten men in the castle and took another twenty into the village. "Nothing too rough, ye understand. Just enough to make them mind." There were only sixteen houses in the village. "Four to a house, I think."

"It's very quiet here, too," said one of his men, more alarmed by the stillness than his captain.

"Search anyway. Rutherford, with me!" Connington went straight to Morag's house. He passed houses with closed doors and smokeless roofs. The old witch didn't come to greet him. He opened the wattle door of her house and peered in. No one. Her cauldron was missing from the central fire. Shona was missing from beside it.

Rutherford shivered in his wake. The witch had tricked them. "The witch, sir. She's vanished them a'." Rutherford turned to go.

"Ye silly bugger! There's got to be an explanation."

"How?"

"They left in the night." Connington spat on the floor. "Probably gied us a potion tae put us tae sleep."

"And who'd dae that? The witch wasnae in the castle."

"D'ye think ma dear auntie had a hand in it?"

Rutherford knew that tone of voice. Connington's aunt might not enjoy a very long life.

Far in the distance, Castle Muirn brooded grey over the loch in the weak autumn sun. Shona didn't know when she'd see it again. Mist obscured part of the fortress and the loch, and wisps lay over the road ahead. She trudged after the cattle into the Strath of Urchie, away from the castle and childhood.

Morag wouldn't tell her whereabouts, and she hoped that no one else had overheard their strategy. The people of the *baile* would be safe if Connington couldn't find the caves and question them. She prayed that Morag's ruse had worked.

And that Priscilla had agreed to hide with them.

Walking was pleasant on a quiet day of autumn with the sun silvering the clouds and glinting on the waterfalls sheeting down from the crags. The herd and herders didn't move fast at all, but every step took her a distance from Connington. Shona counted herself lucky. She was no longer the daughter of the most powerful man in many a Highland district. She was supposed to be one of the younger herd boys on the way to strange parts. However, she was travelling with a man she trusted and loved, and he had promised to take her to her father. Things were headed in the right direction.

They walked five or six miles with the scent of pine following them before stopping at a stance, a grassy sward by a river where the cattle grazed and drank water. She hadn't seen Alasdair all day, but hoped to see him while everyone rested. She saw Ruari speaking to Finlay, the smallest herdboy and the friendliest.

Finlay joined her. "Ruari has put you in my care. I am to make sure you eat something before we start again and teach you things you should know."

"Thank you." She had the feeling that both Alasdair and Ruari were keeping an eye on her, and it pleased her. She'd spend a few agreeable weeks walking to Edinburgh. With any luck the only thing that would happen would be a bit of rain.

They walked another few miles. The cattle were obedient and if one wandered it was efficiently brought back to the herd.

"Come," said Finlay. "Our turn to bring back a wayward heifer. You're worried? A heifer isn't a large cow—she's young yet."

She remembered the cow she had killed. Surely nothing would happen now. She would not use the power because she had not trained sufficiently. She wished she had spent more time with Morag.

"I've dealt with animals before. I can do it. I have a switch."

"Keep her from going into the river. She could break a leg if she moves too fast."

"Right."

Finlay started after the heifer and she ran from him—she was playing!

Shona waved her switch, but the young cow ignored her existence and ran in front of her into the river, where she slowed and picked her way along.

"Don't wave the switch any more. Let her be." Alasdair! He dismounted and walked into the water, talking quietly to the animal as he went along. He put a withy round her neck while his dog yipped to encourage her to return to the bank.

"So glad you're here to help out."

"Finlay, tell Ruari we'll walk another two miles or so to Gleann Caol. We'll stay the night there. Take the heifer with you."

"Right!" And away he went taking the heifer by the withy.

"He's a good lad. He'll do right by you." Alasdair stared at her. "How are you managing?"

"Just fine. I'm so glad to see you." She scanned the riverside and saw no one. "Perhaps we could ... greet each other among the yew trees."

They wandered over and hid themselves among the wide yew trees whose leaves whispered a quiet welcome to her. *We will protect you from your enemies.*

Alasdair's face showed no signs of astonishment at the message of the trees.

He has no ears to hear. He has eyes only for you, woman dear.

So he did. He sang a light tune.

"A beautiful air about a lass lost in the woods," she teased.

"An insignificant air about a beautiful woman here in the woods with me."

A gentle rain pattered through the tree tops, but the yews kept them dry.

"Come to me." He drew her close and removed her bone pin. The top of her *fèileadh* fell down about her hips and legs. He ran his hands down her back. "I've been wanting to come to you, to touch you, all day."

He brushed her ear and neck with his lips. Enough to waken her body. She wanted more. Their lips met, and the kiss was deep and took an earthly lifetime. A kiss—such a wonder.

But it couldn't last. He removed her arms from his neck and stepped back from her. "I will savour these moments."

She'd remember them too, as she walked behind the herd. "I suppose we must return." She felt hollow, a husk that could be blown away in the wind.

"I'll go first. You wait a moment or two and slip in with the herdboys." He kissed the top of her head and left her.

She memorised the place, the yews and the blue periwinkles and purple heather. She would never forget the clean scent of rain-fresh flowers. Then she did as she was told. Gladly—in the hope of many more such moments.

By the end of the first day, her belt rubbed her lower ribs, and the rough fabric of the *fèileadh* scratched her knees. She trudged with three herd boys and one drover behind the cattle. Finlay was the only one to speak to her.

"You're pleased with yourself! Are you not tired?"

"I love it. I love it all." She would not mention her fatigue or the desire for a better quality of wool.

"You love it? Among strangers with beasts that frighten you? You have spirit, I must say. Not too many boys like you around."

No, not many boys like me at all. Hopefully Finlay would never find out she was a woman.

And so the days passed. Ambling behind the beasts, stopping for food and water and walking again. But the rains came, the heavy, sheeting rain that made every *fèileadh* sodden and heavy.

The drovers stopped the herd at a waterfall. Alasdair and the other drovers held the cattle against the rocks at one side of the waterfall while the herd boys made a pen with heather ropes. Shona stood between two cows to take the chill from her body.

"We won't be able to hear anyone coming," said Donall.

Alasdair replied, "And no one passing will hear us—no one will smell the cook fires."

Hot food. After the rain, hot food was welcome indeed. With food in her belly, her legs might hold her up another day or two.

"And we put out sentinels in all directions. The usual,"

said Ruari. Despite the pelting rain, he took precautions—he must expect trouble because of her. The drovers looked as sodden as the herd boys. "If we're attacked, throw off your *fèileadh* for fighting. You can't wield a weapon, weighted down with wet wool." Everyone murmured agreement, then helped to finish the heather barriers for the cattle. The herd boys were too young to have gone to war, but they seemed keen to fight. Shona wished them a long life without great bloodshed.

Shona wished Alasdair would come and speak to her sometime during the evening. Although she wanted to talk, she knew well that they had to be careful. But he kept his distance.

After watching the herdboys mix their meal, she did the same. And when they unpinned and unbelted the *fèileadh*, she did that too. She bundled herself in the wool and fell asleep.

Suddenly she sat up. Connington had appeared from nowhere. The herd had moved on and she was alone by the loch. He seized her as he had in the stairwell and he tried to get under her shirt "for a tasty bite." She tried to evade him, but he caught her and kissed her. She tried to push him away, but he slapped her.

"Ye wait till I get ye home. Ye'll see what I have in mind for ye."

She had never been treated in such a manner. "I am a gentleman's child. You should be ashamed for laying a hand on me."

"I think not, missy. Your father wants rid of you, and I have good uses for your dowry. I shall be King of Scotland. And you will bow—"

His hands imprisoned her. Hard, cruel hands.

With a cry, she woke.

"What's all this?" asked Ruari. "You'll wake the dead."

Shona looked about her. Several herd boys stared at her. "I had a dream."

"So you did." Ruari's voice was not unkind. "No harm done. I told the boys you'd had a hard life before we got you."

The dream was a warning.

The next day the quiet calm of autumn lay over the country, smoothing the rough shapes of rocks and crags. A beautiful country. She went to find Ruari or Gillesbic to find out what she should do. Everyone was pleasant to her as she passed by.

Two of the drovers produced three rabbits, caught in the early morning. After the herd boys skinned the animals and cooked the food, Shona and little Finlay Beag collected cups and distributed them full of rabbit stew. The clothing of the older boys steamed and dried at the cookfire. Her knees chafed in the cold and wet, but she did her duty.

When Alasdair returned from checking the sentinels, she approached him. "Your cup?"

He brought his cup from the fold of his plaid. "I've watched you. You've done well and not a syllable of complaint from you. Regret your decision?"

"Nothing has happened to make me regret it. The weather has been perfect." She took his cup as a squall of wind lifted the folds of her *fèileadh*.

"Journey's not done." He leaned toward her and whispered, "I'd like to take you under my arm and keep you warm." He looked about.

"You know you don't dare."

"I'll have a little gift for you when you've finished your tasks today. See the stone there? Oisean's Stone, it's called." The stone was massive and difficult to miss.

"At day's end I take a walk past the stone. Understood." And away she went.

Wondering what was waiting for her at day's end made the time pass quickly indeed.

"Call of nature," she said to Finlay Beag before he asked.

When she passed by the big stone, she saw Alasdair standing in front of a copse of birch trees. "Follow!"

They walked through birch trees until they reached the other side of the little copse. Masses of white clouds gathered in the sky, but rays of sunshine slid through the narrow passes between them, edging some with ripe gold and others with fiery red as they fell to the loch below.

"I wish we could stay here for ever." Beauty all round her and the man she loved beside her. Heaven could be no different.

Alasdair said nothing, but smiled and nodded. She'd seen that same smile in her little fortress at home. She knew it couldn't last and so did he, but she delayed her future for a time.

"Come." He led her to a little mound of leaf-covered earth—and pulled away the carpet of leaves to reveal the interior of a small tent.

"Wonderful! You have created a paradise for us and disguised it." He knelt and sat, and she crept in beside him. The loch was still in sight.

He reached for a leather bag and drew packages from it. "A little smoked salmon and fresh oatcakes. Sorry, no cream, just a bit of butter."

"A feast nonetheless." The smell of fresh leaves and clean earth mixed with the savory smoke of the salmon.

"Will you have a bit of claret?"

"More claret! Truly a feast fit for kings and the old gods."

He poured a taste into her cup and his own. "We have things to discuss."

An image of him saying farewell and turning his back to her appeared like a bolt of lightning in her mind. *Poof* and gone forever.

"I want to marry you next year."

She must have appeared struck by that lightning.

He put out a hand to her shoulder. "Are you all right?"

"Never better!" Tears came to her eyes. How did that happen? Where did they come from?

"I'll do it properly. Ruari and I will go to your father and ask for you. After I sell the cattle I can prove to him that I'll soon have wealth enough to buy a good house and a bit of land."

She'd go with him without *earasaid* or shoes, without a roof overhead or a garden for food. She said in her most formal voice, "I accept." And giggled.

"I'd take you without a *tochradh, a ghràidh*. I have cattle enough for us. I'll tell your father that too. I don't need your dowry." He took her hands in his and kissed them.

Her heart rippled with sudden joy. She couldn't believe it. But her mind darkened—such joy couldn't last.

"I dreamt about Connington yesterday. That he caught me and put me in prison."

"Say a *seun*, a charm, and put him out of your thoughts."

"I shall."

"Better you do it now so he can't curse you."

"He may already have done so."

"Say it anyway. It may weaken it."

She prepared the *seun* in her mind. Her hands shook and her breathing quickened. She thought about the air moving in and out and slowed it. Then she said the charm perfectly.

Feart sùla dhomh
Feart dùla dhomh
Feart reula dhomh
Feart rùn mo chlèibhe
dhomh an comhnaidh.

Power of eye be mine
Power of the elements be mine.
Power of the stars be mine.
Power of my true love
be ever mine.

"Only walking into the future will tell you what he'll do." He lifted her chin and gave her a gentle kiss. "Ruari suggested that you become my servant. Does that meet with your approval? You'd be near me where I can protect you."

"I shall be your obedient servant in all matters," she said, cheekily.

"The old spirit is almost back."

She couldn't help herself. She reached up and wrapped her two hands round his neck. His skin was cool against her face as he kissed the angle of her neck and jaw. Then she raised his hand to her breast. He gasped. He unbuckled her belt and removed her *féileadh* and journeyed the length of her body. Her *léine* was thin, and little was hidden from him. His fingers explored the shape of her breasts and her back and her waist. She lost herself in his arms. Her breathing became slow and heavy. She pushed into his chest and a thrill passed through her body from breast to womb. She wanted to unbuckle his belt and draw his *féileadh* over the two of them. She wanted to explore him—his face, his skin, and most especially, his male parts.

"Stop. Please stop."

Her heart bounded in her breast. "What's wrong?"

"We cannot go further. If we do, I may give you a child in a dangerous time."

She moaned. "Sweeter than the apples high in the tree are you, and so hard to give up after a taste."

He gave her a light kiss on her forehead and rolled over beside her. "We'll find places to meet on the road to Edinburgh. But it's up to me to make sure there's no child."

"I look for you every day. I follow what you do. I'll spy upon you."

He grinned. "An activity for which we share a common liking. But it will be so very hard when I look at you—when I want to pull you down and make children with you."

"In the roadway! I much prefer this little tent in the birchwood." She turned and lay on top of his chest.

"Sorry. You must sit up. I need to bathe in the stream. Cold water will cure me of lust for you. Stay here while I bathe."

"You're walking oddly. Are you in pain?"

"In a manner of speaking, yes. I'll be fine." His face and neck turned a light shade of pink. "See that no one is looking when you leave the tent. Go ahead of me and find Ruari."

And away he went. She dressed quickly and left for the stance. Just as in her dream, she was back in the world of men and cattle. They noticed her arrival, but no one questioned her. Ruari was making sure the night guards were in place.

"So young—Seathan—you're ready for this venture. We still have a long journey before us." He took her aside. "Right. Where have you been, if I may ask? Did you..."

"No. More's the pity."

"You must stay away from each other. Truly. You endanger all of us."

EPILOGUE

As they travelled down the drove road, Shona was happy thinking about the wonderful things that had happened in the birchwood. His smooth skin over hard muscle was a memory she'd treasure a good long time.

And Alasdair wanted to marry her!

Her father had to allow it. He wouldn't force her to marry Connington when he learned what he had done—that son of the devil.

Shona saw the Crow flying above and craned to see Alasdair. Had he noticed the Crow?

"What do you want, Crow?"

I shall follow, croaked the bird as she descended among the herd boys. *I am charged to watch over you. Fall back so that we may speak.*

That annoying bird would trouble Shona until she listened. She walked more slowly. "I know what you're going to say, Crow. I have a destiny, I have a duty. My destiny and duty's name is Alasdair Dubh—up there in front of the herd."

Morag has looked through the eyestone. Bloody wars and

many deaths, says she. Your task is not complete. You will save lives. As the banshee, your greatest work is yet to come.

"Please, let me be happy—tonight."

Tonight then, and tomorrow, and a few days after that. Then you must face your true destiny. The Crow flew off, leaving two black feathers behind.

That full feeling of joy sluiced from her heart, and it filled with pain. Tears welled in her eyes. Was it so much to ask to do what other women did? Was there no justice in the world?

She watched the ground as she plodded along.

"Hai!"

Shona jumped. She was deep in thought and it took a moment to come back to the world.

Alasdair turned his pony round and walked beside her. "If you don't look up, you won't see what's in front of you. Wolves, marauders and the like. Myself as well." He bent over her and said quietly, "Do you understand what I feel? I love you and I'll be at your side."

They heard a cough. Ruari had ridden back. "I heard. So you will not find a wife among your own people, have children and farm with ourselves."

"I'll stay with Shona."

Ruari said, "Ach, not a good thing. Endless travelling about for a woman you shouldn't have. "

Alasdair said to Shona, "I *will* have a wife with children and land. I'll wait for you—I'm a patient man. I'll help you fight your battles."

"There may be real battles. You could throw your life away." said Ruari. "Or grow old without children. I don't recommend it."

First the Crow and now Ruari. They reminded her of

duty and possibility, and she didn't like it. But still ... "Alasdair, what he says is wise."

Alasdair kissed her hand. "We'll see what happens. Luckless or not, landless or not, you'll always have my love."

THE END

AFTERWORD

Shona and Alasdair's story will continue in The Banshee of the Bright Corrie, releasing in May 2019.

Be sure to sign up for Sheila's newsletter to be the first to hear of her new releases!

www.sheilacurrie.com

AUTHOR NOTES

The banshee, *ban-sìth* as it is in Gaelic, means fairy woman. She has bad PR in the English-speaking world: she is disagreeable, she screeches, she is entirely too noisy. However, in the Gaelic tradition of Scotland and Ireland, the banshee serves a social function, the ability to predict the future—even death which ensures enough time for a proper funeral. Foreigners don't have them or "deserve them". She can protect women. If a man finds a beautiful woman sitting alone outside at night, combing her hair without concern or fear, he will conclude she is a banshee, and not harm her.

This novel is a romantic fantasy, based on historical fact. In the late 1630s Scotland was on the verge of rebellion which would lead to the Wars of the Three Kingdoms. The wars began in Scotland, then spread to Ireland and finally to England where it is called the English Civil War.

In the story Alasdair MacDonald hoped to make a truce with his clan's traditional enemy, the Campbells, and make both clans more prosperous. But he doesn't know about the explosive political situation developing in the Lowlands. He will learn when he leaves the Highlands on the drove to Edinburgh.

Some of the Gaelic names are simplified to make them easier to read for an English-speaking readership. A glossary of Gaelic and Lowland Scots follows.

GLOSSARY

Gàidhlig, Gaelic

alla bhuidhe - St John's wort
bacach - lame, awkward
baile - village, town
ban-sìth - fairy woman, banshee, warns of death, magic powers
bean-shìthe - fairy woman, banshee, warns of death, magic powers
bean-tuiream - mourning woman, keening woman; plural: mnathan-tuiream
Beinn Mhòr - Big Mountain
birlinn- galley, longship, a ship with a square sail and oars,
Caimbeulach - member of Clan Campbell
cèilidh - visit, entertainment
claidheamh mòr - big sword
crùisgean - crusie, oil lamp
cuach - large drinking bowl with two handles
dàn - poem, song, destiny, fate
deiseil - sunwise, clockwise, the right way of doing anything
Dòmhnallach - member of Clan Donald
drama - drink
dubh - black, black-haired
dyke - low wall
geas - spell, enchantment; prohibition
gleann - glen, valley
earasaid - women's plaid of three loom widths, wrapped round the body, belted at the waist and pinned at the shoulder

fèileadh - man's plaid of two loom widths, wrapped round the bodybelted & pinned; great kilt; fèileadhean = great kilts
gall - foreigner; goill = foreigners
gràdh - love; a ghràidh = O love
leac- tall, flat stone: slab, tombstone, flagstone
lèine - shirt for a man, shift for a woman
luadhadh - waulking or fulling of cloth to make it durable
Mac an Donais - Son of the Devil
maor - official, head man of a village, from Latin, similar to mayor
maor taighe - man in charge of the hall, of protocol; steward
mòran taing - many thanks
A Mhuire Mhàthair! - O Mary Mother
Mo mhallachd ort! - My curse on you!
mùirn - delight, joy, contentment
ollamh - master poet, highest grade of poet
plaide - blanket
sealladh - sight, view:
an dà shealladh - the second sight, the ability to predict death through apparitions
seanchaidh - tradition-bearer, storyteller, historian
seun - charm, spell
sgian - knife
sìtheach - fairy
sìthichean - fairies
slàinte - health; a toast
slàinte dhuibh uile- a health to all of you
sporan - purse, wallet
sreath - line, row, circle of people
stad - stop
tànaiste - tanist, second in command to the chief, regent
thugad - watch out
tochradh, tochair - dowry

tràigh bhàn - white sand beach
triubhas - close-fitting trousers cut on the bias, full or knee length

Note: Highlanders speak *Gàidhlig*, a Celtic language called Gaelic in English. *Gàidhlig* is the original Scottish language.

Am Faclair Beag (The Little Dictionary)
http://www.faclair.com/index.aspx?Language=en

Inglishe, Lowland Scots

auld - old
besom - a broom, a bundle of twigs for sweeping, a woman of bad character
bonnet - a head covering for men, a brimless wool cap
brose - watery oatmeal
cauld - cold
chamber - private space in a castle for a lord and/or his lady; a bed-sit
chapman - peddler
claymore - big sword from Gaelic *claidheamh mòr*
crusie lamp - oil lamp made of two iron bowls with a rush wick
daft - stupid, foolish
dais - raised platform at one end of a hall for the table of high-status people
the Deil - the Devil
dram - drink
frae - from
fray - fight, battle
glaikit - foolish
glen - valley from Gaelic *gleann*

gloaming - twilight, dusk
hall - public space for gatherings, meals and sleeping in a castle
hallion - rascal, clumsy man, ragged man
kail- cabbage
Martinmas - 11 November
neb - bird's beak, nose
noo - now
plaid - blanket, shawl; from Gaelic *plaide*
reek - smoke
sporran - purse, from Gaelic *sporan*
stance - resting place for cattle
targe - small round shield
thigger - beggar
tocher - dowry, from Gaelic *tochar, tochradh*
trews - close-fitting trousers, cut on the bias; from Gaelic *triubhas*
vittle - food, provisions from Latin
wattle - stakes interwoven with branches to make a fencing, doors or walls
waulking - a process by which woven cloth was wetted and pounded to shrink and thicken it; to make it warmer and more durable
withy - a rope of slender twigs usually willow, a halter
yett - gate, gateway, entrance, iron gate

Note: Lowlanders speak Inglishe, a Germanic language, increasingly called Scots, Lowland Scots or Broad Scots after 1600.

Dictionary of the Scottish Language
http://www.dsl.ac.uk

DEDICATION

My thanks to everyone who encouraged me to write this novel: my writing buddies, the WIP group, many teachers of craft and language, and of course, those who love reading anything about Scotland.

ABOUT THE AUTHOR

Sheila Currie lives in her world of thousands of books, fiction and non-fiction. Visiting friends worry about an avalanche. Her love of Scotland and Ireland led her to study in Nova Scotia, Canada and then in Scotland where she obtained an M. A. (honours) in Scottish History and Celtic Studies from the University of Glasgow. She was fortunate enough to have a summer job selling Gaelic books door-to-door in the West Highlands and Islands. Going from one cup of tea to the next, she had a wonderful opportunity to talk to local people and hear their stories. Today she teaches history and Gaelic in British Columbia, and at long last she has written a historical fantasy--set in Scotland of course.

www.sheilacurrie.com
www.facebook.com/scottishfantasywriter.ca
www.twitter.com/@sheilacurrie7
www.pinterest.com/sheila70currie
www.instagram.com/sheilacurrie70

23224266R00153

Made in the USA
San Bernardino, CA
23 January 2019